RECONCILIATION

GUY WARE is the author of two novels and many stories. His collection, *You Have 24 Hours to Love Us* (Comma, 2012) included the story 'Hostage', subsequently included in the *Best British Short Stories 2013* (Salt). His first novel, *The Fat of Fed Beasts* (Salt, 2015), was chosen as a 'Paperback of the year' by Nicholas Lezard in the *Guardian*, and described as 'Brilliant . . . the best debut novel I have read in years.'

GUY WARE

RECONCILIATION

LONDON

PUBLISHED BY SALT PUBLISHING 2017

2 4 6 8 10 9 7 5 3 1

Copyright © Guy Ware 2017

Guy Ware has asserted his right under the Copyright, Designs and
Patents Act 1988 to be identified as the author of this work.

First published in Great Britain in 2017 by
Salt Publishing Ltd
International House, 24 Holborn Viaduct, London EC1A 2BN United Kingdom

www.saltpublishing.com

Salt Publishing Limited Reg. No. 5293401

A CIP catalogue record for this book is available from the British Library

ISBN 978 1 78463 104 8 (Paperback edition)
ISBN 978 1 78463 105 5 (Electronic edition)

Typeset in Neacademia by Salt Publishing

Printed and bound in Great Britain by Clays Ltd, St Ives plc

Salt Publishing Limited is committed to responsible forest management.
This book is made from Forest Stewardship Council™ certified paper.

To Major A.C.W. Ware
and R.M. Ware

RECONCILIATION

Contents

An apology

MANY NOVELS BEAR disclaimers: any resemblance, they declare, between the characters depicted and real persons, living or dead, is merely coincidental. But this novel grew from the details of my grandfather's life, passed on in good faith by his son, my father, and I must apologize for the extent to which my characters *fail* to resemble their real-life models, for which I am wholly responsible.

By way of reconciliation, I offer here a few facts the reader might bear in mind during what follows:

My father has never been a lawyer.

He has never had a drink problem.

He has never lived in Scotland.

His father *was* a spy.

To suggest otherwise would be unconscionable.

I
THE GIFT

§

"THAT'S WHERE YOU start."
Being in IT doesn't mean I don't read books. I know how they work.

So I might as well say it started there, on a cold wet Sunday night in February, 2003, with Holly sitting at our attic desk, legs crossed, right over left, twisting from side to side in her office chair - the chair she'd bought when her spine began to ache and she recalled her father nagging on about rowing a boat and having a bad back before she was thirty, which had seemed so far away at the time, but was now so far behind her - and me, kissing the top of her head, the parting in her hair, dropping the typescript on the desk in front of her, my forefinger stretched and pointing to the entry for the 15th of May, and saying:

"That's where you start. Right there."

She knew exactly what I meant, but she asked anyway.

"When you write it, that's where you start."

I held my hands up, palms outward, playing the impresario. "Your granddad playing *Run, Rabbit, Run* on a borrowed accordion. One of the Norwegians chucks a shoe his way to shut him up, and he turns back to his diary" - I knocked my knuckles on the desk - "the sound of soldiers hammering on doors getting closer and closer, louder and louder, and the fog refusing to come."

She didn't answer.

"Or maybe a couple of days later," I said, "National Day. May 17th. When their tiny fishing boat is intercepted by a submarine and the captain is ordered - in rough Norwegian - to line up his crew on the deck."

She looked uncomfortable. I hadn't done the research then. I had no idea that, technically, May 17th is Constitution Day, the anniversary of the day in 1814 when Norway first adopted the constitution of an independent country, even if most Norwegians refer to it as *Nasjonaldagen* (National Day) or just May Seventeenth. I was quoting the diary, the transcript Holly's dad had given her and she'd shown me. That was all I had to go on. I didn't know then that her granddad celebrated the 17th of May for years afterwards, back in England. But she did. She thought she did. She thought she knew this story, her grandfather's story, but perhaps it was only now, with me hamming it up, that she could *see* it: see the small, dirty, working boat, its paint chipped, its winches rusty but serviceable, a boat that did a job, pitching and yawing in a muscular sea as her grandfather climbed up on deck, his face unshaven, his thick, oily sweater identical to Overand's, because Overand's wife had pressed it on him, knowing it was important for them to look as much alike, and as much like fishermen, as possible.

She said it probably wasn't like that, but it was. She knew it was. It was all there, in the diary.

So she said, "Or what about when Overand's family were all dragged off by the SS, Martin? His wife and children. Should I start there?"

If you didn't know her, you might have thought she meant it. You might have taken her literally, as if she were an editor discussing a first draft and wondering how to shape the story. But I knew her.

"Could be," I said. "It's not in the diary, though, is it? And probably not the place to start. You need to establish him first. The hero."

Like I say, I read.

"Who?"

"Albert Charles William. Your grandfather."

She shook her head.

"It's not a story, Martin."

Of course it was.

It had always been a story: her granddad, her father's father, the spy. In Berlin in September 1939, for reasons he never disclosed; in Norway (ditto) when the Germans invaded. Sailed back to England by a brave Norwegian, whose family the Germans killed in retaliation. And he kept a diary.

She'd told me the story years earlier, not making too much of it. We'd been on a demo, which wasn't unusual, then, a demo against the Gulf War. The first Gulf War. Our first, anyway. We were sitting on the wall around the memorial where, normally, there'd be tramps or teenagers with purple hair drinking cider. Someone started in on what could ever justify war. World War II came up - it always did: the fight against fascism - and I was probably giving it my full "glorious sacrifice of the Red Army" spiel - this being 1991 and there still just about being a Communist Party for me to be in - and she told me about her grandfather, and the Norwegian. Just a couple of sentences, she couldn't believe she hadn't told me before. Perhaps she had, and I'd forgotten. We'd been together years by then, after all.

Anyway.

I'd heard her tell other people, too, over the decades we

were together. Her grandmother in domestic service; her grandfather in MI6. A major, no less. She'd barely known him – he died when she was young – but she knew the story, and she told it. It was part of who she was.

This was different, though.

This time she finally had the diary in her hands, or at least the transcript that William, her father, had made.

Stories never start where they start though, do they? Not on a cold wet February night in Cambridge, not in May in the middle of the North Sea, not in a Norwegian cottage listening to the sound of soldiers coming closer, not with the outbreak of war, or before the war – it's always before the war, or after the war, we are always in the middle of things, never the beginning or the end. So we could just as well say this story started the previous day: Saturday – *that* Saturday: 15th February, 2003 – when I shuffled towards Hyde Park, on the look-out for old comrades, and Holly spent the day at her father's house, the house she'd grown up in, helping him clear out the books and papers of a lifetime's work, helping him prepare (as he put it, more than once) to die.

"A bit of a busman's holiday for you, I'm afraid," he'd said, ringing to ask if she would help. Holly said she didn't mind, which I dare say was true. That could be her epitaph: *I don't mind.* Now, as he rummaged in the cupboard under the kitchen sink, looking for dustbin bags, she asked if he wanted to start at the top and work down? Or at the bottom and work up?

It was a tall South London terrace: what it lacked in width, and light, it made up for in stairs that seemed to go up forever. As a girl, she told me, she used to dream of finding whole new staircases leading to whole new floors, familiar but strange. The rooms in these dream-floors would be empty, bare pine floorboards stained black around the edges, patterned wallpaper of the sort her parents had stripped whilst she was still a child and never replaced. Sometimes they contained things that had gone missing from the real house – a battered armchair, a favourite doll, her mother. Now the landings were an obstacle course of half-filled cardboard packing cases, of desk lamps and broken radios, hat stands, board games and kettles, all waiting to be packed or – more likely – pitched into the builder's skip that squatted on the kerb outside, brute and ugly amongst the sleek estates and 4×4s.

Her father straightened up, the black roll of bin bags in his hand like a plastic cosh. "Let's stick with Horace shall we, Holly? It's usually best. We'll begin *in media res.*"

He talked like that.

I'm doing my best.

The middle of things – the very heart of the house – was his study. That's where Holly and Ben always went to find him, the room they were pulled towards, or repelled from, by the shifting tides of family rows. A quiet, crepuscular room at the back of the second floor, overlooking the passage, with a fireplace crowded with books and a portrait on the chimney-breast her father said was of her great-grandparents. They were refugees, emigres: asylum seekers *avant la lettre*. As a child, she'd been fascinated by the man's white beard, which reached down to his stomach; by the straight, tight parting in the woman's hair, which left a luminous white strip of scalp in the middle of her head; and by the way the pair of them loomed over her father as he sat at his desk listening to whatever squabble or schoolwork problem she laid out for his adjudication. The rest of the room was shelved from floor to ceiling. Books, periodicals and files, photograph albums, children's games and jigsaw boxes, telephone directories and ancient briefs were all stuffed and stacked and piled upon each other, without any order or system she could ever detect.

In the middle of the middle of things, with its back to the fireplace, stood a Georgian walnut writing desk, an improbable island of calm amidst the surrounding wreckage. It had been her mother's once, a present from *her* father when she married. She had used it as a dressing table; in bitter moments she referred to it as her dowry. When she left for good, Holly's father threw away the bottles and jars, the lotions and the sprays, and moved it into his study. He had to stand it on blocks – offcuts from the bookcases he was having built at the time – before he could get his knees underneath it comfortably. The Georgians must have been very short indeed, he said – something to do with the diet, no doubt, or the quantity of gin consumed by the wet nurses of the aristocracy. "A beautiful piece of work," the carpenter said, helping to carry it through from the bedroom and sucking his teeth at the sight of nail varnish on the unpolished surface. "You want to look after that."

He started with the top drawer. All the predictable crap of a sedentary working life – dried out ballpoint pens, paper clips, staples, a hole punch and its confetti, business cards, empty cheque books, packets of aspirin and alka seltzer, an appointment diary from 1993, another from 1978, a box of matches, a penknife and a silver and bone ink bottle he'd been given by a grateful graduate student from India. He put his hand inside to reach an invisible catch, and pulled the drawer right out of the desk. He nodded to the roll of bin liners he'd brought up from the kitchen and asked Holly to tear one off and hold it open. He lifted the whole drawer into the bag, and turned it upside down. She felt the weightless plastic snap taut.

"Dad?"

"It's all right. There's nothing there."

When he lifted the empty drawer back out she could see ink-stains like blue-black bruises on the unfinished surface of the wood.

The second drawer contained household bills, receipts, bank statements; there was an old letter from the police about a speeding fine; another from a consultant to his GP outlining the results of blood tests from a few years back when, after four decades of high-to-catastrophic alcohol intake, it looked like there might be something wrong with his liver, but wasn't; and a will in a long, thin manila envelope. He kept the will.

The third drawer contained bundles of letters held together with the faded pink ribbons from barristers' briefs, or with friable rubber bands that snapped at the slightest touch. On some of the envelopes she recognized his handwriting, on some her mother's.

He tossed them all into the bag.

"This is more like it," he said, taking a book from the drawer and passing it to her. Its faded cover was the colour of dead moss. She opened it and read:

THE
STORY OF NORWAY

by

HJALMAR H. BOYESEN

GEBHARD PROFESSOR OF GERMAN
IN COLUMBIA COLLEGE, AUTHOR OF
"GOETHE *&* SCHILLER", "GUNNAR",
"IDYLLS OF NORWAY," ETC.

NEW YORK & LONDON
G. P. PUTNAM'S SONS
The Knickerbocker Press

1886

"It was your grandfather's."

In the middle of the book were half a dozen folded sheets of numbered A4 paper, typed with an old-fashioned typewriter and annotated with hand-written amendments.

"Did you know he was a spy?"

"Yes, Dad. You told me."

"Of course."

She said, "The Knickerbocker Press?"

I got back late that evening, still excited. Holly and her father had already eaten as much as they could of a Chinese takeaway, and her father had opened a bottle of whisky. I insisted we all watch the TV news, together.

"You should have been there," I said. "You too, Bill."

He said the television was still in the living room but there was nothing left in there to sit on. I went to fetch it and returned, a few moments later, struggling backwards through the kitchen door, lugging the absurdly heavy, bulbous TV over to a counter, where, with a grunt, I set it down next to the microwave Holly's father never used. (He said it had been a present from Ben, which meant Alice.)

I said, "Christ, Bill. What's happened in there? It's like you've gone already."

"Ben took a few pieces."

Holly said, "Ben's been? How is he?"

"He's fine. He sends his love."

I doubted that. Not that Ben loved his sister, which I supposed he might, but that he would have said so - least of all to their father.

"And Alice?"

William held out his hands in apology, or supplication. "I didn't ask."

Holly laughed. "Men."

"I know. Where would you be without us?"

I unplugged the redundant microwave, and plugged in the television. "Maybe not about to blow the shit out of Iraq."

William gestured with the whisky bottle, offering me a drink. He said, politely enough, and not as if he were picking a fight: "That's a tad Greenham Common, isn't it, Martin? I thought we'd got beyond war being all the fault of male hegemony." He said it with a smile, not as if he were picking a fight. As if it were the sort of thing he might say, or anybody might say, all the time.

"You should have been there."

"Perhaps."

Holly said, "Did you meet anyone we know?"

"That's the thing. It was too fucking *huge*. I turned up at the Embankment, and it was like one enormous *queue*, all the way to Hyde Park. You know how it is. Every time I thought it was about to get going, I'd just bump into a brass band, or jugglers, or student Trots with a megaphone. By the time I got to the park, there were loads of people already leaving, but it was still packed. And there were thousands more behind me, piling in. Hundreds of thousands."

"Poor you. You hate queues."

But I wasn't listening. I was up on my feet, buzzing again. "It was great. Vast. You should have been there. You really should."

By now I had the TV plugged in, the aerial lead connected to a socket on the kitchen counter William had never used. Even when they all lived there, when Holly and Ben were children and their mother, or the au pair, was making beans on toast for them and a gin and tonic for their father, I guessed the Stantons never watched TV in the kitchen. I switched channels until I saw it again: a million faces, more or less, filling the screen, filling the park.

We watched for banners we might recognize, for unions and Party branches that no longer existed.

I said, "I saw one: *Professors of Jurisprudence against the war.*"

William had spent half his life in cross-examination and couldn't be provoked so easily. He poured himself another drink and said, "It might have been better than that infantile *Not in my name.*"

I knew I shouldn't rise to the bait, but I said: "It's telling Tony Blair he hasn't got our support. It's an unjustified, illegal war and we don't want any part in it."

"Well now," said William, the professor again, "illegal and unjustified? They're rather different concepts."

"There's no UN mandate."

"Which might be another matter again . . ."

"So . . . what?" I slumped back in my chair, more disgusted than defeated. It was more comfortable that way.

William said, "We all know a march won't stop a war."

"So we just do nothing?"

He held up his hand. "There'll be a war. A lot of people will die. But we – you and I and Holly, and people like us (an unfortunate phrase, I know, Martin, but apt, in the circumstances) – people like us won't be killed, or have to kill anyone. At worst we'll be a bit embarrassed about living in a country that does such things, but our guilt helps precisely no one. So what do we do? We get our excuses in first. Like children.

Not in my name is just another way of saying: *It wasn't me.*"

"It's *not* me."

"But who cares, Martin? Really? I don't think this is about your conscience."

"We have to do what we can."

He shook his head. "Perhaps." He swallowed his whisky and held his glass up to the light. "But perhaps this isn't about us."

Watching him, I thought, despite his age, there was still a sense of the strength he had always shown, a combination of tension and stillness that suggested resilience more than stress, like steel wire stretched between secure fence posts. It seemed absurd that he should be retiring, leaving London, preparing to die. Whenever he said that, Holly tried to joke him out of it. Her father wasn't going to die.

He asked if he should open another bottle.

I put my hand over my glass. "Not in my name."

It was feeble, but he laughed.

Then, in Hyde Park, on television, the shot changed, a view up to the stage, and there she was, in Holly's father's kitchen. Cathy.

I had no idea it was going to happen. I told Holly that, afterwards. How could I have known? How could I have guessed that out of all the hours they'd filmed the producers would choose that clip? No one watching would know who Cathy was. But I had been there. I'd seen it at first hand, and she thought I must have known.

I shifted in my chair, pushing it back a fraction from the table, sitting slightly straighter. A union leader wound up his speech, punching his right fist into the palm of his left hand, to muted applause. After a moment's pause, Cathy stepped toward the microphone.

Holly's father said, "Isn't that . . . ?"

And Holly said, "Martin's ex. Yes, it is."

Even her father recognized Cathy. He'd only met her a couple of times, back when we were students – Holly, me, Cathy and a couple of others, sharing a house off Mill Road – and he had driven up to visit. Cathy had changed since then, aged, but not by much: something else Holly could hold against her.

"I thought so," William said. "It's the eyes."

I didn't imagine Holly wanted to discuss Cathy's eyes and neither, then, did I, so we all watched instead, because it was easier to look at the television than each other.

Cathy was on the platform, not one of the speakers, but part of the machinery. Filling a gap, smoothing out some scheduling hiccough, she stepped forward to the microphone and announced that more marchers were arriving at the park, more still were backed up in Piccadilly and Haymarket, some had not yet left Trafalgar Square all these hours after the rally started. There must be a million, two million of them – of *us*, she said – and she was greeted with a cheer, a deep, visceral wall of noise that rose like a wave and broke across the stage, crashing over her, washing away the years and leaving her face a beacon of pure, startled, joy. Which I guess was why, even though her face was not familiar and no one would know who Cathy was – except Holly, of course – why that particular clip made it onto the TV news, and Holly saw her, again, for the first time in years.

And I'd insisted we watch it.

Holly stood up, took her glass over to the sink and rinsed it. She filled it with water to take upstairs, to our room, her old room, the one she'd slept in as a child.

As she left, her father was opening another bottle anyway.

She was asleep, I think, not just pretending, and I woke her, coming in. She rolled onto her side, facing the wall, making space in the single bed. I fitted myself to her, my chest against her back, my knees against the back of hers, like a carpenter stacking timber.

She said, "We're getting a bit old for this."

Holly read the transcript the next day, Sunday, back in Cambridge, while outside the temperature dropped and the sky filled with cloud, dense and grey like steel wool.

We'd driven home that morning, barely speaking – which was not unusual, I told myself, not a sign of anything in particular, just a familiar trance induced by the steady hum of the tyres and the music on the CD player. She'd brought the transcript back, still tucked inside the book her father kept it in, *The Story of Norway*, along with the photographs she'd salvaged from her father's bonfire: one of her grandfather in a folding cardboard frame; one of her mother at seventeen – a studio portrait in a striped silk dress with a broad, tight waist and full petticoats, dated 1958; a handful of family snapshots, leached to chemical browns and inky purples, taken in the family garden, or on beaches around the country, of Holly and her brother, of her mother dressed in Jaeger, in Biba, in increasingly layered and exotic outfits of her own confection, and of her father in well-cut suits, white shirts and thin ties, looking like an associate of the Krays – a diminutive, dangerous one, perhaps – with his fleshy face and hair brushed straight back; none from the last thirty years. Holly said even our physiology seemed to be shaped by fashion. You couldn't mistake these sixties faces for those of any other decade; no one looked like that now, not even her father, whose face it was, not even her mother, she supposed, though she hadn't seen her mother since the early seventies.

She read the diary transcript while I cooked: her, sitting at the kitchen table, turning the pages; me, clattering heavy pans and slicing onions. Neither of us mentioned Cathy.

She knew the story.

She picked up the photograph, the one in the cardboard frame. She said, "I never really knew him."

"No?"

"I was quite young when he died. But I remember he came to stay one Christmas. I think. I can see him – no, I can't really. I can picture the situation. Somehow, I know it was Christmas, but I don't remember him eating turkey, or wearing a paper hat, anything like that. He's sitting in an armchair; I'm looking down at him. He was small, and pale and blond" – she glanced at the photograph again – "I think."

"How old were you?"

She didn't answer for a while. "Six? Eight? It's my only memory of him. Could I have been looking down? Even if he was in a chair?"

"I don't know. You were there."

"Maybe. It was Christmas Eve, I think. We were alone. I told him I really wished I could do card tricks, but wasn't any good at them. His present was a book of magic and tricks with cards. He must have had it wrapped already. It was there, under the tree. Can you imagine how happy he must have been? Listening to me chattering on like that, knowing what was going to happen in the morning, but keeping it to himself?"

I scraped the onions into the pan with a knife that caught the light and flashed like a fish. I said, "I can imagine. But could you? Then?"

"I don't know."

She remembered the story, such as it was, but not the book, or any of the tricks. She couldn't remember Christmas Day itself, she said, the presents in the sack at the end of her bed, more under the tree, her grandfather smiling as she unwrapped his gift. She had remembered a chain of events, a *story*. A story in which she'd accidentally done something good, something selfless. She wouldn't have known it at the time, could only have worked it out much later, as an adult, when her grandfather was already dead. In the end it was a story about her, not him, and she had no way of knowing now how much of it was true.

"I know he smoked a pipe. I remember that. There were racks of them in his house. They were hard and shiny and rather smelly. But, you know, I can't actually remember him with a pipe in his mouth."

Because there wasn't one in the photo?

"But you did know he was a spy?"

"Yes. No."

I turned back to the stove.

"Not at the time. I knew he'd been in the navy. After he died my dad talked more about him. I'm pretty sure that's when I learned he'd been in MI6. That he'd been a spy; that he was in Norway at the start of the war, and had been rescued. That's when I heard about the diary. But, Martin? I didn't really understand it. Not really. Not until today."

After dinner we went up to the attic room and she read the transcript again, while I lay on the sofa watching the new war grinding into gear on television with the sound down low. When she'd finished, she gave it to me to read, while she sat in her chair – the one with the levers and wheels and pumps that would stop her spine curling like a leaf – twisting from side to side, waiting for my verdict.

What was she expecting?

I stood and dropped the typescript back on the desk in front of her, tapped it with my forefinger and said: "That's where you start. Right there."

When she said it wasn't a story, she knew that wasn't true.

When she asked if she should start instead with the SS dragging off the Norwegian's family, she was only stalling.

She said, "He has a name, Martin. I never knew that."

That, when you got down to it, was what she'd understood.

"Everybody has a name."

"Of course. Obviously I knew he *had* a name. But I didn't know what it was. I'd never heard it. Dad never mentioned it. Not once. I'm sure. It was always *the Norwegian*: a brave Norwegian. But the brave Norwegian who sailed my grandfather out of trouble had a name: Overand. He had a wife and children. Who must have been called Overand, too."

"Which is great. You can track them down."

"They were killed, Martin. Executed. That's the point. He, the brave Norwegian – Overand – left them behind to save my grandfather, and they were executed."

Which, actually, she didn't know for sure.

It wasn't in the transcript – how could it be? The diary recorded a successful rescue, a return to Britain – but it was still part of the story. It always had been, as far as she knew. Really, it was the *point* of the story, just as her grandfather's happiness had been the point of her story.

I said, "Their family, then. There must be someone."

She could have verified the story; she could have tried.

She paused, her face blank. I imagined her knocking at

the door of a small wooden house in Stavanger, pictured the door opening and her saying: *Herr Overand? My name is Holly Stanton. I wrote to you about your great uncle?* She may have been thinking something similar, thinking she could not possibly do that.

She said, "I wanted you to understand. That's why I showed it to you."

I understood it was an opportunity. A chance for her to do something other than the job she always moaned about but always – when I told her to do something else, then – said she didn't really mind.

I said, "I understand. I do. It's a gift."

She didn't respond.

"For a book. Think about it, Holly. Family memoir. War-time resistance, heroism and atrocity; post-war reticence and suppressed memory. A total gift."

I'm no expert, but I could see *that*.

When she said she couldn't do it, she didn't mean she *couldn't*. She meant she *wouldn't*. That she didn't want to. That she was afraid to. She said her father would say she had no *locus standi*, no standing, no rights in the case. But did she believe it? Or was it simply that she didn't have the stomach for it, the splinter of ice in the heart?

She said, "It's not my story."

She must have known that wasn't true, either.

I said her father had given her the transcript for a reason; she just said it wasn't her story. She said she wouldn't (*wouldn't*, you see – not *couldn't*) appropriate other people's tragedy.

I laughed. It sounded so pompous.

She said, "It's not about me. I won't be a hyena, Martin."

I told her it would be a crime to waste it. That she owed

it to her grandfather. To Overand. I said, "He sacrificed his family for your grandfather. For you, in a way. Don't you think you owe them something?"

All the same, she said she wouldn't do it.

She said, "It's not about me."

Over the weeks that followed, we had three conversations, many times.

We talked about the coming war, its legality, the existence or otherwise of weapons of mass destruction, and whether or not Hans Blix and his UN inspectors should be withdrawn or allowed to complete their task; about oil, and the criminal and irresponsible fatuity of linking Saddam Hussein with Al Qaeda. It was the easiest topic for us to discuss in those weeks: it reinforced our preconceptions and comfortably indulged our millennial doom. Holly and I - and people like us - would not die; but we would be right.

The second conversation, more fleeting and fraught, concerned Holly's approaching birthday and what, if anything, she wanted for a present. She said, "Nothing." She always did. It was an almost-joke between us. Every birthday, every Christmas, I'd ask, and she'd say: "Nothing," and I'd wind up getting something not too far wide of the mark, until the year I saw it through and bought her nothing. I expected her to be upset; but she was relieved, which was worse. This year, however, she was going to be forty, a big, round number. And still, when I asked, which I did, more than once, she said: "Nothing".

Finally, most difficult of all, we talked about her grandfather's diary. I started it over and over again, despite myself, despite her.

I'd say, "How come you never found the diary?"

The question must have occurred to her – how could it not?

She'd say, "It's a long time since he died. Dad must have lost it. Or maybe Mum took it by mistake when she left. Or burned it. How do I know?"

She would be no more convinced than I.

"So your dad keeps the transcript for thirty years – right there, in his desk drawer, at his side for all that time. He asks you round to help clear out and – bingo! – there it is, in practically the first place he looks – but he loses the original?"

"It's possible."

"Anything's possible."

❧

As February bled into March, we saw less and less of each other. When I wasn't at work, I was at a meeting, a committee, a demonstration, or I was upstairs, in the attic, hammering away at the laptop.

One evening when she came home late from work, I was still in my dressing gown, lit only by the glow from my computer screen. I hadn't shaved or washed, or, to be honest, moved much from my desk since morning. She asked if I'd had a good day. I knew she was trying to keep the sarcasm out of her voice, because she didn't really want to fight, so I said, "The firewall crashed, we think it was a deliberate attack." She laughed. I knew she couldn't help it, that it didn't mean much. She said I made it sound so melodramatic, like something orchestrated by Al Qaeda via satellite from a laptop in the Tora Bora. She didn't obviously assume that I was lying.

"And you saved the world in your dressing gown?"

I tried, even then, to pull her down onto my lap, but there wasn't enough room, and she bumped her hip against the edge of the desk. I pushed my chair back, and she stood up. The streetlamps outside daubed the attic skylights chemical orange. She switched on the lights, turning the panes to liquid mirrors, reflecting the room back on itself. In the sloping glass above her head I watched her notice that the photograph of her grandfather – the photograph in the cardboard frame that had been on the bookshelf in her father's study all her life, until she brought it home and placed it on her side of the desk, beside her computer – was now on my side, beside *my* computer, my laptop. She picked it up and moved it back. I said: "Why would there even *be* a diary?"

Which she said made no sense at all, although she must have known it did. There had always been a diary.

"How could there not be one?"

I got up and walked across the attic room, dropped into the sofa.

Holly remained standing by the desk. "There's always been a diary."

I pulled a cushion onto my lap, leaned forward with my arms pressing it into my bare legs where the dressing gown hung open. "I'm just saying, Holly. There's your grandfather, right? He's a spy. The Germans invade and he burns all his papers. He's on the run. And he starts writing everything down. Why? Why would he do that?"

She might have said: *Because that's what people do*, because he did. We know he did. Instead she said, "I don't know."

"You don't know?"

"I don't know, Martin. Because it was interesting, maybe.

23

Because he was hanging around with a lot of time on his hands and he was probably scared."

"But he's a *spy*, Holly. Isn't he supposed to eat the fucking evidence?"

I was curled tight, squeezing the cushion on my lap, my arms wrapped hard around my legs. Wound tight. The way I used to be, the way I had been more and more, since I'd started to get involved again.

She said, "He worked in signals. He wasn't James Bond."

She said, "Martin? You should spend less time on the Internet."

She came and sat next to me. She picked the remote up off the coffee table, turned on the television, and together we watched the news. We heard UN weapons inspectors say they could not be certain what had happened to all the weapons they'd catalogued in the past: the weapons might have been destroyed, but might not; they wanted more time to look. It was clear to us then, as it must have been to the inspectors, that there would be no more time. The news ended and Holly switched the television off.

I said, "They're going to do it."

"Of course they're going to do it."

"And then what?"

She shrugged. "Tea?"

She said she was going to bed, was I coming?

There was a diary. She had read the transcript. I had read the transcript.

She took her tea and a novel about Bombay and went to bed. I went back to the desk and was still there when I heard her switch off the bedroom light, still there when she left for work the following morning.

§

SOMEWHAT AGAINST THE odds, Aleks Overand had a good war.

A year before it started, he had volunteered to fight for Finland against the Soviet Union, an enemy that would soon become an ally. He was a little over one metre sixty-five, had flat feet and a hint of rickets; tests indicated possible undiagnosed diabetes. Even a volunteer army did not want him.

The letter was waiting on the table in the hall when he returned from court. "Pompous little beggar," he said, when he had read it twice.

"Who, darling?"

"The under-secretary of stationery, or whatever he was. At the consulate. You'd think they'd be grateful."

Kirsten told the children to sit down and watch out as the maid cautiously bore a vast iron pot into the room and placed it on the table, trailing an aroma that spoke of long preparation and rich ingredients.

"I told them if I couldn't fight, I could at least drive a truck. I could run guns and bandages across the border."

"You?" Elda laughed. Elda Overand was thirteen; already she wrote plays and read Russian novels. "A smuggler?"

"He can sail a boat," Oskar spoke up in his father's defence.

"It's not really smuggling," Overand said, in the voice he reserved for explaining the real world to his children, and to others less *au fait* with its complexities than he. "The government knows. They can't admit it, of course, because we're not at war, but they've told the police and the army to turn a blind eye."

Oskar was ten, and wanted to be a lawyer like his father. He said, "Where do the guns come from, Pappa?"

"England, Oskar. Lee-Enfield rifles. Very reliable."

Elda sighed and rolled her eyes. "Why do men love guns so much? Men who've never fired them?" (Prince Andrei was a soldier, it was true; but, despite his dream of shooting Napoleon, Pierre Bezukhov did not love guns: he loved Natasha.)

Her mother smiled but said, "That's enough." And, as the maid lifted the hot lid and released a cloud of steam, she added: "And I can't say I'm sorry."

She asked the maid to thank the housekeeper. The reindeer casserole was excellent.

In the year that followed, Aleks Overand became increasingly distracted and irritable.

No one was more surprised, Overand suspected, than the Finns themselves when Finland fought its vastly more powerful enemy to a standstill. ("You see," Kirsten told her husband, "they didn't need you.") Everywhere else, however, war looked inevitable, He attended meetings where men, mostly less well dressed and less articulate than he, told him that the future lay in his own hands. That he was not powerless, but time was running out. He joined committees, signed letters. He learned to argue that only through rearmament and universal conscription – through a general mobilization of the whole people of Norway – was it possible to maintain neutrality and peace. ("Conscription? They still wouldn't take you," Elda said, and was sent up to her room.)

"Are you so determined to be killed?" Kirsten asked, when she believed the children were both asleep. "Do we make you so unhappy?"

"Our happiness is not the point," Overand said. "There are greater questions at stake."

Kirsten was not convinced.

"The question of freedom, of sovereignty," Overand said, "is not about us."

"Then whose freedom is it?" Kirsten asked.

His business did not suffer. Men still robbed and raped and murdered for all the old reasons, and the courts still tried most of them, but Overand felt his pleas and legal arguments were more and more beside the point. What good were depositions when all of this was about to be swept away?

Could no one else see that?

That year, as Christmas approached, Kirsten did everything she could. "If there is to be a war," she told everyone, "we might as well enjoy ourselves now." She started in November, instructing Fru Jennsen to pickle pears and beetroot. She persuaded the children to cut up strips of paper to make chains. She ordered a pike, and a goose, claret and brandy. She bought a portable Olivetti for Elda, a bicycle for Oskar. We are not poor, she told herself, again and again. Our life is not over. Norway is not at war with anyone. She bought her husband a watch the dealer said had once belonged to a minor Romanov, and ordered a waistcoat with a fob pocket for him to put it in. On Christmas Eve, when they opened their presents, he wore the waistcoat and slipped the watch into the pocket, but it was obvious he was not comfortable. He kissed Kirsten briefly, and offered to help Oskar adjust the saddle of his bicycle. Oskar pulled out the watch and weighed it seriously, still chained to his father's new waistcoat, in the palm of his hand.

"Is it gold, Pappa?"

"Yes."

"You already have a wristwatch."

Overand took it back and pocketed it again. "Your mother thought this would be . . . more special."

He had given Kirsten, who always said she never wanted anything, a pair of gloves.

On Christmas Day they ate goose and listened to the wireless. The King said the situation was bleak, but, with God's help and the continued efforts of his government, they would survive. Pray God, he said, there would be no war in their country.

"God!" Overand shouted. Then, in English, "Bugger God!"

Kirsten rose and switched off the radio.

Oskar did not understand, but Elda, whose English was already impressive, was delighted. She rolled a fresh sheet of paper into her new typewriter. Slowly, unevenly, with the thwack of the metal arms against the paper filling the room, she picked out the words: Bugger God, a Comedy, by Elda Overand.

The following day Overand rose early and left the house before breakfast. The National Defence Union had called a rally at the War Memorial. The trams were not running and he walked in his precise, flat-footed way to the city centre, buttoning his overcoat against the vicious cold. There seemed to be more people than usual in the dark, icy streets, and he allowed himself a brief sense of optimism, of unaccustomed fellowship. When he arrived at the monument, however, he was surprised to find only a few score of people gathered doubtfully around it. Half of them seemed to be holding back, suggesting through their posture, through the lightness of their gestures and conversation, that they were merely curious, pausing to observe events and prepared, at any moment, to wander on if what they heard proved insufficiently amusing. The mood hardened, however, when a phalanx of young men in khaki shirts lined up in front of the makeshift platform and a handful of speakers demanded that the King do more than pray, that he make treaties with one nation or another, that he instruct the generals to arm the people, to create militias for their defence. When the organizers passed through the small crowd with buckets, Overand threw in his new gold watch.

At the first signs of spring, Kirsten suggested a holiday. Overand did not refuse, exactly. He simply did not answer, just closed his eyes and blew air sharply through his teeth.

Kirsten persisted. "We could go to the coast."

Overand said he had cases to attend to.

"You have assistants."

He said the National Defence Union was planning an Easter demonstration.

"You don't have to be there."

"I'm on the organizing committee."

This was news to Kirsten, although hardly a surprise. The new-fledged party would naturally have been quick to identify and exploit her husband's abilities. She sighed. They faced each other across the dinner table, the children upstairs, the dessert plates and wine glasses not yet cleared away. She leaned her elbows on the table, and, as she did so, heard her mother's admonition: she always was a willful child, her mother's voice said, and she took strength from that. She always had. She pressed her hands together and rested her chin on them.

"I'm going, Aleks. I'll take the children."

"And I will join you. After Easter."

They would not discuss the matter again.

§

ON THE 9TH of April, 2003, the day US troops entered central Baghdad, Holly woke to her fortieth birthday alone. Parsed by the wooden blinds, late winter sunshine sliced viciously across the vacant expanse of bed where Martin should have been. Her head had been hollowed out in the night, stuffed with newspaper and old socks. She rolled over, pushing her face into the duvet. Martin's half still bore his faint warm ghost. Without looking at the clock on the bedside table she could tell – she would like to have thought from the angle of the sunbeams across the bed, but really just from the state of her hangover – that it was too early for Martin to have left for work. He would be in the kitchen, padding around in bare feet, making breakfast, making a cup of tea, at least. She listened cautiously for the familiar domestic sounds, for running taps and clicking mugs, Martin trumpet-farting without restraint, supposing himself alone. But she heard nothing and must have imagined that he was already upstairs, at his desk. How could he? He'd had at least as much as her to drink.

She rolled from the bed with a grunt, pulled her dressing gown around her and, with one hand supporting her head, the other brushing the wall to steady her progress, she shuffle-stepped her way up to the attic, where, on her side of the desk, in front of her PC, she found a parcel, about the size and shape of a shoe box, perhaps a little wider, wrapped in offensively cheerful red-and-white striped paper. The words

"Happy Birthday" and the silhouettes of balloons were printed in red on the white stripes, and in white on the red. She contemplated it suspiciously. This was not how birthdays worked. On birthdays they brought each other's presents to the bed, sometimes with a Bloody Mary, more recently with tea. She pulled the parcel towards her. It was lighter than she'd expected. She opened it and found a typewritten note that said: *When I ask what you want, you say "Nothing."*

§

BEFORE THIS GENERATION, before Elda and Oskar, the Overands had all grown up in a small port town where for a thousand years men had built boats and landed fish. Aleks' father descended from a line of fishermen and sailors that stretched further back than anyone could remember, or see any point in remembering. When the past was no different from the present, what did it matter? At the cost of family rifts that never healed, however, Aleks' father chose to stay on land, and set up as a chandler. He kept a boat, though – a stubby, ugly fishing boat that differed from the others in the harbour only in that it did not stink and the decks were not slippery with fish oil – and laughed whenever his wife suggested he might prefer a yacht.

"This is a real boat," he told the young Aleks over soft diesel thudding as they slid past the harbour bar on quiet Sunday mornings and felt the swell rise. "Your mother wouldn't understand."

Aleks understood. He was sure of it.

He learned to sail, to read the weather and the tide, to strip and rebuild the engine. He liked it best when the sky was overcast, the water sleek, solid, the colour of the herring it bred. For a while the sea was real, everything else an interruption. But, unlike his father, he was small, clever but never strong. When he read the books a trusted schoolteacher encouraged him to try he quickly learned to see his father differently. Ibsen, of course. Hamsun. Kierkegaard.

Now, he thought, *now* he understood. Better than his mother, better than anyone.

Now he saw the bad faith, the inauthenticity, of keeping a fishing boat that never landed fish, the guilt of the newly rich. Comfortable, his mother said; and when she died, unexpectedly, at forty-two, Aleks came home from university and clashed with his father at the funeral. He returned to his studies, determined not to be held back by petty-minded shame about his own success.

He established a practice in the capital, opening an office with distinctive bravado on Møllergata, within spitting distance of the police headquarters. He secured his reputation by defending the beautiful young mistress of a famous writer who had been accused – by the writer, by the press and subsequently by the police – of murdering the writer's wife in a misplaced bid to preserve his waning affections. The defence concocted by the young, unlikely-looking lawyer not only satisfied the jury of her innocence, but raised serious doubts about that of the writer himself. When the case returned to court the following year, Overand had already wooed and married the former mistress, Kirsten. He promptly changed clients and secured the acquittal of the writer, too, convincing a second jury that the victim had, after all, taken her own life in an access of ennui. He remained on friendly terms with the writer – it was a talent he was conscious he possessed – and built upon the connection to good effect, meeting many other writers, artists, scholars and journalists. He became known as a lawyer with opinions on matters outside the law. Once he could afford it, he moved into the house on Inkognito gate: he could not resist the address, he said, or the location just behind the Palace. People who had professed themselves unable to understand what Kirsten could possibly see in this peculiar – some even said ugly – little man, began to understand. He was charming, they said, he was nobody's fool. There was a spark about him that you wouldn't expect, but which, in his presence, was unmistakable. Life with Overand, they said, would at least not be boring. And there was no sin greater than that of tedium.

Business was brisk.

When his father died, Aleks' life was in Oslo. He could have sold the chandlery on the quayside along with the apartment above it; he could have sold the boat; but he was wealthier than his father had ever been and did not need the money. When children came along, he told Kirsten, it would be good for them.

It was. Elda and Oskar spent their holidays exploring the mountains and the rocky coastline. They played shops at a real counter with a brass bell that clanged loudly when you hit the button on top. When the courts closed for the summer, their father drove out to join them in the English motor car he'd bought with a roof that folded down and a chrome rack on the boot to which he tied his small leather suitcase. Together they would drop mackerel lines from the back of the blunt-nosed tub their farfar had always called a real boat. They'd never met their grandfather, and Elda asked endless questions about his life, about the business he had run and its ghosts, which surrounded them every day; her father's answers were as brief and vague as he could contrive, until, eventually, unwilling to concede defeat, Elda took to making them up for herself. Oskar loved the rocks, the salt air, the suck of the sea as the waves retreated, the weight of endless skies over the water. He loved being out on the boat with his father, loved sliding just far enough around the curve of the world to lose sight of land; he loved to think they might never go back. But his father somehow always managed to have them home in time for dinner; and after dinner he would go downstairs to work, using the old shop counter as a desk, surrounded by the cleats and lines and rotted canvas sails he never cleared out.

As the children grew, Overand spent less and less time at the coast and, when he was there, less and less time on the sea. It was not just that he was busy – he *was* busy: there was no shortage of work, and, as his practice grew, he became increasingly embroiled in managing a staff and a business in addition to representing his clients – but rather that there seemed to be less and less point in doing anything else. The bright start he'd made in the salons of Oslo had settled into ritual, emptied of meaning, the same faces mouthing the same anecdotes, arguing the same issues, their lines as predictable as the liturgy; only the cocktails changed. Overand still held opinions – he was not quite as far gone as some of his acquaintance – but he came to regard even his own opinions as mere curiosities, objects he could turn over in his hands and hold up to the light for admiration, bearing no practical value or application in the world. He could no longer see why anyone else would take any interest in what he might have to say, and so said less and less. By 1939 he had long since given up writing the letters and essays that, earlier in his career, had made his name familiar well beyond the legal profession. And, as a result, he spent less time, not more, with his family; more time, not less, with his work, with his accounts and with Herr

Prytt, the junior partner who was, in fact, rather older than he.

Then came the Finnish war, and his opinions mattered again, if only to himself. After that, the German war with France, with Poland, with Britain, and what he thought and said - changing what others thought and said - became of paramount importance to Aleks Overand.

§

I T WAS A Wednesday, but she was not at work, and now
had nothing else to do.

She wouldn't have chosen to take the day off, if she'd had
any choice in the matter. Being forty was no different from any
other day. It was not a milestone in any sense that mattered.
But lately she'd been working a great deal of overtime and
Walter - who despite being her boss, and a man, was basically
all right, even if he was called Walter and had a strip of facial
hair no wider than a cigarette running vertically down his
chin from his lower lip, just a millimetre or two off-centre, a
strip that, once noticed, drew the eye unwillingly, like some
terrible disfigurement, but all the more powerfully for being,
in a sense, *voluntary*, there being no need for such facial hair
at all, she'd told Martin, much less for such asymmetry, and
was therefore impossible to ignore, no matter how hard she
or her colleagues tried - Walter had told her there was no
more money in the project budget for overtime and would she
mind taking time off in lieu instead? Not that he was actually
asking. Think of it as my gift to you, he said, smiling.

Happy Birthday.

She made tea and burned toast.

When the postman came he brought a card from her
brother she could see at once had been chosen by Alice. She
knew her father's card would have been delivered a couple of
days ago. Martin would have hidden it away to bring out this

morning, but now Martin wasn't there and she didn't know where he'd put it.

There would not have been a card from her mother, obviously.

She'd have a bath, a long bath. She would read one of the small crate of books her father refused to take with him to Scotland because, he said, they were all books she really should have read by now. She would walk across the Green into town: it really was a perfect morning for a stroll, she told herself, clear and bright and just warm enough. She would treat herself to lunch somewhere moderately expensive. There was an exhibition at the Fitzwilliam for which she had seen countless posters – or the same poster countless times, perhaps – but which she had nonetheless assumed she would never visit. Well, now she would. Walter had done her a favour; he was basically all right.

Martin had done her a favour, too. When she returned, he would also have returned from wherever it was that he had gone so early. He would be bearing whatever gift it was that he'd really bought for her birthday, which must have required collecting at some ridiculously early hour, in order to return, in time, to wish her a happy birthday; plus, in all likelihood, he would have a bottle of champagne (another bottle: they'd drunk the first, together, in anticipation of her birthday, before she'd drunk the whisky) along with something frivolous and expensive, something fashioned out of sterling silver and semi-precious stones, or even precious stones, and there would be a reason for all this.

The restaurant had a sheltered courtyard that was just warm enough to sit in, now that it was spring. The food was only moderately preposterous and the wine adequate, but she felt the eyes of the waiter and the other diners upon her, a woman eating alone, her father's *Tristram Shandy* weighed flat against the table with the salt and pepper mills, the half bottle empty before she'd finished her main course. She skipped dessert, asked for coffee and the bill. She left a substantial tip.

The exhibition was interesting, but no more. After forty minutes she had seen it all and became conscious of the other visitors, their whispered conversations, their clothes, their ages, and of the sound of her own heels on the wooden floors.

She left and went shopping instead. She tried on a pair of earrings, but did not buy them. She spent an hour in a bookshop, but found nothing she wanted to read she did not already own. She bought a cheap box set of Mahler symphonies. Martin had never liked Mahler.

She walked home with the gnawing sense that she had wasted the unasked-for gift of a day off. She had been free to do anything she chose, and couldn't help feeling all her choices had turned out wrong.

When she got back, Martin was not there. She watched the TV news without him, watched without his commentary as a concrete statue of Saddam refused to topple properly, the steel rods in his legs bending, not breaking, leaving the dictator leaning improbably horizontal from the top of his plinth, one outstretched arm pointing straight at the ground.

Martin did not return that night, and was not there the following morning. In the bed, the warm ghost cooled.

§

THE SNOW HAD begun to melt early in the spring of 1940 when Kirsten wrote to the children's schools. She apologized for the trouble she might be causing: as a rule, she did not approve of taking pupils out of school during term. However, for "family reasons", they would be away until after Easter. Elda and Oskar were both doing well with their studies, and she would see that they kept up their reading; no great harm would come of the break, which was, she wrote, unavoidable.

She directed trunks to be packed with clothes and books and toys. Elda would not allow her mother to pack the typewriter or her blue notebook: she would carry them with her on the train. Oskar's bicycle could go in the guard's van, he said; he would ride it from the station while his mother and Elda took a taxi and someone – probably the man who fixed things and painted the windows – brought the trunks on by cart. Fru Jennsen telegraphed ahead to make sure there would be a taxi, and a cart.

Overand barely noticed the preparations. Kirsten was right, he thought: his assistants could handle most of his cases. At this moment the National Defence Union was more important – nothing, in fact, could be more important. There was the Easter demonstration to handle, of course. But there was also the King, who had agreed in principle to meet a delegation from the Union to discuss the demand for national mobilization. Overand had been chosen as one of the delegates. For the first time in several years he knew precisely what he wanted to be doing, where he wanted to be, and it was not skulking about the coast *for family reasons*.

When it first become apparent that his father was seriously ill, before the children were born, they had installed a telephone he never used. Now, each Sunday evening, Overand rang the house on the coast. Oskar told him about the weather, the high spring tides, the ships - not fishing boats, real ships, he said: British battleships - that moored outside the harbour, and about the mines they left behind. Elda barely spoke, leaving Overand mouthing inanities into the mouthpiece. Was she having a nice time? What had they eaten for dinner? After a while, he gave up trying. Kirsten asked when he might be able to join them. Then she, too, stopped trying. Overand would hang up and pour himself a glass of vodka. Each Monday he woke early, looking forward to the week ahead.

Like the thaw, Easter came early that year. At the demonstration there were clashes with the police, a number of arrests. Overand secured the demonstrators' release, and wrote about it for the Union's newspaper. But the King's advisors and the Ministry of Defence dragged their feet, politely contesting the points that could be raised should the delegation take place; they still had not agreed a date, and Overand stayed on in the capital. What choice did he have? Kirsten would just have to understand. And if she didn't? It scarcely mattered. Securing the peace - that was what mattered.

He was still in the capital, two weeks after Easter, when the first bombs fell. It was about four-thirty on a Tuesday morning, the 9th of April. Overand woke at the noise, but soon went back to sleep. By daybreak the capital was full of foreign troops installing checkpoints and requisitioning government buildings. The maid, who slept in a small room under the eaves, and had been awake since the first explosions, told him the news; Fru Jennsen had not yet arrived.

Overand dressed quickly and made his way towards the office of the NDU. It was a clear, bright morning; spring softened the air. There was blossom on the trees he had not noticed before. At an alley off Akersgata, he turned a corner and found the road blocked by a tank. Its driver had misjudged a bend in the narrow stone street and the tank was wedged in, inching and grinding slowly back and forth as he tried to work it free, to the cheers and laughter of his comrades, which Overand could barely hear over the screech of metal scraping granite; the tank itself and the surrounding street were strewn with dust and chunks of masonry gouged from the walls. He doubled back. There were soldiers in grey uniforms every-where, but they seemed occupied about their own business. He was not stopped and no one asked where he was going.

At the Union office he found a fellow member he knew only by sight. The man was big, with broad, coarse features and a suit that was too tight; he looked like a plain-clothed policeman. He was emptying the filing cabinets, carrying armfuls of paper out into the little courtyard behind the office, where a second man – an altogether more dapper individual in a double-breasted blazer and co-respondent shoes – was patiently, methodically, feeding pages into a makeshift brazier.

They told him he should leave, get out of the capital if he could.

"What about the delegation? The King?"

They laughed, the big man tipping back his head and

43

braying like a donkey. The King had fled, the smaller man said. He and the whole Government had slipped away in the night and were probably on their way to England even as he spoke.

Overand glanced around the courtyard, nodded towards the burning papers. "And the Leader?"

The two men exchanged glances. The man in the blazer nodded. The big man said, "Our Leader" – he paused just long enough to qualify the word – "is paying his respects to the commissioner. He is offering our assistance."

Overand said, "Is that wise?"

The small man said, "He believes so."

There was a pause during which they fed more paper into the flames.

Overand said, "Can I help?"

The two men looked at each other again.

"Do you have anywhere to go?"

He told them about the house on the coast, about the boat. They said he should go there as soon as he could, and wait.

They told him they might need his help.

He told them about the telephone; they said he should not try to ring them.

They said somebody would be in touch.

§

WALTER WAS NOT all right at all.
He had stupid facial hair and he was a cunt.

That was what she told him on the morning of Thursday, April 10th in his office that had a window overlooking the quad and smelled of soap.

It was raining; the wind had shifted during the night and now declared that winter wasn't giving up without a fight. She had wrapped herself in a long woollen coat and returned to work unusually eager to get stuck in to the backlog of Sisyphean tasks that had piled up during her recent focus on the digital media project, and the subsequent day off she had been forced to take – and had wasted; she was unusually keen to get back in control. Which made it all the more difficult to respond with any measure of restraint or professionalism when Walter called her onto his tiny – but, now that she thought about it, suspiciously *tidy* – office, and, with his back to the view of the oak tree almost as old as the college itself, told her that, as she knew, the budget situation was difficult and they had overrun the end of the financial year with no additional resources allocated; that, while she was away yesterday, the Departmental Management Team had met and, reluctantly, concluded they could no longer afford to retain two archivists and had no choice but to make her post redundant; that he knew there was never a good time for bad news, but he wanted her to hear it from him, personally, as soon as possible;

and that he *understood* – he understood this would be very difficult and traumatic for her. None of this was about *her*, he said: it was the *post* that was redundant, and the decision in no way reflected any criticism of her performance, her attitude or her contribution to the team. He would be happy to write her a very positive reference. Holly, for her part, suspected that he knew nothing at all about just how fucking difficult and traumatic this was for her, and said so. He said he understood – which was when she called him a cunt.

It was a word she had not used aloud in almost twenty years – not since, as a student in the same university where she now suddenly no longer worked, she'd engaged in heated debates about whether to re-appropriate sexist language or to police it out of existence: on the whole, she had favoured the latter, the re-appropriation route being adopted mostly by women she found, frankly, rather tiring – and she was as surprised as Walter himself to hear it bursting from her mouth. She had not *chosen* to call Walter a cunt; she had simply done so. And whilst a small part of her brain screamed that it was not appropriate, that she would regret, if nothing else, the loss of moral high ground, of the opportunity to look back with satisfaction at the dignity and poise with which she had handled a difficult situation, that small part was drowned out by the righteous roar of indignation, the certainty that, without in any way reflecting any negative, self-hating or culturally hegemonic views she might hold about vaginas in general, or her own vagina in particular, the word captured with a precision for which there was no adequate substitute the sheer, inexcusable *loathsomeness* of Walter, of his facial hair and his unnaturally tidy, soap-scented office, of his hideous lapse into undigested management bullshit and his wholly misconceived claims to understand how she might feel about anything at all, much less about the fact that he had comprehensively fucked her over and was now so lacking in shame or basic human decency as to offer her his *sympathy*. Remorse would come, of course, but at that moment there was no doubt whatsoever that Walter was a cunt.

He told her to go home again, she was clearly too upset to work, and for a moment she wondered if she was also going to have to hit him with something hard and heavy: the telephone on his desk, perhaps; or a car. He understood (the cunt). The overall savings package, of which Holly's post was one small part, still had to be consulted upon, and agreed by the university council – although they both knew that was something of a formality – and she would be given two months' notice. But right now, he knew, it was all something of a shock, and she should definitely go home. She should take the rest of the week off. He would see her on Monday. They would talk then.

She said nothing more. Without agreeing or disagreeing, without another word, she turned her back on Walter and walked out of his office. Without a word, she picked up her bag, slung it across her shoulder and headed for the stairs. On the way, she bumped into James, the other archivist who still worked at the library and whose post, apparently, was not redundant.

"Holly?"

She knew, even if James *was* younger, and a man, and still had a job, that none of this was actually his fault.

"What's going on?"

It wasn't James' fault, but that didn't mean she could talk to him. Or that she had to. She turned to see Walter standing in his office doorway, sadly shaking his head, his furry chin strip waving from side to side as if wishing her farewell.

She kept going. Out and down the stairs, out into the quadrangle, past the oak tree beneath which opiate-riddled poets and natural philosophers of vast repute had changed the world for ever; past the surly porters; past the tangled undergrowth of bicycles and out into the street, which the morning's rain had left slick and cold and as nearly empty as a street in this tiny crowded city ever could be at nine o'clock on a weekday morning out of term time.

Which was pretty fucking empty, to her eye.

Nine o'clock.

It was nine o'clock in the morning and she had another whole day free in which to do whatever she chose. Another day? It was worse than that. Far worse. She had two days – Thursday and Friday, and then the weekend, and then the weekend after that was Easter, Good Friday and Easter Monday making it another four-day weekend and anyway, what did weekends matter now? She was forty years old. She had thirty, forty, fifty more years of this, this *freedom*.

She had left her coat behind.

Fuck the coat. It was nine o'clock and she wanted a drink.

She did not want a drink.

This was an opportunity, a chance to sort herself out. She had never really wanted to be an archivist, never really liked the job, never really chosen it. It had happened to her. She had never really chosen Martin, either. Her life had simply happened. She had been stuck in a rut; she needed a change. Getting dumped and getting fired were the best things that could possibly have happened to her. All was for the best in the best of all possible worlds.

48

This was the first day of the rest of her life.

She winced.

She had reached her tolerance limit for self-deluding happy talk.

She wanted a drink.

She turned off the street into a shopping centre, bright with false daylight. It was by no means empty, but it was quiet. Those who would pass through on their way to work had passed through; many of the shops were not yet open. Apparently no one bought shoes at this time of day. Or expensive chocolate. But they did place bets, and drink coffee. She found the sort of café Martin always objected to politically and ordered a moderately enormous coffee with an extra shot of coffee in it and no chocolate – because she was not a child – and the largest pastry she could see, because she nonetheless craved sugar.

Of all of the lies she'd just told herself, the least untrue was that she'd never chosen the job. She'd been an archivist for twenty years – longer than James, far longer than Walter – and that, she knew, was a form of choice in itself. But she'd never actually decided that preserving books and manuscripts would be her life's work.

She carried her coffee and pastry over to a table at the back of the café, where it could have been midnight, or four in the afternoon, but there were plenty of the deep leather armchairs free. They were never quite as comfortable as they looked, but still. She felt like hunkering down.

She had fallen into the job with no destination in mind. At college, the librarian had regarded her as some sort of project, like a bird with a broken wing. When an economist friend of Harold Wilson who'd been at Bretton Woods died, and bequeathed them his effects, the librarian offered her a temporary job. She'd accepted, in the absence of anything else, and spent the summer after finals – when she wasn't out with Martin, collecting for the NUM – in a windowless basement cracking open tea chest after tea chest, transcribing onto index cards the title, author, publisher and date of countless dirty, dusty books, journals and manuscripts, many in languages she could not read, or even recognize. When the new term started, she had nowhere else to be, and stayed on, sticking magnetic security strips down the spines of countless books. Three months later an eminent historian had died, followed by a philosopher. In the years that followed she had qualified, specialized, changed libraries, changed back, but none of these moves had arisen from any plan, or even any tangible intention on her part; rather, they'd all been the result of a push, a shove – sometimes gentle, sometimes not – from someone else.

And now she'd been shoved out.

She watched a man at the counter waiting for his drink. He wore a bright blue raincoat, of the sort designed for walking up mountains, over a suit. He had a large black brief-case-cum-laptop bag hanging from one shoulder by a long, padded strap. She knew without looking that his shoes would be well polished, and have rubber soles.

No one ever knew what they wanted to do, and just did it. Did they?

Her father had wanted to be a lawyer, and had been a lawyer.

And Ben. Ben had wanted to be an accountant. He was sixteen when he first said he would put his financial skills at the service of the public. Sixteen. None of them – Ben included – ever quite knew how he'd come by this revelation. Now he told people he earned a "six-figure salary" – much less, he would add, than he'd get in the private sector – as Finance Director for one of the London Boroughs, though Holly could never quite remember which.

Was it a male facility, then, this ability to tune in to the wavelength of vocation? Or at least to admit of no doubt?

Her mother had had no ambition, as far as Holly knew. Now she simply wanted to stay alive. Perhaps that was all it took? She'd made quite clear that cancer was a challenge she was dealing with: health was a matter of conviction, dying an admission of failure.

Holly sipped her coffee. This was *her* day to feel sorry for herself. She uncurled a length of pastry and put it in her mouth. It tasted like cardboard steeped in lard.

Martin had never known what he wanted from life, either.

The man with the rubber-soled shoes squeaked across the polished floor towards her. He bent down to put his cup on the low table, his laptop bag swinging forward clumsily, and gestured towards the armchair opposite hers.

"Do you mind?"

For once, she did. There were plenty of other, empty, tables. But she said nothing. He sat down and shrugged out of his raincoat. He had thin, greasy hair that seemed to grow from his neck as well as his head. His shirt had been ironed so often and so brutally that the outline of the collar stiffeners showed like tidemarks on an oily beach. He said, "Do you like this place?" She didn't answer, and he said, "Only, I think I've seen you here before." She found it hard to believe that he would actually say that. Had he read it somewhere?

She'd been dumped and sacked and she wanted to kill

somebody, or at least cause someone – someone male, for preference – a great deal of pain, or failing that at least to have a drink. Instead she had coffee and this . . .

She said, "If you say another word, I'll scream 'rape'."

They both looked around the quiet coffee shop. She said, more quietly, "I'll tell the staff you exposed yourself."

He opened his mouth, but she said, "I mean it."

He stood, and took his coffee to another table.

She called out: "You've forgotten your coat."

He came back to pick it up and mumbled something that might have been "thank you".

She finished her coffee, but couldn't stomach the rest of the pastry. She should probably ring somebody. Someone who wouldn't pretend to understand and wouldn't take offence.

Martin?

She couldn't call Martin.

Her father?

Not now. Not today. She was forty years old. Her father couldn't be the first person she rang. That would be too pathetic.

Who, then?

Alice.

The idea was so unlikely that it made her smile. And from the smile it was a short step to the thought: why not? She'd call up Alice and they'd have that heart-to-heart she'd often said they ought to have, one day, but had never really meant, or expected to happen, and she'd find there was more to Alice than met the eye, and Alice would find that Holly didn't despise her just because she read the *Mail*, and they could be friends. They'd have lunch, and a glass or two of wine with lunch, and that afternoon Holly would help collect the girls from school and take them to the park – no, it was raining, and cold – she'd make them hot chocolate and help them with their homework, and play games; by the time Ben came home from work she and Alice would have had a couple of early evening gins and would share a joke Ben wouldn't get and he'd be peeved and Holly could tease him a bit before saying, lightly, that she'd just got the sack. He would be horrified, but Alice would say, "You don't care, do you Holly?" Alice would say it was the best thing that had ever happened to her, and Holly would sip her gin and agree and watch her brother's eyes as he stared at his wife and wondered if she had somehow lost her mind since breakfast.

She'd do it. She'd call Alice.

She didn't call Alice.

She didn't want to call Alice.

What she wanted was a drink.

It was the middle of the afternoon when she got home from the pub. She ate nothing, read nothing, listened to none of her new Mahler CDs and did not turn on the television. She did not hear Donald Rumsfeld declaring that, while the war was certainly not over, the degree of success so far was "nothing short of spectacular". She did, however, have another drink, a gin so stiff there was barely any room for ice, much less tonic, and then another. She finished the gin and moved onto the wine left over from the night before her birthday, when Martin was still there, before he left. The telephone rang. She picked it up just as the answerphone kicked in. Over the sound of her own voice saying she was sorry she was out, she heard her father say:

"Happy Birthday."

"It was yesterday, Dad."

"Was it? Sorry. Did you get my card?"

"Yes." She did not feel like explaining. "Thank you."

After a while, he said, "Forty, eh? Did you have a good day?"

She took a deep breath, a mouthful of wine. She swallowed and said, "Dad, could I come up to see you?"

"Of course, sweetheart. When did you have in mind?"

"Tomorrow?"

§

OVERAND RETURNED HOME by the back streets, pressing into doorways to avoid armoured cars and squads of infantrymen. He picked his way past men – fellow citizens – hauling furniture out into the street and lashing it purposefully to wooden barrows or the roofs of cars. He saw families carrying suitcases towards the railway station, the children excited, or apprehensive, their parents not meeting his eyes. He saw poorer families filing into the city from the south and the east, carrying little, some of them injured and supporting each other. He heard, through an open window on Kristian IVs gate, a woman's voice, quite loud and very clear, saying: "And do what?" He saw young men, alone or in knots of two or three, standing at corners, in alleyways, smoking, calculating, watching people pass.

The house was empty. The maid had left a note listing three of his colleagues who had called, and explaining that she had gone to look for the housekeeper, who had still not arrived for work. Overand knew Fru Jennsen was a widow – her husband had survived the previous war, but died of influenza shortly afterwards. If he had been pressed, he would have guessed that she was in her early fifties. She lived with her sister in an apartment in a neighbouring district, but he'd had no call to know the address.

The long case clock in the hall ground out the third quarter. He was surprised to realize it was not yet ten o'clock. He hung up his hat and rang his own office. Nobody answered. He called his junior partner, at home. He was pleased to hear that Fru Prytt and the children were safe. The office would remain closed today, of course. He would be grateful if Herr Prytt would contact the members of the staff to let them know.

"And tomorrow, Herr Overand?"

Tomorrow they would see.

He went up to his bedroom, took off his jacket and hung it on a peg on the back of the door. He unbuttoned his waistcoat; then he sat on the bed to unlace his shoes. He lay down and closed his eyes, but the light was bright in the room and he was not tired. He opened his eyes again, and felt more comfortable. He studied the ceiling, noticing that the paint had clogged and softened the outlines of the plaster mouldings, and, at last, faced the question that had been hovering at the periphery of his mind. The woman's voice floated back to him: *And do what?*

He had been asked – ordered, really; that was how it felt – to leave the city. But was there nothing he could do here? Nothing he *should* do?

He heard troops and machinery on the street outside, heard his neighbours shouting, banging trunks into the staircase walls, apparently preparing to join the exodus. He heard, from some way off, the arhythmic stutter of small arms fire. A burst of noise – six? seven shots? – followed by silence, then three or four more. Was there resistance after all? Or merely celebration?

Which would he prefer?

He was still on the bed when the maid returned. He must have fallen asleep – despite the light, despite the noise – for it was now early afternoon. He sat up and put on his shoes, went down to the hall. Oslo was full of soldiers. Norway had been occupied, and his reaction was – to sleep?

The girl said she was sorry she had been out so long. Fru Jennsen's sister said she had left that morning as usual. But she had never arrived.

Overand reassured her that he was not cross.

"But Fru Jennsen, sir?"

"Yes?"

"I've been to all the hospitals I could think of. I went to the police station. They laughed. They said they had other fish to fry."

Overand smiled. "I'm sure they have."

"They said I could try the barracks, sir. Said *they* might know. But I didn't dare, sir. So I came back, hoping she'd be here. But she isn't, is she, Herr Overand?"

Overand realized that his waistcoat was still unbuttoned. He strained for the girl's name, but it would not come. "Fru Jennsen is either dead or she is alive. Either way," – it came, at last – "either way, Abi, I can't imagine she would be of particular interest to our new friends."

(He was sure – fairly sure – that he had heard Kirsten call the girl Abi.)

She looked up, saw him fastening his waistcoat. "Friends, sir?"

"I choose my words carefully, Abi. I suggest you do the same."

She looked at the floor.

He tugged the points of his waistcoat taut with both hands, then patted his stomach. He had slept through lunch. "Is there any food in the house?"

§

S HE WAS STILL there three months later when Dr.
David Kelly took a non-fatal overdose of painkillers and
slit his left wrist. And when her father died.

Those three months had not been altogether easy, although
they had started well enough. When she arrived at Inverness,
her father had been happy to meet her in the ancient Land
Rover he'd justified to himself now that he lived half a mile
up an unmade road. He drove her across to the west coast,
to his new, last home, as he called it, playing host along the
way. The journey was noisy, slow and cold – the Land Rover
was of the old school, its windows leaked, the seats were hard
and the vibrations jarred her bones like some vicious, palsied
chiropractor. She wondered how much use it would be in the
winter. But her father was too busy naming mountains, shouting out to her the ones he'd already climbed, the ones he was
saving for the summer, to notice her discomfort. The road was
a sleek grey vein threading through the muted purple moor;
she could not believe how empty it all was. Here and there
mercury lochs punctured the scoured landscape like polished
armour glimpsed through spear holes in a muddy, bloodied
tunic. The view stretched for fifty miles, a hundred: apart
from the road itself, she could see no trace of humanity at all.
Then the road turned and dropped. Great grey mountainsides
and granite screes hemmed her in, filling her vision, stopping
her breath. She was frightened, then exhilarated. At the head

of a deep glen her father pulled off the road. They sat side-by-side listening to the cooling engine tick.

"Doesn't it scare you?"

He turned from the windscreen to look at her. "Should it?"

"You've always lived in a city. To be this far from any sign of human life . . ."

"It only looks this way because of people."

She stared out at the mountaintops. A hawk of some sort circled, its five-fingered wings black against the grey sky. She thought nowhere could be less human, less concerned with anything so petty as our lives and fears.

"There used to be people here, Holly. Hundreds would have lived in a valley like this. Until other people cleared them out. Look hard enough, you'll see the signs . . ."

She looked but could not imagine living there, couldn't imagine anything as soft as human flesh bearing the weight of those rocks. But people had, of course. She knew that. It was the story of the place.

Her father wrestled the Land Rover into gear and began the steep descent towards the valley floor. It began to rain. Water leaked through the perished rubber around a window vent and puddled at her feet. She spotted the ruins of a cottage, walls no higher than her waist, where a ewe and two lambs sheltered from the wind, their pale ghost faces staring mutely from the gap that would once have been a doorway. They reached a river and then a loch, passing more ruins but also, here and there, low small houses, with whitewashed walls and slate roofs tight against the weather. As they followed the lochside, the houses thickened, marshalling themselves into a village, a small town, with a pub and a post office. She said, "Is this it?" But her father shook his head.

"It's another hour, hour-and-a-half from here."

In an hour and a half she could have driven from Cambridge to his old house – the family house – in London, though she rarely had.

The rain had stopped by the time they arrived, replaced by sunlight washed through clouds. Her father's cottage was like the others, sharp-edged and monochrome with small, pinched windows like puncture wounds: it squatted the land but did not belong to it. A small garden had been harrowed from the hillside by sheer force of will – not her father's, she knew, some previous occupant. A rowan tree leaned hard to the east, away from the sea. Below – a good way below, but walkable, her father said, if she wanted to build up an appetite for breakfast – a small village sprawled along the banks of a sea loch that opened towards Skye and, beyond Skye, just visible now in the liquid light, the isle of Lewis.

He stood beside her, watching her taking in the view. "You see now?"

"Not really, Dad."

"No? Truly?"

She turned away, back towards the house. For a holiday, maybe. It made sense for a holiday. In the summer, it went without saying. Or at least in the spring, as the evenings started to lengthen. But as a place to live? A place to come to die?

He said, "It's your loss."

That evening, she unpacked the few things she'd brought with her and stowed them in the small pine wardrobe in the second bedroom. She put the books – her father's *Tristram Shandy* and a new one, *The Line of Beauty* – on the fragile-looking table beside the bed. She gave her father the bottle of whisky she'd packed.

"Like coals to Newcastle, I suppose."

He said it never hurt to have another.

In the morning the bottle was empty, but there'd been two of them drinking. That wasn't so bad. The house was empty, too. She kicked around, wondering why she'd come.

Her father returned at lunchtime. He'd climbed the hill behind the house. He said it cleared his head and reminded him, every time, why he'd moved. He'd thought she would prefer to sleep in, but recommended she try the hill that afternoon. He had a review to write.

"You're still working?"

She was surprised, perhaps a little hurt.

"Just odds and ends, you know? For Blackwell's, or the University Press."

When her father shut the door of the living room that she only now realized was also a study, she thought she might as well take his advice and go for a walk. Once outside, she decided the hills could wait. She would head down, into the village. Down would be easy enough, she thought, but she was wrong. Living in Cambridge for so long, she had forgotten what it was like, the strain in one's knees, in one's shins, the unaccustomed effort of walking steeply downhill.

At the village, she was relieved to reach level ground. She found a small shop and bought a newspaper, a bar of chocolate and, after a moment's hesitation, another bottle of whisky. She sat on a wooden jetty with her feet dangling over the water, her thin plastic grocery bag placed carefully beside her, watching birds she didn't recognize – they were too small to be gulls – wheel and dart across the loch. Every few seconds one would shrug a shoulder and plunge diagonally into the water, but they never brought anything back up that she could see.

When she was six and Ben not much more than a toddler they had found a dead crow on a beach, its black, irides-cent plumage and glass-eyed stare incongruous against the warm golden sand of – where had it been? Dorset, possibly, Cornwall. Or Wales. They'd spent a fortnight in a caravan in Pembrokeshire, once, the three of them. Her mother had stayed at home. She threw the corpse at Ben; it hit him full in the face. She'd been trying to make it fly, she told her father, who didn't believe her but didn't make much of it, either.

On the walk back up to the house she could feel the stretch of the hillside in her calves and thighs.

"Terns," her father said, when she described the birds she'd seen.

She said, "How do you know?"

He shrugged. "You can't mistake them."

"I mean, how do *you* know? You don't know the names of birds. What have you done with my real father?"

He looked pleased. "I've been here six weeks," he said. "It must rub off."

§

THERE WAS HALF a leg of lamb in the pantry, left over from the weekend. To the girl's obvious surprise – which Overand found he rather enjoyed – he suggested they eat together in the kitchen. "You must be hungry," he said, carving thick slabs of cold meat, which they ate with rye bread and pickles. "You've had a trying morning." He poured a glass of wine, and, after a moment's hesitation, offered it to the girl, but she declined, dropping her eyes to the backs of her hands as they lay in her lap.

He watched her across the table, offered her another slice of bread. She was young, perhaps twenty, and slim. A little flat-chested, Overand thought, but not unattractively so. Her hands seemed large, however, and the skin red. He said, "What are you going to do now?"

"What do you mean, Herr Overand?"

"I mean" – what did he mean? – "do you have any family?"

"There's my mother, sir. And my brother."

"Where do they live?"

"In Nordland. A small town north of Bodo."

Bodo itself was beyond the Arctic Circle. A southerner himself, and now a city-dweller, Overand found it hard to imagine anyone living still further north.

He said, "What about your father?"

"He volunteered, sir. Same as you. We haven't heard from him for nine months."

Overand put down his fork. Had the girl been here nine months ago? He wasn't sure, but thought on balance that she probably had. He said, "I'm sorry. I didn't know."

"No, sir."

There was a silence. Overand sipped his wine, replaced the glass on the bare wooden table, twisted it by the stem. "Perhaps you would be better off in Nordland. With your family."

"Are you giving me notice, sir?"

Overand looked up quickly. He hadn't meant that. But what else had he meant? He said, "I'll pay you, of course. A month's wages." He realized too late, when he looked up, that she had been smiling. Why was he so slow this afternoon? At his words, her smile collapsed.

"Or . . . you could come to the coast. It would be a bit of a squeeze in the apartment. You might have to sleep in the shop. But I am sure Kirsten would welcome the help."

"Are you going to the coast, then?"

Was he? Was that what he was going to do?

He said, "I imagine so."

Although there were no further disturbances, no repetition of the earlier gunfire, Overand spent much of that night awake, conscious for the first time of the width of the bed, the space where Kirsten slept, conscious that a young woman was sleeping, alone, in the attic room above his own.

When Hector Prytt telephoned for instructions the following morning, Overand observed that there seemed to be no reason to panic. The city had been quiet overnight, as far as he was aware. He instructed Prytt to open up the office as usual. He should accept no new clients, however, until the legal aspects of the current situation became clearer, and should seek to resolve current cases as expeditiously as possible. The staff was to be retained, at least for the time being.

"And you, sir?"

"I may have to go out to the coast, Prytt. For family reasons. You do understand?"

"Yes, Herr Overand."

§

A WEEK LATER - a week in which her father walked
alone in the mornings, and worked in the afternoons,
in which they passed each other at mealtimes and drank a
bottle of whisky or thereabouts each night without either of
them once mentioning Martin, or her job, really, other than
to say she no longer had one - it was obvious that her father
was becoming impatient with her presence. He switched off
Newsnight and asked what she was planning to do. To which
she had no more answer now than when she'd arrived, no more
than she'd ever had.

This was *his* retreat, his last home, even if he hadn't retreated quite as much as Holly had assumed. She couldn't blame
him for not wanting her there, cluttering the place up with
her own lack of future.

She said, "I suppose I'll get another job."

"You won't find one here."

"I didn't . . ."

"Not much call for archivists up here."

"No."

She stayed, all the same, because - because what else was
she going to do?

Then her father fell off a rock face he had no call to be
climbing at his age - at any age, she said - there was a perfectly
good path he could have used. He said that wasn't the point,
that wasn't why you climbed things, and she wondered again

what had happened to her real father. His leg was broken. It was a complex, nasty fracture – several fractures, in fact – and would have incapacitated anybody, but his age would extend and further complicate the process of recovery. So it was just as well she was there to help him around the house, wasn't it?

It was June, and never really dark, not even at midnight, a different sort of not really dark from the sodium gloom of cities she was used to. They ate meals together, in silence, mostly, other than the familiar voices of Radio 4. The news continued to wash over them. President Bush had declared "Mission Accomplished", though it wasn't; he'd told the world "We found the WMD", although there weren't any and they hadn't. A journalist had said the British Government knew its claims about weapons of mass destruction were over-egged, even when it published them, eight months earlier. Ben came to visit. The kids were in school, and Alice had to stay with them, so he came on his own. He'd flown to Glasgow and hired a car. It had taken all day.

"Christ, Dad," he said, after he'd unpacked his small suitcase, laying out his pants and socks and tee shirts in separate drawers, "I *started* in Glasgow. I didn't know it was possible to drive that far in Britain and not fall off the edge."

Then Holly and her father teased him a little and it was like it had always been, except her father's leg was in plaster and they were both a little drunk. Ben wasn't.

In the morning, once he'd set his father up with a pile of books and papers on a bench in the garden, Ben came to find her in the kitchen. He reminded her he'd always said this place was a mistake.

"That's right. You did, didn't you?"

"It's a good job you were here." Sarcasm had never been Ben's strong point.

She carried on washing plates, balancing them carefully on the rack to dry. Ben leaned against the draining board, holding a mug of coffee in both hands.

"If you hadn't . . . Are you going to stay? I mean, after his leg's better?"

One thing about Ben – having him press her to stay might make it easier for her to leave.

"I don't think so. He doesn't want me here."

Ben made a noise in the back of his throat. "He doesn't know what he wants."

"Yes he does, Ben. He's like you. He's always known."

Ben took that as a compliment. Not knowing was a sign of weakness, always.

He said, "So what are you going to do?"

"Find another job."

What else could she do? She had enough money to live on for a while, but eventually she'd have to earn more. Besides, drinking away her savings with her father wasn't exactly what she'd had in mind. Not that she'd had anything in mind. The cash had just silted up for lack of things to spend it on.

"In Cambridge?"

She thought about that for a moment, then shrugged. She didn't know.

Ben said, "What about Martin?"

There it was.

She said, "I think he's worked out what he wants."

"And it isn't you?"

She had finished the plates. She tipped up the plastic bowl and emptied out the greasy water. A slew of knives and spoons she had forgotten clattered against the stainless steel sink.

"Always subtle, Ben."

When he left, thirty-six hours later, her father relaxed, at first, but then, unable to walk, unable even to get out of the house without her help, he became impatient for his leg to heal.

§

OVERAND DID NOT leave, however, or not immediately. He checked the car, thinking that it might now
be difficult to obtain petrol, thinking already of the sharp
young men he had seen in the street; he found the tank was
almost full. He packed a suitcase. Kirsten had taken nothing
of his with her when she left, and there was far too much to
carry now. He scooped up shirts, some socks and underwear,
a couple of books that came easily to hand and strapped shut
the leather case with a belt. He carried it downstairs and
placed it in the hall.

He straightened up and a woman's voice, the voice he had
heard through an open window the previous morning – the
morning of the invasion: was it only yesterday? – came to
him, as clearly as if she were there in the hall: *And do what?*

Leaving the suitcase where it stood, he found another and
began the task all over again, more slowly: a dinner jacket, a
spare suit, six white shirts and collars. He put a pair of shoes
with built-up heels, stiff and heavy with the wooden trees
still inside them, into a velvet drawstring bag and slotted it
under the appropriate strap on the suitcase lid. He packed
an ingenious leather travelling case that had come from his
father's shop – it had been designed, he supposed, for life in a
captain's cabin – with hairbrushes, collar studs, cufflinks, tie
pins, razors, shaving brush and a bowl. He took the folding
alarm clock from his study, the silver letter knife and the

framed certificate that confirmed his right to address the country's higher courts. He packed them all carefully in the second suitcase, wrapping the certificate in a cotton hand towel. Then he carried it down and placed it beside the first, next to the hat-stand in the hall, where they would both stay, untouched, for six more days.

§

THERE FOLLOWED SEVERAL weeks of helping her father up and down the stairs, to the desk in the living room, to the garden bench and back - although helping a little less each day as he became increasingly proficient with his crutches - several weeks of walking down the steep path to the village, alone, for groceries whenever the milk, or the bread, or the whisky ran out - which was most days, because she couldn't carry much, not back up that path, no matter how often she did it and, besides, she had to do something with the time on her hands - until one July morning, when it had already been light for hours, she was woken by the sound of a car horn bleating over and over like a lamb lost on the hillside. Her head ached and was set not quite straight on her shoulders. Her throat was dry. She looked out of the window to see her father sitting in the passenger seat of the Land Rover, leaning over to press the horn. When he saw her at the window he shouted: "Drive me to the village!"

She dressed as rapidly as her morning head allowed and went outside. She rested her hand on the high roof of the Land Rover, spoke through the open passenger window. "I can't drive this thing, Dad."

"Course you can. It's not like you're going to meet anything coming the other way. Get in."

He slapped the seat beside him. It made a dull sound where the vinyl had split.

Reluctantly, she walked around and climbed into the driver's seat. She put her hands on the wide, hard wheel, looked down at the pedals. The accelerator was flat, clean and shiny, like a fish. The rubber on the brake had worn through on one side, exposing a steel skeleton.

"I can't."

"Yes, you can. It's like riding a bike."

"I live in Cambridge, Dad. Riding a bike is easy."

"Come on. We need more food."

She pushed at the clutch with her foot. It went down a long way before it hit the floor. It reminded her of the machines she'd once tried in the University gym and quickly given up.

"Come on."

By the time they reached the village and parked outside the shop, she had managed to get into second gear a couple of times. Her fingers and wrists and shoulders ached from grasping the steering wheel, there was a cold sheen of acidic sweat on her forehead, and she felt just a little proud of herself.

She reached over to the back seat to pick up her father's crutches. As she lifted them awkwardly, she hit his head. They were light, aluminium, and could not have hurt much, but he said, "Trying to bump me off, now?"

"That's right. I'm after the inheritance."

It was a lame joke, but didn't deserve the slow, painful silence in which her father let it die.

"Right," he said at last. "Let's stock up."

In the shop he chose breakfast cereal, chocolate, beer and whisky – a case of each. Holly bought bread, sausages, bacon, tinned tomatoes, pasta, coffee, tea, milk, rice, cheese, frozen peas and such fresh vegetables as she could find. He introduced her to the woman at the counter and Holly asked for all the ibuprofen and paracetamol they had. The woman said everyone thought he must have died, or gone back to England, which would be worse. She asked about his leg; he told her Holly had tried to club him to death with his own crutches. The woman laughed and said, "She'll be after the inheritance, Bill." They both seemed to find this very funny. Holly felt as if she were ten again, when her mother had talked about her to friends, or to people she met in queues, as if Holly were not there, and she'd had no choice but to stand and wait and hear whatever it was came into her mother's head. But her father had never been like that. She couldn't blame Scotland for the change, or small village life: she had come to the shop herself most days for several weeks now, and not shared this many words with anyone. Afterwards, when her mother finished talking and dragged her off towards another shop, another market stall, Holly would ask why she said things about her that weren't true, and her mother would say, "It's just a bit of fun, sweetheart. Nobody cares."

She loaded the groceries into the flat metal back of the Land Rover, and her father said it was time for lunch.

It was eleven o'clock.

He swung himself rapidly on his crutches towards the pub, and she followed. Inside, she found floral carpet, a bar panelled in pine and small, uncomfortable wooden seats. Some of the tables were round, with beaten copper surfaces; others were square and shone with the gloss of reproduction furniture. It looked like a 1970's teashop, Holly thought. It was not just the landscape that made this place another country.

There was a stag on the bitter pump. She ordered two pints, and carried them over to one of the larger, wooden tables. There was no food menu. Lunch was sandwiches, crisps or nuts. There was a glass case on the bar for pasties and meat pies, but it was empty. Holly said she'd have a cheese sandwich, and nuts.

"Salted or dry roasted?"

"Oh, the tyranny of choice!"

He laughed at that, at least.

She offered to order, but her father levered himself to his feet with more dexterity than she had seen in weeks. When he swung back from the bar – where he'd chatted to the barman about his leg, and to another drinker perched on a stool who spoke in an accent so thick she could not make out a word – he said: "There's no good you looking at me like that. I'm not moving."

"I didn't say a word."

He shook his head.

"But I still want to know what you've done with my real dad."

"He retired, Holly." He took a mouthful of his beer, swallowed slowly and screwed the glass back into the beer mat. "He made his peace with the world."

"All by himself?"

"What do you mean?"

"Your peace doesn't seem to involve the rest of us."

He looked down at the table. He picked up his glass again, swirled the beer in it until the bubbles rose, and took another mouthful. She was about to change the subject when he said: "Isn't that what peace means?"

After lunch he said he needed to walk. Or, at least, to hobble. He opened the back of the Land Rover and told her to get a bottle from the case.

"For a walk?"

"Round here, you never walk without it. Might be dangerous."

By planting both crutches well ahead and swinging himself between them, pivoting on his solid plaster leg and winging both crutches forward again, like a lolloping clockwork toy, he could now, on the level at least, cover the ground faster than she could walk. He headed out of the village, Holly trailing behind. But he could not keep it up for long. He cut off the road, negotiating the smooth rocks, and headed out towards the jetty where, on her first morning, she had watched the seabirds whose name she hadn't known. He let one crutch fall, lowered himself carefully with the other, his broken leg held awkwardly out before him, until he was close enough to drop safely to the weathered planks. When she caught up he said, "That'll be enough for today." She placed the bottle next to him and walked slowly to the end of the jetty. The water looked grey, still, solid – as if she could keep walking straight out across it.

§

THE MAID WAS watching him, when he brought down the second case. He realized she was not wearing her uniform. Instead, she had on a simple grey dress that hung to her knees, cinched at the waist with a broad black belt. Without her cap, he noticed that her hair was cut short and styled in waves close to her head like Kirsten's, although the maid's hair was black, where his wife's was blonde. The girl's mouth was sharply drawn in dark lipstick.

As he straightened up a second time, she said, "Are we leaving now, sir?"

We?

He had said she might come with him to the coast.

And do what?

He said, "Perhaps we should look again for Fru Jennsen?"

She said something quietly that he did not catch.

He said, "Do you want me to?"

He took a step towards her. In heels she was perhaps five centimetres taller than he.

He said, "It might not be safe. Asking questions, I mean. And she may have her reasons . . ."

He said, "If we're going to leave we might as well eat something first. There's still a little of that lamb."

This time she accepted the wine. Her lipstick left marks on the glass.

The man at the NDU – the small man, he thought, though

he himself was shorter – had ordered him to go to the coast.

And do what?

And wait.

Someone would be in touch, he had said.

When they finished eating, Abi stood and walked around the table towards him, her heels clicking slowly on the wooden floor.

§

"I'M SORRY," HER father said, and it was so unex-
pected that, at first, she could not catch his words. She
walked back along the jetty and sat beside him.

"I'm sorry. I've been a bully."

She linked an arm through his. "You're allowed to be
grouchy."

"Because I'm old?"

"Because you've broken your leg."

He uncorked the whisky and poured it slowly into a silver
flask she had never seen before. He drank, then wiped the flask
with his hand before passing it to Holly. "A little less sordid
than drinking straight from the bottle, I think." She wasn't
sure what difference it made, but she drank anyway.

He said, "I meant something more than the leg. More than
today."

A movement at the shoreline caught her eye. Amongst what
she had taken for pebbles were a dozen small black and white
birds. They scurried together towards the water, stopped,
scurried away, turning together like fish in a school.

"What are they?"

After a moment, he said, "Oystercatchers."

She smiled. It wasn't that she wanted to know: she was
happy that he knew. She said, "Why did she leave?"

He did not seem surprised at the question.

"She said she was dying."

"Even then?"

"Oh, it wasn't the cancer. Not that sort of dying. Suffocating. She said I was suffocating her. It was a fashionable word at the time. Crushing her creativity, or some such." He paused to let that sink in, then added, "Actually, she said *we* were suffocating her."

Holly supposed there must have been a moment, between the second wave of feminism and the cult of parenthood, when a mother could say something like that. She said, "She blamed me as well?"

"And Ben. Ben, especially."

He took another drink and passed the flask without looking at her.

"I always thought Ben was such a Mummy's boy."

He did not reply, but simply held his hand back out for the flask. He drained it, and then refilled it from the bottle, pouring slowly, licking the whisky he spilled from the neck of the flask and the back of his hand. When he had finished he looked up, out over the water, not at Holly, as he said: "So."

"So?"

"Martin."

When her father called, the day after her birthday, the day she lost her job, and she'd asked if she could come to stay, she would not have believed it possible to live with him here, alone, for three months and not once mention Martin. Yet it had happened. Between his impatience and her reticence it had been easy – easier, certainly, than explaining why she was there. Now he was asking her outright: now, here, with his plaster leg cantilevered out over the loch, crutches laid beside him and a flask in his hand, with nowhere else for her to be, and no way out.

She said, "He left. He disappeared."

She did not mention the empty gift.

"Why?"

Sometimes it was possible to forget her father had been a lawyer all his life. A lawyer, he'd often told her, never asks a question to which he does not already know the answer. In court you don't ever want to be surprised.

"He got so tied up with the war."

"You surely didn't fall out over politics? After all these years?"

"We didn't disagree, or argue. I . . . just didn't have his energy."

Her father passed her the flask again. He probed gently, "He didn't leave because you missed a demo."

She shook her head. Above her the terns shrugged and dipped. On the far bank she could see a van, tiny and white, passing between trees on the lochside road.

"Dad, if you mean: was it Cathy? Or someone else? I don't think so. It's possible, I suppose; it happened before. But, no. I don't think so."

He turned from the loch to look at her without speaking. It was an old cross-examination trick, a trick she'd known was a trick even as a child, when, sitting at the walnut writing desk in the gloom of his study, he would meet her half-concocted evasions with a silence she could not help toppling into. Now, however, she thought she could give him an answer he wouldn't be expecting.

"He wanted me to write a book."

"And you didn't want to?"

"I couldn't."

"I see. Most unusual grounds for a divorce, I must say. Possibly unique."

"He wanted me to write about Norway. About Granddad. He said it was a gift. He said that was why you'd given me the diary."

"Did he now?"

She knew a lawyer should never ask a question like that, a question that gave away more than it sought.

She said, "I couldn't, Dad. When I read it, he had a name."

"Your grandfather?"

"Overand."

He took another drink from the flask. His eyes were closed.

"You'd never mentioned his name."

"I must have forgotten. My father never mentioned it, either. I only found it in the diary. It's been a long time since I typed it out."

"Martin asked about that, too. He asked why you only found the transcript, not the diary itself?"

"I think your mother . . ."

Grateful, Holly said, "That's what I said."

She looked for the oystercatchers, but they were gone, or still. She said, "Then he asked why there was a diary at all."

"Did he?"

She waited. This was her silence.

Eventually, he said, "I imagine he said your grandfather was supposed to be a spy - that he shouldn't have been writing all this down?"

Holly took the flask again, tipped it to her lips. She waited.

"I expect Martin said he should have eaten the evidence?"

"Shouldn't he?"

"He was in signals. A radio operator. He wasn't James Bond."

She handed back the empty flask. Her grandfather was a

major; in the navy that would have made him a lieutenant commander - just one rank below Commander Bond, as it happened. She didn't think they'd have made him a major for operating radios, however dangerous the circumstances. She said, "That's what I said."

He held the empty flask up, catching the last drops in his mouth.

"There you are, then."

The oystercatchers were still there after all. They ran like paparazzi to some imagined excitement, and then ran back. It looked as if the stones themselves were shifting.

"Help me up."

Her father planted one crutch upright, and tried to haul himself up to his feet. Holly stood quickly, and, for a moment, found herself too dizzy to see. When her head cleared and her breath returned, she took his outstretched arm, her hand under his armpit, and lifted. Over the last few weeks she had grown used to the lightness of her father's body, to its lack of substance.

Back in the village, outside the shop, he propped his crutches against the side of the Land Rover and leaned back towards the passenger seat.

She thought, now, about the whisky they'd both drunk and said, "I can't drive."

"Of course you can. This isn't Cambridge."

"I don't think I can manage the hill."

"You made it down."

"That was down. And I was sober."

He knocked his knuckles on the plaster up above his thigh. "Well I'm certainly not doing it."

"We could get a taxi."

He looked around, and shrugged.

She climbed into the driver's seat and reluctantly started the engine, but never got as far as the hill. They were still on the flat lochside road, no more than thirty feet above sea level, when a car coming too fast for the bend made her swerve hard to the left. Before she knew it, her nearside wheels were spinning over empty air. There was a moment when nothing seemed to move, when the earth stopped turning, then they were upside down, the bare metal roof under her head scraping and grinding on the rocks as the Land Rover ricocheted down the hillside. There was a jolt, a lurch, and she was hanging sideways, above her father, when they hit the loch. Water burst through broken windows, through the floor, spraying them both. The car was on its side, the driver's door uppermost, clear, milky sky still visible through the window. With an effort she pulled herself upright, completely sober, kneeling, then standing on her father, her left foot on his right shoulder, in order to push the door up and open. She clambered on to the steering wheel and hauled herself up through the door. The car settled, inches above the surface of the loch. She lay down and reached an arm back through the doorway. Her father was scrabbling against the passenger door, not trying to open it, but just to pull his head up as water filled the car. Gently, silently, the water outside rose. When it reached the threshold of the driver's door where she still lay, hands grasping at nothing, it flowed suddenly past her and down, instantly filling the body of the Land Rover, which sank like a brick, hesitant, ungainly, sucking her down, then spitting her free to tread the black cold salt water of her father's grave.

§

IT WOULD BE six more days before Overand left Oslo, and two more before he arrived at the coast.

§

B EN AND ALICE came up for the funeral, but left the
girls with a neighbour. It was term-time and Alice said
they'd find it too upsetting. Her mother did not come. It was
a long way from New Mexico and, besides, she and William
had not spoken in thirty years. Martin did not come, either.

At the inquest the pub landlord confirmed that Holly had
drunk half a pint of bitter – he'd have remembered if a woman
drank a pint, he said, it would have stuck in his mind – and
eaten a sandwich, some hours before the accident. Nobody
mentioned having seen Holly and her father on the jetty,
drinking whisky. The obituaries concentrated on William
Stanton's considerable courtroom reputation, and his work
on human rights. Mostly they were printed below – and were
far shorter than – those of Dr David Kelly, whose body had recently been found in the woods near his home in Oxfordshire.

When she went to sleep – or to bed, at least: she slept little
– she could feel her father's body, light but already waterlogged
– on the soles of her feet.

At the solicitor's office in Ullapool – two buses and three
hours away – she discovered her father had updated his will
since she'd come to stay. She would inherit the cottage and the
books, Ben the remaining pictures that were worth keeping.
They would share with Liberty and Amnesty International
the remaining estate, including considerable savings and the
sale proceeds of the family house in London.

"Liberty?" said Ben when she told him. "Can't we contest that?" But he didn't really have the stomach for a fight.

Holly stayed on in the cottage. She sold her flat in Cambridge and bought a car, a Land Rover - a new one, that didn't look as if it had fought a war or ever would. She drove down to the village to buy whisky. She bought walking boots and waterproofs, explored the hills and mountains. She learned to use a compass, and to name the birds, trees, rocks and winds, the soughing of air through an empty valley.

One afternoon, after a long, stiff climb, she sat with her back to a triangulation point, looking at fifty miles or more of coast and mountain after mountain, and there below her, not thirty yards away, she saw an eagle, a golden eagle, she was sure, its wings stretched effortlessly on the whisky soft salt air. Her father's voice was as clear as if he'd been there on the rock beside her. She'd come down from the hill behind the cottage once and told him she had - maybe - seen an eagle. He said it was possible, but unlikely. "Because eagles, if you'll pardon the demotic, Holly, are *fucking huge*. They're monstrous. They're bigger than anything you'll ever see in the air without a pilot of its own. When you see one, you'll know." And now it turned out he was right. Now she finally had seen an eagle, so close she could almost step aboard and ride it. Now she knew that he'd been right, but he was dead, and she couldn't tell him.

It could not last. She could not last.

The following April, on her forty-first birthday, she drove down to the village and parked at the foot of the jetty. She took a flask - a new one she'd bought after her father took his to the bottom of the loch – and sat on the weathered planks, watching seabirds, watching the light shift on the mountains across the water. When the flask was empty she climbed back into the car. She put the CD player on and turned the volume up. She drove slowly, steadily, onto and along the jetty, insulated from the sound of splintering wood. When the car toppled into the water she closed her eyes and pressed her feet hard against the pedals, feeling soft flesh, hard bone. But the car was new and, although heavy, more watertight than her father's.

In the time before it sank she could not help saving herself.

When the taxi dropped her off from the hospital, there was a parcel on the doorstep of her father's cottage, her cottage. She carried it into the kitchen. It was dense, hard-edged, like a ream of printer paper, or an old-fashioned clothing catalogue, wrapped and sealed with yards of tape. It had been addressed – with a printed label – to her flat in Cambridge, and subsequently re-directed.

She opened it, eventually.

Inside, she found a manuscript – a typescript, to be more precise – printed in a font that seemed chosen to resemble that of an old-fashioned manual typewriter. The first page read:

The Gift
A novel
by
Paul Overand

She flipped through the pages. A small, cheap business card fell out onto the kitchen table. It was blank apart from a name - Paul Overand - and an email address. The package must have contained five hundred pages - a whole ream - she guessed, but only about a hundred had been used. The rest were clean and crisp and blank.

2
NOT IN MY NAME

§

L ATE IN THE morning of April 10th, 2004 – the
Saturday of the Easter weekend, an island of secular calm
between the Passion and the Resurrection, and the day after
my forty-second birthday – I returned to my flat in Albert
Street, just north of Jesus Green, where, for the first time in
at least a year, I had not spent the night. Lisa, the woman
who lives on the ground floor of our little house, and who
must have left for work at her bookshop much earlier that
morning – had gathered my mail and left it on the table in
the hall. The unpromising pile included a birthday card she
had left for me – I knew without opening the envelope that
it would feature a humorous depiction of cats – along with a
bank statement, a charity circular, and a red Post Office slip,
on which 'Hannah Stanton' was scribbled below the printed
message: *Sorry you were out.*

I admit I was intrigued.

I had spent the previous evening – Good Friday, my birthday itself – with Walter, who had given me a pair of bright,
plastic, but evidently expensive earrings I would never have
chosen for myself but which were already growing on me. Ben
and Alice would be driving up to Cambridge on Sunday to
take me to lunch, and would doubtless bring toiletries with
them. ("Just some smellies," Alice would say. "We all enjoy a
few smellies." Personally, I don't, much.) My father had finally
moved to Scotland a few weeks earlier, and had left behind a

small parcel, which he had instructed me not to open before my birthday. Naturally, I had opened it the moment he left, and had found, as I suspected I might, his second edition of Volumes I and II of *The Life and Opinions of Tristram Shandy, Gentleman* – the Dodsley, from 1760 – inadequately wrapped in tissue paper with an acidic content I did not care to contemplate. In time, I would have to pass the book on to the University but, for the moment, I was enjoying its unashamed presence on the coffee table in the converted attic room of my flat.

Who, then, could have sent the package that the postman had been unable to deliver?

I cautioned myself against childish optimism. Whatever it contained, whoever had sent it, the contents were unlikely to stand up under the weight of a long weekend's foolish speculation. The last time I had received one of these slips the resulting package – once I had presented myself at the sorting office and then retired, in expectation, to a local café, ordered cappuccino and forced myself to wait until it was brought to my table (and sent away to be re-made, without chocolate powder, which I had not ordered) – proved to be nothing more exciting than a box of low-energy light bulbs of quite extraordinarily ugly design, sent to me by a power company in fulfillment of some regulatory obligation of which I had been wholly unaware. When fitted in the lamps in my attic, they cast a Stygian gloom one could stir with a spoon.

I knew that no harm – and little disappointment – came of lowering one's expectations.

That afternoon I tidied my flat. I threw out the weight-less, desiccated freesias Walter had brought two weeks earlier, and stirred the dust along the edges of my bookshelves. I telephoned my father, who was out. I left a message affecting surprise at his gift and told him – not untruthfully – that he really should not have made it. Such objects are not ours to dispose of as we will.

I spent the evening alone. Occasionally, carefully, I re-read a favourite page or two of *Tristram Shandy*; mostly I listened to music: Purcel. I drank a glass of wine with supper, and another in front of the television. I tried to watch *The Sopranos* – an American programme about which Walter had been unaccountably evangelical, pressing a video collection of the first two series on me early in our relationship – but I found both its violence and its psychoanalysis unbearably mannered.

Walter and I were still – I found myself beginning to hope – *early in our relationship*. We had spent the night together precisely twice, although only one of those occasions – the previous night, my birthday – had involved sex. The first, after an evening of wine and conversation and unaccustomed marijuana – I had not smoked since I was a student, and, even then, had barely inhaled – we lay awake together, fully-dressed, until, with the dawn, common sense returned and I made him up a bed on the sofa. Among his many attractions – he was genuinely clever, for example, and neither unusually proud nor (and this, I think, is rarer) ashamed of his cleverness; he was also kind in a way clever people often cannot be – there remained things about Walter I found less appealing: one was his capacity to make me act younger than my age.

"There's nothing wrong with being forty-two," I'd said, when we were discussing plans for my birthday.

"Of course there isn't," he replied, from the vantage point of forty-nine. "There's nothing wrong with allotments, either. Or macramé. Or golf."

"I don't want to play golf."

"Exactly. But there'd be nothing wrong with it, if you did."

"You think?"

"Just as there's nothing wrong with ecstasy or hip-hop or enjoying the sound of Italian-American actors saying *muthafuckin' muthafucka*. Age has nothing to do with it."

"It's just a number?"

Walter mimicked shame. "I apologize."

I accepted the apology; but I still insisted on a restaurant, not a nightclub, for my birthday. At dinner I discovered Walter could not only drink, but could do so with discernment; my guard lowered another notch.

It had been a year since I had slept with a man.

The following day, back at my own flat, I showered and drank coffee. There would be no time to work before my brother arrived. At noon, as advertised, I opened the door to Ben and Alice and – *surprise!* – their children. Ben apologized, and Alice pretended to be offended on their behalf. I told him not to be ridiculous; I said I much preferred the company of the girls to that of their father. Which was true. My nieces – ten year-old twins – were capable of unselfconscious joy and an originality of thought that escaped their parents. (Which I did not say: I am not wholly without self-awareness.) Ben announced, dispiritingly, that he had already booked a table at Brown's. I wondered how far down the list towards the real wines I would be able to push him.

Alice asked if I had heard from my father. I said I had, and that he seemed to be settling in well. In reality, I had only spoken to him once; the rest of the time we had left messages on each other's answerphones; this was not unusual. Ben snorted. He regarded our father's move as insane, or at least, demented – as *prima facie* evidence that he was no longer capable of making informed choices for himself. I had pointed out before that an "informed choice" was not by definition one that Ben agreed with, but it had little impact, and now I held my tongue. "He gave me a book for my birthday I can't possibly keep."

"A book?" Alice's tone suggested the notion of giving a book as a present – or perhaps that of a relatively wealthy father giving his adult daughter a book as a present – was simply incomprehensible, as if I had said "a box of staples" or "a bag of coal".

Ben said, "It'll be some priceless first edition he was chucking out."

"Second edition. But, yes, invaluable."

Alice appeared mollified; Ben did not.

In the restaurant I scored a Chateau Musar from 1995, mostly by playing on Ben's ignorance of the Bekaa Valley ("I thought it was all terrorists," he said. Ben's support for Israel was purely instinctive, untainted by any actual knowledge.) The wine cost him something over £50, and was a minor victory of which I became ashamed as soon as the bottle was empty. Not sufficiently ashamed, however, to refrain from asking Alice if she were going to have a glass of Sauternes with her sticky toffee pudding, obliging Ben to ask if I would like one, too. He could afford it.

With the twins I discussed the relative merits of JK Rowling and Philip Pullman. I was interested to find that Milly, the older by twenty minutes, preferred Harry Potter, while Molly preferred Lyra Belacqua and the fighting polar bears. (Burdening their near-identical twin girls with near-identical twee names was not, in my opinion, the least of their parents' casual cruelties.) Milly said Philip Pullman was too busy attacking the church to concentrate on telling a good story. He was too *didactic*. I asked her where she learned such words. She looked at her hands, then up at me, her brown eyes sly. "You said it, Auntie Hannah." Molly said Harry Potter was just *pastiche and plagiarism*. I didn't ask.

That evening I pecked at an overdue piece for the *London Review of Books* on two biographies of Smollett that had appeared within weeks of each other – the odds against which one might have thought to be incalculably high. I would concentrate on the more egregious and error-riddled of the two, which would at least make the review more amusing to write.

After an hour or so, the fun began to pall. I poured myself a brandy and logged on to Wikipedia, where I spent another thirty minutes inserting subtly inaccurate biographical details into the Smollett page: it would tell me which of my students, despite the University's shrill warnings to the contrary, had begun to use the site uncritically for research. On one hand, petty vandalism; on the other, a service to scholarship. Posterity could decide. I was going to bed.

Two days later I awoke with a familiar, imprecise, unfocused sense of possession: I owned something new. It was an apprehension I recognized from childhood. A few days after each Christmas or birthday I would lie in bed, waiting for the house to wake around me, for my father to pad down stairs to make tea, for Ben to begin his inane boy-games, and my mother to ask him to please, please be quiet. A warm sensation would creep over me, at once soothing and exciting. I could feel it in my arms and legs, if I could only work out what it was. Ah, yes, I had . . . I had . . . *I had a new bicycle*. And an image of the bicycle – or radio-cassette player, or fountain pen, or typewriter – would form slowly, in perfect detail, in my mind. Still in bed, my eyes closed, I would turn them over, feel their weight, their sheen, I'd climb aboard, plug it in, write. Over the years, the objects changed, but the sensation didn't. I had it then, that Tuesday morning four days after my forty-second birthday: I recognized it at once. But why? Why?

Because I had a card from the Post Office that said: *Sorry you were out.*

Disgusted with myself, I pushed back the duvet and swung my legs out of bed. I am ashamed to say that I have always been quietly pleased with my legs. Even at forty-two. With an effort I stood and reached for my heavy dressing gown. That had been a present, too, though not the sort I had ever woken to daydream about. Padding barefoot through to the kitchen, I heard my father's footsteps in my own. I thought of Hardy: it was not only the family face that could pass trait and trace over oblivion. I made tea.

I had received no card, no gift from my mother. This was no surprise. The last time she sent anything was my twenty-first (a jumper from the Isle of Arran, where she'd been living in an holistic therapy commune, coming to terms, she wrote, with the break-up of her first major post-marital relationship, and eradicating all the biological, mental and spiritual toxins with which she had clogged her energies over the years.) The parcel would not be from my mother.

Perhaps Walter had sent another present – besides the earrings – which he had not mentioned on Friday, not wanting to spoil the surprise? It was possible, even if it would have been a little too much. Walter seemed eager to please; so eager, in fact, that I doubt he could have refrained from mentioning it, however obliquely. I told myself the parcel would not be from Walter; I hoped it wasn't. His not having mentioned it would have been just a little creepy.

Who, then?

I told myself I would not think about it now. I was not six years old. I could get on with the business of life without being distracted by the prospect of a birthday present. Besides, anticipation would only guarantee that it turned out to be more low-energy light bulbs. Or a clothing catalogue I had accidentally failed to tick the box to refuse. Something unsolicited.

I turned on the radio. The Interim Iraqi government said the informal ceasefire would be extended for another twelve hours. An American general said their mission was to capture or kill Muqtada al-Sadr. President Bush had said it had been "a tough week". Vitamin E protected men from prostate cancer. Cloudy with rain later. Or was that Wales? I could never concentrate long enough to know what was happening where I lived. I made toast and drank tea.

I put my plate in the sink. I poured a second cup and carried it upstairs to my desk. Before anything else, I would finish that review.

Thirty minutes later, review unfinished, I stood in the sorting office waiting for the man who had taken my "Sorry you were out" card to return with my package. It seemed to be taking a very long time. He returned to the counter, still holding the card.

"Did you say Friday?"

"Maybe, but that was a holiday. It must have been first thing Saturday. It says on the card."

He disappeared again. I wondered how much space there was back there, how they organized the undelivered parcels. By name? By date? By address? From the time it was taking to locate mine, I suspected it might be by word association. *Hannah Stanton.* Stanton. Stand-on. It would be stood on something. My address was Albert Street. There'd be a postman called Albert, surely? The parcel would be standing on Albert's locker. When the man returned again, still empty-handed, I almost said it aloud. *Have you tried Albert's locker?* Almost. He went back for a third attempt. No one was called Albert these days. Not even postmen.

My grandfather's name was Albert. Albert Charles William. When you said them all together like that it sounded less like a name than a radio code, the sort of thing he must have used when sending messages home from Occupied Europe. My grandfather had been in the navy, had lied about his age to fight the First World War, and then got into signals. Which was how he wound up in MI6. A spy. Or so the family story went.

Finally, the man in the pale blue shirt with the red writing that said *Royal Mail* – I bet he's not, I thought, word-associating again – came out with a large jiffy bag. "Sorry about that," he said. "Some joker put it on top of the lockers."

He slid it into that inexplicable air-lock contraption all post offices have, and I waited while he slid shut his doors and opened mine. It had sounded heavy. The address was a printed label. Not hand-written: no clues there. Nothing to get excited about. When I picked up the parcel it felt like a ream of paper. I took it to the café just around the corner and waited until they'd brought me a cappuccino (twice) before tearing open the gummed flap, not caring enough to reuse the envelope, and found it was indeed a ream of paper. Clipped to the first page was a small, cheap business card, blank except for a name - Paul Overand - and an email address.

I rang my father, praying for once that he would answer. When he asked what Martin had got wrong, I said I hardly knew where to start.

I didn't want to say: *he killed you off*. Much less: *he made me kill you off*.

Of all the instances of Martin's license with the truth - some important; some, like the way he'd shaved a year off my age, but added rather more to my father's, seemingly trivial - it was this that struck me as the most gratuitous. I dare say he hated me. I dare say he had persuaded himself that it was I who had mistreated *him*: it would be only human, after all. But to kill a man who was still alive to read it, to have me tread him down into the water - and then try but fail to kill myself - felt vindictive. And not to put his own name to the deed, to hide behind that of a fictional descendant of the fictional characters he had created out of the reality of my family's history seemed peculiarly craven.

I had no doubt whatever that Martin was the author.

I have never been the suicidal type.

So, for the record:

My name is Hannah Stanton. (I can't see myself as a 'Holly'. I suspect Martin's choice had more to do with a fascination for Miss Golightly, or, more accurately, for the young Audrey Hepburn, than with anything to do with me.)

Martin was Martin.

Ben was Ben, my brother; he has a wife called Alice and two daughters.

I have a friend, Walter, who had recently become more than a friend. What other word can I use? At forty-two one cannot say *boyfriend*; at this stage it would be presumptuous to say *partner*; so, *lover*, perhaps? But even lover seems preposterous and, above all, Walter is my friend. He has never been my manager; he has no facial hair. If I ever felt the need to describe someone as a 'cunt' I would do so, I hope, without the prudish self-justification Martin attributed to me, but it is not a word I can imagine applying to Walter.

Cathy had been Kath (again, not much of an alias), when Martin and I knew her. Martin did not leave me to return to her; the last I heard, she was happily married to a Labour MP whose toehold on the lower rungs of ministerial preferment had slipped as a result of his opposition to the invasion of Iraq.

I was not – am not – an archivist. Holly is barely an archivist, either, of course. In Martin's mind, there must have been some connection to be made with the preservation and resurrection of my grandfather's diary and its transcript. But, if he were going to make such a change, might he not at least have put in a little more effort? Some perfunctory research into what archivists actually do, how they train, the qualifications they hold – the MA, for example, in Archives and Records Management one can study for at University College London, or the membership requirements of the Society of Archivists – so that he could drop in a few more plausible and authoritative details into his narrative? It wouldn't have been hard: with the World Wide Web it is easier than ever. I have just done it myself in minutes.

My father was alive.

It was true that he had recently moved to Scotland, but he

had never, to my knowledge, broken his leg or driven a Land
Rover into the loch.

My grandfather was a spy. He was in Norway when the
Germans invaded. For the following six weeks he kept a
diary; my father transcribed it. It begins on the 9th of April,
1940, the day of the German invasion; it ends at dawn on
the 18th of May, the morning after Norwegian National
Day (Constitution Day, if you will). It describes how, with
a handful of colleagues from the British Consulate, actively
aided by many Norwegians and protected by the silence of
many more, he made his way by night in motor boats that
slid between rocks in oily blackness, in cars that broke down
on rough country roads and, guided by torch-bearing children, on foot over mountainous goat tracks from Stavanger
to Hjelmeland to Forre and on to Haugesund where, billeted
in a trawlerman's house within sight of the German GHQ
they had their first bath for five weeks, ate well and prayed
for fog. The barest bones of this story had been with me for
many years: the details I learned only when my father became
possessed by the idea of *preparing for death* – along with the
ridiculous notion that such preparation required wholesale
relocation to the northwest of Scotland – and I agreed to help
sort out his books and papers. It was then, as Martin correctly
had it, that we came across the transcript of the diary I had
heard much about but never actually seen: before that I knew
only that my grandfather had been in Norway and had been
helped to escape. Although I knew the story and had told it
myself, often enough, I knew none of the details a storyteller
needs, that Martin had needed.

Overand was Overand: at least, that was the name in
the transcript of my grandfather's diary. He was not Aleks,

however, his son not Oskar: this was 1940 and the men had no first names.

Martin did say *it was a gift*: I distinctly remember that. He did say: *it would be a crime not to use it*. I did not agree; we had argued. I may indeed have said something about my *locus standi* – or lack of it. I may even have said I was not comfortable *appropriating other people's tragedy*. But the fact of the matter was that I was squeamish. What would my father think? What, if such a book were ever published, would the surviving Overands think? *Especially if the book were not good?*

I had enough history to work on – eighteenth-century literary history – not to have to worry about my own.

On the phone I laid out for my father a few of Martin's more egregious economies with the *actualité*, a little more of my resentment of this man who had simply disappeared from my life a year ago, and had now reappeared in such a fashion. I did not mention to my father his supposed death or my supposed part in it. I did not ask why, after years in which the story of my grandfather was simply a story, he had found and given me the transcript only a year ago. I did not ask why it was the transcript he had found, and not the diary itself. I did not ask why there was a diary at all.

My father said little, and nothing at all about what I might do with Martin's story, with *The Gift*, now that I had it.

The conversation moved on. I thanked him for the Sterne, but explained I could not keep it. I told him about Alice's smellies; he asked, unusually, about Walter.

"Earrings?" he said. "Diamond?"

"Plastic."

"Ah."

"But very stylish. I like them."

He told me he'd been climbing the mountain behind his cottage and thought he'd seen an eagle.

"You're not sure?"

"It was a long way off."

I told him to be careful, walking alone.

Over breakfast the following day, and at work, while I ate my lunch at my desk, I found myself wondering not about Martin, not about my grandfather, but about Overand.

What did he think he was doing?

I didn't know Aleks Overand, hadn't heard of him before yesterday, and did not now believe in his existence. Nonetheless, I found myself thinking more and more about him, thinking there could be any number of reasons why his suitcases had stood, untouched, in the hall of his house on Inkognito gate for six days, and why it had been two more days before he pulled up at the house on the coast, alone, and unfastened the leather straps that bound the cases to the chrome rack on the boot of his car, carried them indoors and placed them amongst the coiled ropes and polished wood of his father's old shop.

A lot would depend, I thought, upon whom you asked.

That afternoon, during a departmental meeting of excruciating dullness, I thought it might be possible that, when she reached his side of the table, Abi had bent over the still-seated Overand and kissed his mouth. That she took his hand and placed it against her soft - or flat? - breast, before leading him up to the bedroom - his and Kirsten's bedroom? - to her room under the eaves, where he may have struck his head gently on the sloping ceiling before laughing and falling backwards onto her bed, pulling her down on top of him.

Walking home, I thought it possible that the following morning they might have searched diligently – or perfunctorily, but in any case unsuccessfully – for Fru Jennsen, before returning to the attic room, and that, in the days which followed, they rose late, drank much, ate what they could find, made love repeatedly and enthusiastically, wore whichever of each other's clothes came to hand and talked, when they talked at all, about freedom and sacrifice, or about food.

Overand may have thought he looked particularly fetching in the grey shift dress that came down to his shins and which might actually have been Kirsten's.

It was also possible, I thought, unlocking the door and checking the table in the hall for belated birthday post, that Aleks Overand caught hold of the maid's hand as she walked around the table and pulled her down onto his lap. That he reached for her breasts with one hand while pushing the other up the grey dress in search of stocking top, garter, bare slim thigh. That she resisted, or did not resist. That they made love, once, unsuccessfully, and that little love was involved.

It was possible that they searched diligently – or perfunctorily, but in any case unsuccessfully – for Fru Jennsen, or that Overand sought out other members of the National Defence Union while Abi tracked down the few shops that remained open and still had food to sell. That, as the early spring sunshine broke and the weather turned cold again and the coal ran out, they burned furniture and wore every scrap of clothing they could lay their hands on.

Booting up my computer, I thought it possible that it was mostly food they talked about, and it was mostly Abi talking.

Later that evening I made a salad, drank a little wine,

and watched *Newsnight* – Iraqi militants threatening to kill an Italian hostage; a tape of Osama Bin Laden apparently offering to end terrorist attacks in return for withdrawal from Muslim countries; the ANC re-elected in South Africa, with an increased majority – without following any of it.

Overand had saved my grandfather's life. Was that what mattered most? Was that the story?

The following day, in the college library, I conducted a little research of my own. I found, with little effort, that during the first week of the Occupation, while Overand remained in the capital, shots were fired at the new commissioner's car; that a bomb exploded outside the barracks, killing nineteen soldiers of the occupying army, along with a handful of civilians; that, in coordinated attacks, mines tore apart the runways at three airports, one just outside the capital, one in the north and one on the west coast of the country. It is a matter of record that, on the evening of the fourth day, Vidkun Quisling, the leader of a small and previously unsuccessful fascist party, was allowed into a radio studio to broadcast a speech in which he lamented the King's desertion of his country, and then called upon party members and fellow citizens alike to cease all attempts to obstruct the legitimate exercise of authority by his – Quisling's – new government and its allies. There was no war, and there should be no fighting.

I could not be certain that Overand or Abi heard the broadcast.

It is possible that they were making love at the time, or talking about freedom, or arguing about food.

I decided, however – I became increasingly sure in my own mind – that on the afternoon of the fifth day, Sunday, Aleks Overand telephoned the house on the coast and spoke to his children and his wife. He told them he had been busy resolving certain matters at work, and would be with them soon; Kirsten told him to hurry, that he was needed, that something had changed.

It could not have been otherwise, I knew.

She may have told him that two men who said they knew him from the NDU - the National Defence Union, they would have explained - had arrived at the house the previous evening, together with a foreigner, and had insisted she let them in and allow them to sleep in the shop-cum-office; that, having little choice, she had chased the children back upstairs, to their own room, and made the men as comfortable as she could with blankets and a few cushions and had given them soup and bread and carrots; that the men were expecting Overand to return and to help the foreigner escape the country.

It was perhaps more likely, though, that on the advice or instruction of the men she had said no such thing on the telephone to her husband in the capital, but simply pleaded with him to come as soon as he could.

I thought there could be many reasons why, having decided to leave the capital, it had been a further two days before Overand reached the coast and hugged his children and kissed his wife.

The roads were, in all likelihood, clogged with checkpoints and refugees and armoured convoys - so clogged that Overand would have done well to cover the distance - some three hundred miles - in only two days.

It was also possible that he had not left the capital alone. That he and Abi spent a night in a small hotel on the road out towards the north, not the coast, a hotel which, despite the exodus, still had one vacant room, and where Overand had signed them in as man and wife and the landlady, the proprietor, whose sharp eyes had noticed the absence of a ring, had reasoned that, at a time like this, it couldn't do much harm and it was probably kindest not to ask too many questions.

The following morning, Overand may have come down to breakfast alone, to eggs and smoked fish, and may have told the proprietor he would be leaving soon and would she please prepare the bill.

When asked, he may have hesitated for a moment before confirming that no, Fru Overand would not require breakfast.

It was possible.

It was also possible that the men from the NDU did not, in fact, turn up until after Overand had finally arrived at the house on the coast, alone, and had unfastened his suitcases from the chrome luggage rack on the boot of his car and carried them through the empty shop and up into the apartment, after he had hugged Elda and Oskar, and heard all about the ships Oskar had seen in the harbour and the soldiers who had marched into the little port two days before, until after he had kissed Kirsten and been kissed in return and had felt her arms pull tight around his back and the fullness of her breasts against his chest. After he'd heard her ask why it had taken him so long to come.

It was possible: which is why I had not wanted to write the book in the first place. It was not my story. I had thought it was not was not my place to speculate.

But how could it not be?

Overand had saved my grandfather's life, at the expense of his own family. Martin had changed a great deal, but not my grandfather. I'd feared that might be the worst of it, worse even than having me kill my father, because less obviously fictional. But if he had not changed my grandfather, it was only because he had not even mentioned him. He'd begun the story so far back – in Oslo, on the Norwegian coast, in Overand's childhood – that he had not even reached my grandfather.

He'd made Overand real: that was the worst of it.

§

EARLY ON SUNDAY, before his father telephoned,
Oskar heard a knock at the shop door. He was downstairs,
practising knots with his grandfather's old ropes. His mother
and Elda were upstairs, folding clean sheets. Oskar opened
the door to find Herr Marthinsen standing on the doorstep
holding an umbrella and a clipboard. Marthinsen owned the
greengrocer's shop; his son had taken Oskar out bird trap-
ping once or twice and made jokes about Elda that made him
blush. Standing beside Herr Marthinsen was a soldier. The
soldier's face was soft, and red, as if he had been out in the
cold too long. He wore a helmet and carried a rifle; he had a
polished black belt; beads of water stood proud and distinct
like costume jewellery on the gleaming leather. From the belt
hung a collection of bulky, awkward-looking pouches. One of
them, Oskar thought, the long thin one, would be a bayonet.

His mother stepped up to the door, beside Oskar. She put
her arm around his shoulders.

She nodded. "Herr Marthinsen."

"Good morning, Fru Overand."

She waited.

Eventually the greengrocer gestured with his clipboard
towards the soldier at his side. He said, "Our . . . friends are
settling in. There will be more of them soon. They will need
to be" - he paused - "accommodated."

"I see."

She looked him in the face. His eyes dropped to his clipboard.

"How many rooms do you have?"

"Three. Two bedrooms and the kitchen. And the shop, of course."

She gestured over her shoulder at the empty counter.

The greengrocer ticked a box.

"How many people are here?"

"You know our family, Herr Marthinsen."

The greengrocer paused, his pen hovering above the form. The soldier looked at him expectantly.

"How many?"

"Three. The children and I."

Marthinsen lowered his clipboard. "Is your husband not with you, Fru Overand?"

"Four." She laughed and pulled Oskar closer to her. "I meant four, of course."

The greengrocer ticked another box and, with a polite farewell, moved towards the next house, followed by the soldier.

Eight days later, when Aleks Overand finally arrived from the capital, alone, and unfastened his suitcases from the chrome rack on the boot of his car, he was surprised to find the door not only locked, but bolted, and to have to knock loudly and call through the letterbox before it was opened by a smiling and obviously excited Oskar. He handed the smaller, lighter case – the case he had packed first – to his son and asked him to carry it upstairs. Oskar led the way, calling to his mother: "He's here! Pappa's here!"

At the top of the stairs Overand stopped, and placed his case down carefully. He stood in the doorway of the kitchen, patting Oskar's head. He watched his wife hang up the tea towel with which she had been drying glasses, smooth the front of her dress, and walk across the kitchen towards him. They embraced; he kissed her and was kissed in return.

"Where's Elda?"

She was in the children's bedroom. Since coming to the coast, Elda and Oskar had had to share, as they had for holidays for as long as they could remember. Both children complained about this arrangement, but only Elda meant it. Now Oskar pushed open the door.

"Elda! Pappa's here!"

She must have known this. The flat was small, the bedroom opened straight off the kitchen. She could not have failed to hear her father's voice.

She was sitting on her bed, her shoes slipped off and her feet up on the eiderdown, writing. She made a point of laying down her pencil and shutting her notebook carefully, pulling a rubber band around it to keep the covers closed, before she stood, slipped her shoes back on, and welcomed her father.

Overand grinned. "Come here!" He hugged her. She did not resist, but neither did she participate. It was like grappling a bag of curtain poles.

"What are you writing, sweetheart? Another play?"

Elda said it was just her diary.

Oskar said, "The Germans are here, Pappa." He told his father about the soldiers in their grey uniforms, about the ships in the harbour, and about watching them lay mines.

"Mamma says we can't go out."

Kirsten said, "He means on the boat. He's been so impatient for you to come. But I told him you wouldn't be able to sail. Not now. Not with the mines."

Overand said, "We'll see."

He turned away, picked up his suitcases again.

"I'd better unpack."

He carried the cases into the other bedroom, the one he shared with Kirsten: the one where his father had died. A small bottle of Kirsten's make-up and a pair of mother-of-pearl hairbrushes he had given her before the children were born were arranged neatly on the dressing table. Kirsten followed him into the room. He swung the suitcases, one after the other, up onto the high bed, where they sank into the heavy covers.

"You rang. We've been expecting you all week."

He opened one of the suitcases, and began fussing with the shirts inside.

"I know. I'm sorry. I couldn't just come at once. There were things I had to finish."

"Things?"

"Yes."

She waited for him to say more. He took out the small leather case that held his own hairbrushes, his combs and cufflinks and razors, and placed it on the dressing table next to his wife's toiletries.

She said, "Of course."

She left him to finish his unpacking, thinking she should have offered to do it herself. He would be tired. Still, she could prepare dinner.

In the kitchen, Elda was sitting at the table, her notebook open in front of her.

That evening, when she was sure the children were asleep, Kirsten said, "Is Fru Jennsen still at the house?"

Fru Jennsen had been with them as long as they'd been married. Overand shrugged. "She disappeared."

"Disappeared?"

"I haven't seen her since . . . She wasn't there the morning of the invasion."

"Did you try her house? Her sister?"

"I couldn't remember where they lived."

"Oh, Aleks!"

Overand turned back to his clothes. He lifted a pair of trousers from the case and held them by the cuffs, letting them hang, pinching the creases together.

"You know the woman. If she were alive, she would have come to work."

"You . . ."

"What could I do? The girl asked at the hospitals; she even tried the police station. No one knew anything, or would tell her anything."

"Her, no. But surely, you could have . . . ?"

"Could have what?"

"With your contacts?"

Overand shook his head. He was still holding the trousers. "Don't you understand what's going on here? We're at war. My contacts are nothing!"

"But the NDU?"

"Is the Government. Is nothing. I don't know."

It was clear that he did not want to say anything more. Kirsten knew that she should let him be. She said, "So what *have* you been doing for the last week?"

"I told you."

He had told her nothing.

"And the girl?"

He threaded the trousers onto a hanger and carried it over to the wardrobe.

"I gave her money. She's gone back to her family."

"To Nordland?"

"That's what she said. Somewhere up past Bodo, apparently."

The men arrived that night. It was as if they had been waiting for him, Overand would say later.

The rain had become heavier. Just before midnight Overand opened the door expecting soldiers but found, instead, four men who – in their wet, muddy clothes, with collars pulled up and caps pulled down against a puddle of weak lamplight – looked like crudely drawn fugitives in the sort of comic book he might buy for Oskar. He knew one of them – it was the man he had met at the NDU offices just over a week before, the big man with the tight suit, the one who looked like a policeman, not the dapper Treasurer. He introduced himself as Morten Sher, and introduced a second man – equally large but who otherwise looked not in the least like himself – as his brother, Peder. Overand understood that he was not to take these names too seriously. That is, too literally. The anonymity was serious enough.

The man who called himself Morten Sher said that, pleasant as it was to pass the time of day, they really should get off the street before they were spotted. Overand stepped back from the doorway, telling the children, who had been drawn to the bottom of the stairs by the knock at the door and the sound of voices, to go back up to bed. The children lingered, fascinated, as four men slipped silently into the shop. They heard their mother call from upstairs, "Who is it?"

Elda said, "Men."

"What men?"

"I don't know."

Overand said, "Friends. Go back to bed."

The children passed their mother on the stairs.

Kirsten nodded at the men, but spoke to her husband. "What's going on, Aleks?"

"It's all right, darling. These are my friends."

"It's almost midnight."

"I don't imagine they'd be here if it were not important."

The man Overand knew stepped forward. "Your husband is quite right, Fru Overand. My name is Morten Sher," - he held out his hand for her to shake; she ignored it - "and this is my brother, Peder." He seemed keen, Overand thought, to practise unfamiliar names.

Sher gestured towards the two men for whom he had so far offered no names, plausible or otherwise. "Our friends are from England. It is important - essential - that they are not found, and that they return to England as soon as possible."

Kirsten said, "You want us to hide them?"

There was a pause in which both Morten and Peder Sher looked at Overand.

"I told Herr Sher - Morten - that we have a boat."

Kirsten laughed, a harsh sound that came from somewhere in the back of her throat.

Overand spoke to Sher. "We have a boat. We will sail your friends to England."

Sher said there was no need. He gestured to one of the Englishmen, the smaller of the two, a pale man with watery blue eyes. "This man - Jan - was a sailor, before . . . In the last war."

Overand thought: *Jan?* It was a barely credible name for an Englishman but, again, he supposed they were all of them new to this subterfuge; Sher was merely practising. To Jan he said, in English, "We will sail you to England. Sher says you are a sailor, and I am sure that will help. But it is my father's boat. We will sail you and your colleague home."

The Englishman nodded. "Thank you."

Sher said, "If you are sure?"

In Norwegian, so that there could be no misunderstanding on Kirsten's part, Overand said, "We will sail them to England." He paused just long enough to make clear no discussion was invited, then turned back to the four men whose dripping clothes clung thickly to their legs and shoulders and around whom small puddles had gathered.

"And now, I imagine you are hungry, no?"

To Kirsten he said, "Is there any food in the house?"

When the men had eaten, Overand led them back downstairs. He watched as, without turning on the lights, they laid out blankets and bed rolls amongst the decaying lines and canvas, dividing the shop between them, marking territory with the few personal possessions they had brought - a photograph, a notebook, a pack of playing cards, a small accordion. Then he returned to the kitchen and stood looking out towards the harbour while Kirsten washed plates and rattled cutlery in the sink. There were no lights outside, and he found it hard to see anything past his own reflection.

It was after two o'clock by the time they got to bed, and Overand had been on the road, arguing with soldiers around a hastily assembled checkpoint, at six that morning.

Sitting upright, her back against the headboard, Kirsten said, "When you said *we* would sail the Englishmen home, what did you mean?"

Overand rolled onto his side, his knees curling up towards

his chest. There was nothing he could do now but sleep.

"We'll talk about this tomorrow."

"You want us *all* to go?"

Overand was not sure himself what he had meant. Probably he was just trying not to sound as if he were excluding them, not being selfish. He had not pictured the whole family on the boat, pitching and yawing across the North Sea. But now that Kirsten had raised the idea he said, "Why not?"

It was as if he had slapped her. She said, "We live here. Our home is here – in Oslo. You have a business."

Reluctantly, Overand sat up. "Not any more. Do you not understand? By now our house will be home to a herd of fat, cabbage-coloured oberleutnants and their blonde concubines. My business is defending criminals. But the criminals are running the country now. Who is going to put them on trial? It is finished. We are finished."

They should wait for fog, Sher said, but there was no fog. They waited three days, during which Kirsten never once relented in her opposition to her husband's plan. Perhaps as a result, Overand spent much of the time down in the shop with the Sher brothers and the Englishmen, or away from the house altogether, preparing the boat, he said, reconnoitering the mine laying and the troop arrivals. Whenever he returned, however, Kirsten would quietly, patiently, without ever raising her voice in the small apartment, explain all over again – ignoring Overand's brusque dismissals, his heavy sighs and rolling eyes, his languid wave of the hand as he sought to swat away the tiresome irritant she had become – and again, without respite, but without apparent effect, that he was being selfish and cruel, that they would all be captured, imprisoned or killed, that they would die at sea, that, even if they made it to England, they would be refugees, without resources or friends, their children torn from their home, and for what? To help two Englishmen they did not know, whose presence and activities in their country they refused to explain.

Overand reminded her that it was she who had taken the children out of Oslo for their own safety and – he had to admit – she had been right.

"It is not the same," Kirsten said. "Out of Oslo is not out of Norway."

"Norway is not Norway any more. It is finished."

Kirsten allowed a pause just long enough for Aleks' own words to sink in, long enough for him to wonder if he really meant it.

She said, "You can't say that. The Germans will not win. They won't be here forever."

Aleks shook his head, allowing his wife the luxury of consoling herself, like a child in the night who needs to know the monsters are not real.

She said, "The British will not abandon us. British soldiers are in the North and they will . . ."

"It is the British I'm trying to help. Those men downstairs. Who do you think they are?"

"They don't need your help, Aleks. They can take the boat and sail themselves. That man, Jan, he is a sailor, Sher said so."

Aleks drew himself up. "One man can't sail that boat alone."

"But you have sailed it before, with Oskar, and he is just a boy. A boy. How much use could he be?"

"More than his mother, it seems."

It was late when this was said, and Oskar was asleep. But Elda had been reading by torchlight, until the drama in the adjacent room eclipsed that on the page. She lost little time in waking her younger brother and repeating their mother's words.

Oskar would not cry. He would confront his cowardly mother. Even if she was too scared to do her duty, he was not. He would sail with his father and they could leave the women behind. It was, in any case, a job for men.

Oskar went back to sleep, clutching to his chest the hank of rope in which he had tied a loose, complicated hitch. He saw himself standing in the prow of his grandfather's boat – a *real* boat – eyes scanning the surface of the water for telltale signs of the mines he had seen the British and then the Germans lay, calling instructions firmly, calmly, to his father in the wheelhouse. The Englishmen were not visible in this scene.

At breakfast the following morning, when his mother began again to explain why they would not be leaving Norway, Oskar announced, "Father, I wish to sail with you to England."

Overand, who had just taken a sip of coffee, pursed his lips hard to keep his laughter – and his coffee – under control. When he had swallowed and replaced his cup he said, his eyes not on his son but on his wife, "You do? Good for you, little man."

Kirsten said it was not possible.

"Why?"

Kirsten was a mother: this was a question she had faced countless times, and she responded with practised calm. It was not safe. They would all be killed. It was not necessary.

Oskar longed for his father to intervene, to tell his mother how things were going to be, but his father merely allowed her words to rise and fall and pour around them, like smooth waves combing seaweed over rocks on the shore. In the end Oskar said, "Please, Mamma, stop. I *want* to go." Then, after a moment: "I will go."

She stood then, and hugged him, pressing his face into her soft belly, but she did not stop.

Her words – quiet, insistent – filled the apartment.

His father ignored them. Oskar wanted more than anything to hear him say, "Don't worry, son. I wouldn't go without you." He wanted his father to stand and step towards him, his hand outstretched. Oskar would feel his mother's grip tighten around his chest, then feel his father ruffle his hair and say, "We'll be all right, won't we? You'll look after your father, won't you, little man?" Oskar would pull away from his mother, and his father would say, "A job for the men, eh?" as he had so often in the past.

But his father said nothing and he stayed put, the closely woven wool of his mother's cardigan soft against his cheek as she spoke on, words following words without anger or sympathy, dropping endlessly into the pool of his father's silence.

Eventually Overand finished his breakfast, thanked his wife for preparing it, and left.

At times throughout the day, when his father was not there – or when Morten and Peder Sher or the Englishmen *were* there, when she was feeding them, or heating water to fill the zinc tub they had carried down to the shop and fetching clean towels for them – at these times, she said nothing about Oskar going, about the danger, about his age, about the selfishness of his father. She was relaxed with the children, polite – even friendly – with the visitors. But when his father returned – when the visitors, after thanking her warmly for the food, or the water or the towels, had descended again to the empty shop – she would take up her theme, quietly, patiently, as if there had been no interruption.

They would be caught before they left the harbour. They would be captured. They would be tortured and shot. They had never sailed in fog. They would hit a mine. They had never really sailed anywhere, either of them. They would get lost. There would be a storm and they would drown. There were submarines. The boat would be spotted and torpedoed.

On the second night after the men's arrival, the sky was clear and although the moon was old, its light tired and attenuated, it was still bright enough to make out the insignia on the grey ships in the harbour. Pinpoints of reflected light on the far side of the bay shifted lazily on the flaccid water. The hills behind the town loomed dense and black, seemingly impenetrable.

In the flat above the empty chandler's shop, the soup was thick with lamb and potato and cabbage. Sher offered to lift the heavy iron pot onto the table for Kirsten, but she said she could manage. ("Where's Abi when we need her?" Elda said, and was shushed.) Seven people squeezed around the table that was tight for four. One of the NDU men – the one Overand had not met before in the capital, the one who had been introduced as Peder, but had not said much himself – was not there. Sher said his colleague had other business to attend to; he would not be back that night.

Overand said if they were going nowhere now, they might as well have a drink with their supper. He said there wasn't any decent wine out here, but there was plenty of beer and a bottle of aquavit he'd been given by a grateful client following an improbable acquittal. Sher translated for the Englishmen, who said they would like beer very much. Overand apologized for not asking them in English. He drank beer, too, and talked about boats to the Englishman with the improbable name. He realized the man was wearing one of his old shirts. Sher drank aquavit; to Overand's surprise, Kirsten drank aquavit too. He allowed the children small glasses of beer: Oskar was eager, Elda uninterested.

Elda had kept her distance, avoiding, as best she could at the crowded table, bumping elbows with the Englishman beside her as she ate. But when he asked her, with Sher translating, what she had been writing in her notebook before supper, she replied in English that she had been writing a play.

The Englishman sat back, putting his spoon on the table. "You speak English?"

"Some."

"I'm sorry, I can't speak Norwegian."

"No."

Elda took a mouthful of soup, sipping carefully from the side of her spoon.

"And what is your play about?"

Elda paused for a moment, as if weighing the options. "You could say it is about truth."

"Truth?" Sher, who had returned to telling Kirsten about how he had come to join the NDU, now interrupted himself to exclaim: "What a big subject for such a small girl!" But the Englishman ignored him and asked Elda if she had read any Chekhov, after which Elda contrived both to relax and to sit taller at the same time, becoming more animated than she had been all evening.

It got late and Kirsten suggested that the children go to bed, but did not insist.

When the soup and the bread were all gone, they stayed at the table, drinking and swapping stories as best they could. At some point Overand became aware that one of the Englishmen had fetched an accordion and was playing softly. The other, with a napkin and Elda's help, was trying to describe knots to Oskar. The music was a cheap dance tune Overand thought he recognized, but played slowly, wistfully, it acquired a sentimental power he would not have anticipated. He looked up at his wife. She noticed him watching her, but bowed her head, turning back to Sher, who asked how she and her husband had met. Overand waited, straining to hear her answer through the hubbub of gentle music and bilingual conversation.

She said, "You don't know?"

Sher shook his head. "How would I?"

Kirsten raised her eyes to meet her husband's, but spoke to Sher. "I thought everybody knew."

Overand called across the table, "It was a long time ago. You can't expect anyone else to remember the details of our private life."

Sher said, "I am intrigued. What should I remember?"

Overand spotted Elda reaching for the notebook she had placed under her seat when dinner began.

Kirsten raised her glass to her mouth, swallowed hard. She said, "I was a grateful client."

Overand said, "You used to say I saved your life."

"Really?" Sher's eyebrows lifted, his eyes round in his broad face like a child's drawing, pennies on a dinner plate. "I must hear more."

Overand said, "It is true she was a client. She might have hanged."

"Aleks." Kirsten nodded towards Elda.

Overand sighed. "But it's ancient history. Last year's snow. You don't want to get a lawyer talking about old cases."

He opened more bottles for himself and the Englishmen. Sher poured aquavit for Kirsten. Overand poured and drank a glass of beer, then turned to the accordion player. "More music!" he said, loudly. He clapped his hands. "Faster. Dance! Dance!"

Sher said, "Not too loud!"

"It's all right. Nobody will hear! Dance!"

Sher said something to the accordion player who, finding himself caught between the two of them, played faster, but not much louder.

Overand turned to his daughter. "Come on Elda. Put that book down and dance with your Pappa."

"No thank you."

"Come on."

Kirsten said, "Aleks . . ."

"All right. You?"

She did not reply.

He sat down heavily. "You dance with her, then," he said to Sher, and, to Overand's disbelief, the beggar actually asked her. She said no, but she smiled as she did so.

Jan, the Englishman in Overand's old shirt, asked if they could use the radio. Overand gestured towards the set he'd bought his father not long before he died. Jan rose and switched it on; a warm yellow light filled the circular tuning dial. He waited for the valves to come to life, then turned the dial carefully, his ear close to the fabric of the speaker cover. As the radio warmed up, the accordion player stopped, the instrument emitting a final, discordant wheeze, the buttons clicking tonelessly as he packed it away. Jan said the wireless was a beautiful set. When he found what he was looking for he sat back down, squeezing between Oskar and his mother.

They heard a flat, monotonous voice, speaking English steadily, precisely, with no emotion or interest in what it had to say and, as far as Overand or Elda could detect, making no sense at all. After a while the voice stopped and music came on. The Englishmen stood, scraping back their chairs, their hands clasped behind their backs and their chins held up until it finished. Overand and Sher exchanged a glance and watched in silence. When the music ended, Sher proposed a toast. To the King. They raised their glasses. To both their kings.

Elda said, "Father says it's all our King's fault."

Later, Overand climbed into bed without a word. Kirsten said, "If you go what will happen to us?"

"Then come."

She would not, he knew that.

The following morning, while their father drank coffee, Oskar teased Elda, trying to interrupt whatever she was writing. Kirsten told him to stop, and then told Elda to put the notebook away. Elda folded the cover closed, making a wedge where a pencil, caught between the pages, marked her place. She said, politely, "Father, can I come?"

Oskar watched her father turn slowly towards her. "What?"

"I can sail, too. Can I come with you?"

Their mother said, "Elda, please . . ."

"No."

Elda made a familiar sound, a rapid exhalation through her nose, like a horse. Oskar had heard it before: it was the sound his father made, a sound of disapproval.

128

"Why not?"

"You'll stay here with your mother."

"We could all go."

Oskar understood she was provoking their father, taunting him, somehow, but was not sure how; after each point she seemed to feint and dart at things from different angles.

"We could all go. To England. Then we wouldn't have to come back. We could live there."

Their mother said, "We can't simply leave. We're not refugees."

"Why not?"

"What would we do?"

"We could be safe. We could live there."

"And do what, Elda?"

Oskar saw his father straighten, his chest filling.

Elda began to say, "Anything we . . ." But her father's voice rose, crushing hers with its intensity. "Apparently we *can't* do anything we want. Apparently that's . . . childish."

Elda smirked. "So why are *you* going?"

He stood, knocking his chair over, and started towards her.

Kirsten said, "Aleks . . ."

He grabbed his daughter, both hands gripping her upper arms, lifting her up on her toes. She was as tall as he, then.

Their mother's voice rose finally to a shout.

"Aleks! That's *enough* . . ."

He released the girl. She sank down, rubbing her arms.

He said slowly, "I will sail to England. Then I will come back. I will leave as soon as there is fog."

But there was no fog.

129

In the end they went anyway.

Later that day, the one who had been introduced as Peder Sher returned. He said the English would have to leave tonight, fog or no fog. There was a troopship in the harbour; the men would need billeting. Also, he said, there had been an incident the previous night. Kirsten asked what kind of incident, but the men ignored her. The army would probably start house-to-house searches. They had to leave.

That night there was still no fog, but there was a little cloud. The moon was a day older, a day weaker. It would be dark enough.

The Shers and the Englishmen packed the little they possessed. Kirsten tried one last time to persuade Overand not to go, not to leave his family, and Overand tried hard to ignore her. In the shop was a wooden stepladder his father had used to reach goods on high shelves. He carried it up to the apartment and, having summoned Oskar to hold the ladder steady, he stepped up and lifted the hatch into the attic. Beyond the hatch, where Overand could just reach it, was a trunk that he and Kirsten had stored away when his father died and they had decided not to sell the shop. Now, reaching awkwardly above his head, Overand dragged the trunk one-handed across the bare joists. It was heavy, but the surface of the trunk was lacquered and it slid more easily than Overand had feared it might. He dragged it to the lip of the hatch, then, pulling down hard with both hands, he managed to pivot the dead weight upwards until something shifted inside and the trunk fell down; he stepped back to take the weight against his chest and missed the ladder's rung. When Elda came out of the kitchen to investigate the noise, she found Oskar still holding onto a stepladder on which was balanced a polished wooden trunk, while her father was wedged between the ladder and the wall, his feet caught up in the rungs, higher than his head. She went back into the kitchen and told her mother, who said: "Your father knows what he is doing."

Overand untangled himself and lifted down the trunk. It contained his own father's clothes, the clothes he had worn when out on the boat - Farfar's fancy dress, Elda called them - thick, greasy woollen sweaters that smelled of camphor, heavy canvas tunics, leather gauntlets stiff for lack of oil from all the fish they had not cleaned. Overand dug out three sweaters; there were only two jackets, but they would have to do. It was important, he told Oskar, that he and the Englishmen look as much alike - and as much like fishermen - as possible: their lives might depend on it. He pulled on a sweater and a canvas jacket and took the other clothes downstairs for the Englishmen. They took a sweater each and tossed a coin for the jacket. Jan won, but offered the jacket to the other man, the one who had played the accordion - Overand realized that even now he did not know the man's name; not even the name he was using - but he refused.

Kirsten came down to the shop; Elda hung back on the stairs, listening. Kirsten asked Sher if they had everything. Overand said, "We're fine."

There was a knock at the street door.

Silently, faster than Overand would have believed possible, the Englishmen and the faux-Shers swept up their belongings and disappeared behind the long, wooden counter. Only the paraffin heater, now cold, was out of place; and that, Overand thought, proved nothing.

"Herr Overand? I see you have come from Oslo."

131

It was the greengrocer. He was holding a clipboard. Beside him was a soldier. Overand said nothing.

"Only your wife did not seem certain when you would arrive?" He nodded towards Kirsten, who did not greet him.

"As you can see, I am here."

"Good."

The greengrocer made a mark on his chart. He said, "A troopship arrived this afternoon."

Overand said, "It would be hard to miss." The square grey bulk of the ship filled the harbour.

"It brought two thousand men. You . . ." he paused for a moment to consult the clipboard, ". . . will take six."

"Six?"

The greengrocer leaned towards Overand conspiratorially. "If you had not been here, Herr Overand, it would have been eight." He stepped back. "They will come later tonight. I am sure you will make them welcome."

When Overand closed the door and turned back into the shop, Kirsten said, "When they come, you must be here. Otherwise . . ." But Overand ignored her.

Slowly, still silently, the men emerged from behind the counter. Sher said, "You must go now. As soon as that man has moved on."

"It is not really dark."

"There is no choice."

They lined up at the door. Kirsten walked past her husband. She embraced each of the Englishmen in turn, kissing them on the cheek. She wished them well; she would pray for them. To Overand's surprise, Elda ran from the stairway and hugged one of the Englishmen, the one who had talked about Chekhov, the one wearing his father's jacket. As she stepped back, Overand reached out to hold her, but she shrugged him off. She ran back upstairs, into the flat. Oskar stepped up, held out a hand for his father to shake. "Good man," Overand said.

Sher, too, shook Overand's hand. He said "Good luck. Bon voyage."

"And you? What will you do?"

Sher said, "We'll be in touch when you get back."

That wasn't what Overand had meant, what he'd wanted to know, but he said, "How?"

"Don't worry. We'll find you."

This time, when the tiny boat slid far enough around the curve of the earth to lose sight of the lights winking on the shore, there was nothing there.

The cloud had thickened and the darkness was absolute. Overand felt as if they were sealed inside a vast black dome. Even on deck, he could see nothing, could only feel the boat pitch comfortably, hear the thudding diesel and the slap of water against the hull. The sea smelled, strangely, of animals and dry sweat.

A small yellow light flicked on, startling him. In the wheelhouse – he had always called it the bridge, with a knowing edge to his voice, although Elda always said it looked more like a shed, a small but sturdy greenhouse bolted incongruously to the deck – Jan, the Englishman who had been a sailor, was shining a torch on the boat's large brass compass. The light reflected weakly and lit his face from below: a disembodied clown mask glowing spectrally in the dark.

Overand stood in the doorway of the wheelhouse and said something curt, no more than a word or two. The Englishman said something, a single word. It might have been 'south'.

Overand made that noise, air blown forcefully down his nose, the noise he made to express the infinite incompetence of others; the noise Elda had made when he had said she could not go with them. The torchlight swung from the compass to the chart table and the clown face disappeared. A hand – Overand's hand – entered the funnel of feeble light, jabbing a finger at the chart. A second hand floated over the chart from the left, forefinger tapping gently at a point a little lower down. Overand snorted again, a little more muted this time. Then the light clicked off. The wheelhouse door opened, then slammed shut. The light flicked on again, just for a moment, bouncing off the glass. Jan adjusted the wheel a couple of points. A few moments later, Overand felt the boat pull, gently, to port.

It was Overand who first saw the whale that turned out to be a submarine.

The morning had dawned still and grey, the sky an unbroken canopy of thin, high cloud that might, he said, burn off, or might just thicken up. The Englishmen shrugged, as if it were all the same to them. The water was smooth and greasy, the same dull grey as the sky. A flat, directionless light had penetrated the night's black dome, but otherwise nothing had changed. Only the diesel thud and the propeller's churn – both so familiar now he had to listen consciously to hear them – told him they were making progress, moving from one point to another.

They ate breakfast – the bread and cheese and boiled eggs Kirsten had given Jan – and brewed coffee, though none of them had much appetite.

Then Overand saw it – a slick black smudge five kilometres off their port beam. (Five kilometres? Two? Fifty? In truth he had no idea, found it impossible to judge distance in the featureless greyscape.) Overand focused hard and saw a massive dorsal fin. Or perhaps it was a flipper, because the whale seemed to roll and dive, to be swallowed by the sea.

"A whale!" he shouted, hurrying back towards the wheelhouse. "I saw a whale."

In his excitement, he was speaking Norwegian. The Englishman without a name was just coming up on deck. He looked blank.

"*Hval!*" Overand said again, as clearly as he could, his mouth unnaturally wide, as if the man might be able to lip read a language he didn't speak.

The Englishman smiled and said something Overand couldn't catch, then shook his head and went below.

Overand went to the wheelhouse, where Jan was carefully turning the radio dial, one degree at a time. "I saw a whale," Overand said again, more calmly this time, and in English.

"Really? Did it spout?"

"No. It rolled and dived."

Jan said, "Take over, please. Keep a steady course. I'd better go below."

Overand took the wheel. The boat turned to starboard; the straight line of their wake curved gently behind them.

An hour later Overand saw the whale fin break the surface no more than fifty metres astern. It rose, followed by the terrifying bulk of its sleek black body, water cascading down and off its flanks. On the side of the fin, in stark white paint, they could see numbers and a letter: "68T".

A hatch opened, then settled with a clang. A man's head appeared. He seemed to hesitate, as if testing Overand's reaction, then climbed up to his waist out of the hatch. He wore a dark uniform with buttons that glinted dully in the weak grey light. He had a gun in one hand. Overand couldn't say what sort of gun. Not a rifle, but it was bigger than a pistol. He cut the engine and went astern. There was no choice.

Over the roar of sudden silence the man shouted, "Where from?"

The man sounded foreign. He had an accent of some sort, but, with him shouting like that across the water, Overand couldn't pin it down.

Overand shouted back the real name of his town. Then he pointed at the winches he'd never used and shouted, "Fishing. Herring."

The man shouted, "How many?"

Overand shook his head ruefully, an exaggerated gesture, as if he were in court, wooing a jury. "None yet."

The man shouted something short and guttural Overand couldn't make out, then: "How many crew?"

He paused. The two Englishmen were down in the hold. Invisible for now. But would a man go fishing alone this far out in a boat this size? If they were boarded the men would be found.

"How many?"

"Three."

"All on deck. Quick. Now."

The man climbed out onto the deck of the submarine, followed by several members of his crew, all armed. They lined up, weapons ready.

On the fishing boat, the two Englishmen climbed out of the hold and lined up with Overand, facing the submarine, now no more than twenty metres off.

It is hard to write this stuff without coming over all *Boys' Own*.

In reality, according to the diary transcript, there were seven men on the boat: four Brits and three Norwegians. I have cut it down to three because the story needs no more. Besides, it is difficult to orchestrate a cast of seven in a confined space, especially when most of them have no names and no identities. But when the boat set sail, my grandfather presumably had more time to write: it is as if his diary fills its lungs and rouses itself to life, the telegraphic prose replaced by something altogether more expansive, working by turns the dramatic and the lyrical potential of his situation.

They line up on deck. My grandfather enlisted in the Navy to fight the First World War as a child of fifteen; in September 1939, he fled Berlin at the declaration of the second. But this, he wrote, waiting on the deck of a small Norwegian fishing boat a few yards from a submarine and its armed crew, this was the most fearful moment of his life.

All the same, in the diary, it is he who spots the blue serge coat and the red badge on one of the submarine crew, who sees the number painted on the conning tower, and wonders why it nags at him, nibbling away at a corner of his mind, until sudden revelation crashes through the tiredness and the fear and he yells, "The TRUANT. She's British!"

His colleagues laugh and wave and shout, asking to go aboard; my grandfather tries semaphore but, in all the excitement, the signalman does not get his message. The Submarine Captain will not allow them to board, but sends them on their way towards Orkney, zigzagging ahead of the sluggish trawler before making off northwards.

There are still U-boats to worry about, though; and when, that evening, an aeroplane circles low around them and makes off quickly westwards they guess - and hope - that it too is British.

As the fear and its release recede, the diary's prose contracts, conserving energy once again: the remainder of the trip, a crawl across open, contested sea at a feeble two knots, is *tedious though anxious*.

The following morning they land, not at Lerwick, as they had planned, not in Orkney at all, the diary says, but a hundred miles north, at Kirkwall, in the Shetlands.

It is 7.00am on the 18th of May.

There are no goodbyes, no kisses and prayers, no handshakes, even.

§

T HE DIARY ENDED there: it was as far as I could go. It had been more than two weeks since my birthday, since I'd had dinner with Walter, since I'd collected the parcel that turned out to be *The Gift*. It was still the Easter vacation. Walter was walking in the Lake District; my students would be at home, I hoped, reading, researching, preparing, if they were in their final year, for their examinations. After twenty years of teaching, I doubted this was true, but, all the same, I knew that if I'd ventured out I would have found Cambridge unnaturally quiet, the bicycles outside each college temporarily abandoned, tethered to each other, layer upon layer, like mussels on a rope. But I had been no further than the corner shop. When I had eaten at all, it had been porridge and white bread and pasta and tinned food. If a vitamin passed my lips it was pure happenstance. The newspapers I'd bought remained unread, the recycling pile higher than ever. I had unplugged my phone and disconnected from the Internet, as I generally do when I am trying to work. For two weeks I had neither read nor answered email. I half-heard, but did not listen to, the radio from time to time. I was aware that the war in Iraq, which ended a year earlier, had not ended; I was aware that a great many people had died in a train crash in North Korea, one of the very few things anyone knew about North Korea; but, if I am honest, I cannot say that I had been paying attention. These human tragedies are just the oxygen we breathe.

Today was different, though. Today I had reached the end of the diary, and run out of things to write. Today I would go into town, eat lunch, visit a gallery perhaps; when I came home I would watch the news, I would switch back on the modem in my attic office, listen to its electronic chirrup and reconnect with the world.

But first, a shower.

When I was clean, I dressed and left my flat, locking the door with care and treading quietly lest Lisa in the flat below was not at work. Outside, clear spring sunshine lit the street with forensic clarity. I walked across the Green into town. I spent an hour in Heffers bookshop. I browsed the criticism section but chose nothing. Barely conscious of what I was doing, so automatic had the action become, I moved a copy of my essays on the philosophy of taste from an obscure shelf to the display table. I drifted to fiction, and picked up *The Line of Beauty*. I didn't know the book, or the author, but when I saw it on the display table I realized with a jolt that in *The Gift* Martin had placed it beside my bed in Scotland, a year ago. A year before it was published. I browsed a *New York Review of Books*. There were three headline articles about Islam and Iraq, but I flipped past them to one on Hannah Arendt. It dated Arendt's political awakening to the Reichstag fire. "I felt responsible," it quoted her as saying. For what? I wondered. Not for the fire, of course. Because she had no choice? Because she was human, and had to be at the heart of the story? I put the periodical back on the shelf and bought the novel.

In Russell & Bromley I tried on a pair of high-heeled sandals, in which, I thought, I would be almost as tall as Walter. I bought instead a pair of low black court shoes, similar to those I was already wearing.

I bought a bottle of malt whisky.

In a café I sank into a low, leather sofa and opened my new book. A man in a waterproof coat the weather did not call for placed a coffee on the table in front of me, spilling a little into the asymmetrical saucer, and lowered himself heavily into the armchair opposite. Without speaking, he opened his newspaper and held it up, covering his face – like a spy, I thought, childishly: it should have had two holes cut out right there, right where I could in fact see a blurred photograph of a man standing on what appeared to be a crate, his arms outstretched, his body draped in black cloth, his face covered by a black pointed hood, in which were crudely cut two holes for his eyes. I thought of the Ku Klux Klan in negative, of lynching and – perhaps because of the arms – of Crucifixion. Then I saw the wires.

There was something evil about this photograph, I knew, even before I knew what it was.

I thought: I am not responsible for this.

I ate lunch in a pub and read *The Line of Beauty*. I went to a supermarket; I got a taxi to drive me and my groceries, my book, my newspaper and my new shoes home. I put perishables in the fridge, the shoes on the rack by the door and the box in the recycling. I poured myself a drink and went upstairs. By the time my computer had booted up and the modem had stuttered into life and – finally – connected me to my email service, by the time two weeks' worth of messages had dropped, one by one, into my inbox, I had finished my whisky and poured another.

By the standards of my contemporaries, I understood, I did not receive a great deal of email. I encouraged my students to talk to me. I routinely "unsubscribed" from any mailing list I inadvertently found myself upon. Those emails I received from people I did not know and suspected might not exist – emails offering me insurance or drugs, or to deposit unimaginable but precisely quantified sums of money into my account if I would only supply the details – I cheerfully deleted, unopened and unread. And when I emptied my electronic trash and was asked whether I was sure, I clicked "Yes" without a qualm. That evening, however, when I had finished – or had gone as far as I could – and when, after my day of relaxation and reward and minor self-gratification, I was almost certain I knew what I was going to do, I found myself hoping, scanning, trawling the junk for an email from a man I knew without a shadow of a doubt did not exist.

It was not there.

The card that had come with *The Gift* two weeks earlier, however, was blu-tacked to the wall above my desk.

I opened Netscape and searched for "Paul Overand". I got no results at all, which surprised me, notwithstanding his non-existence. I removed the quote marks and searched again. I got a hundred million results, not one of which re-ferred to Paul Overand. I had no idea how the Internet did this. Or why. Martin would have known. The third result was a quote attributed to Oscar Wilde: "If one cannot enjoy reading a book *over and* over again, there is no use in reading it at all." It was not my period, and I did not recognize the source.

I switched off my PC and turned to the silt of unread newspapers. Muqtada al-Sadr had threatened suicide bomb attacks if the US moved against Najaf; car and truck bombs had exploded in Baghdad and Basra, killing hundreds; the US had been shelling Fallujah. And, in that morning's paper, the photo of the man in the hood was there again. It was an Iraqi prisoner of war. Another picture showed a young white woman in combat fatigues standing in front of a row of naked but hooded men, one hand pointing at a penis, the other giving a thumbs-up. A stark white overexposed and unlit cigarette protruded from her grinning mouth. A third showed the same woman holding a leash, the other end of which was tied around the neck of yet another naked man, lying curled on the floor. This man had no hood.

A Gallup poll showed 71% of Iraqis regarded the US as "occupiers".

I turned the pages and read about a new wave of anti-Semitism sweeping through French schools; the article referred back to France's war-time experience, to the 750,000 French Jews deported by the Germans and the Vichy French to Nazi death camps; I turned to the culture supplement. There was a review of *The Line of Beauty*. I tried to resist reading it, but failed. It told me the drug-taking scenes were frequent and boring, the sex was worse, and when the two were combined the results were "dire", but it said there was much else to enjoy, and I wondered about that. I had bought the book: I should never have read the review.

I booted up my computer again, and finished another drink. I re-read what I had written.

I had gone as far as I could go, as far as the diary went. Surely he would see this?

I closed down my computer once again.

It had grown dark in the attic room, and, without the screen's antiseptic glow, I could see little. I checked my watch: it was two-thirty in the morning. Tomorrow, I told myself, tomorrow I would return to the diary, to my father's transcript of his father's diary, which, I realized now, to my surprise, I had not consulted once during the past two weeks.

I went downstairs to bed but could not sleep. I turned on the art deco bedside light that Martin had found in a skip, and read the first two pages of an article on Lovelace in the *Times Literary Supplement* without taking in a word. I picked up my phone and re-read the text I had received from Walter two days earlier – *Wish you were here* – to which I had not yet replied. Walter was the only actual, non-corporate person from whom I had ever received a text message. I did not give my mobile number to my students; Ben called once in a blue moon; Alice had rung a couple of times in all the years she had been married to my brother. My father did not text.

Two days seemed to me an appropriate time to respond: it was the time it would have taken the Post Office to deliver a letter and its immediate reply.

Dear Walter, How are the Lakes? Hannah.

I put the phone down on top of the pile of books beside my bed but, to my surprise, it vibrated urgently before I could re-open the *TLS*.

Wet. How are you?

I fell asleep with the phone in my hand and woke an hour later to find that I was accidentally calling my father. I hung up before he could answer, although I knew he would not have done so anyway.

April 9th.
  Up all night.
  April the 9th: the day the Germans invaded Norway. That's how it started. I knew this.

2000 Completed my destruction.

2100 All personal papers burnt.

Except this one. Except this new personal paper, this diary.

It was morning. I was back upstairs, a mug of tea on the wall-to-wall desk Martin and I had built across the attic room. The transcript was buried in the papers piled at Martin's end of the desk, and took me a while to find. The end that used to be Martin's.

I thought I knew this story.

1500 Left Bergs. kiss(?) Miss & Munthe.

What?

By the evening of April 10th my grandfather reached Hjelmeland, where, with two colleagues, he stayed in a Pension and noted the *Proprietor's nice eyes.*

From the transcript I see now that he initially wrote *Landlady's nice eyes,* but then crossed out *landlady.* My father, in transcribing the diary, preserved that indecision.

Why? Had he perhaps considered *proprietor* more accurate? More respectful? Less suggestive?

It seemed he was concerned about the impression his words would make.

But on whom?

If he was concerned, why record her eyes at all?

I lowered the typescript, pushed up my spectacles and rubbed my own eyes with the back of my hand. Because it was true, I told myself.

Because the woman had nice eyes.

The diary named names.

When the decision to run had been taken, and his destruction completed, why record the names of his colleagues and the families who helped them?

Because it was true.

Because they helped.

Some were protected. H.E. might or might not have been His Excellency the Ambassador.

But the family whose bath my grandfather so appreciated after five weeks on the run (along with the *frequent and glorious food* they provided) was there for all to see.

As were the Overands: husband, *his wife "Bina" and boy.* No girl. Bina was in inverted commas. *"Bina".*

Why? Was that not in fact her name?

At 23.45 on the 16th of May, after the Germans found a transmitter at Kopervik and began house-to-house searches, my grandfather left with Overand; his wife, "Bina", kissed him and said that she would pray.

The second or third time I re-read this passage, I paused. I no longer knew whether Bina Overand kissed her husband, my grandfather, or both:

23.45 Mrs kissed and said she would pray.

Does it matter? Why have I even noticed the elision?

But I have noticed; nothing can change that.

I feel unclean.

I cannot escape the conclusion that my grandfather wrote as if it mattered what his readers thought.

As if he would have readers.

As if he knew.

I returned to the transcript once more, and noticed the strangest thing. I had read these pages countless times. I had interrogated them for clues, for inconsistencies. I had transcribed many of the words myself, had plotted my grandfather's movements on a map of Norway pinned to the wall above my desk. And yet now I saw a detail I had missed every time: *7.00pm In car to Overand's at Aland, his wife "Bina" and boy.* I'd seen the wife, I'd seen the boy, I'd even seen the quotation marks; but somehow I had placed them all in Haugesund, where my grandfather had arrived after a *hair-raising drive* and a burst tyre. I'd never before noticed Åland. I checked the map again. It took me a while to find, because it was nowhere near where I expected it to be. Åland was eighty miles inland.

If my grandfather wrote as if he knew he'd have readers, it seems he thought those readers would know little about Norway.

The following morning I received a text from Walter. *Back this evening. Dinner?*

I was in the café again when I read it, turning the pages of the newspaper. There were more photographs from Abu Graibh. I did not want dinner with Walter.

I returned home, stared at my grandfather's diary, at the pages I had written. It is not enough. It does not end, just stops. But I can go no further. Each time I try to see past this point, there is nothing.

All personal papers destroyed.

The men parted on the Kirkwall quayside. Jan - Albert Charles William - must have turned south, must have made his way to England, to London, or to whatever anonymous location they used for his extensive de-briefing, to wherever he called home, to meet his future wife, my grandmother, all the while carrying his diary, guarding the small navy blue notebook, keeping it safe to pass on one day, but never adding another word. That must have been what happened.

I could not see it, however. I could not write it.

I re-named the file 'Not *in my name*' and emailed it to Paul Overand. I said that I could go no further, he must see that? I signed the email 'Holly'.

§

Re: Not in my name
Ask yourself: what would MY grandfather have done?
Paul

§

T HE REPLY CAME before lunchtime, before I had finished the bottle I'd bought the day before, before he could even have read all I had written.

It came from 'Paul Overand', from the imaginary grandson of a man who existed only in my grandfather's diary, and now in *Not in my name*.

That was not true.

This man I did not know, had never met, not even as a child, this Aleks Overand, whose part in my family story I knew, but whose name I had never heard until a year ago, this man nonetheless existed – or had existed, sixty years ago. He had had a wife, a family he was prepared to put at risk, to sacrifice, perhaps, to save my grandfather's life, and that of his companions.

How could I know what this man would have done?

And yet, the more I thought about it, the more I found I could see what happened next, precisely because I did not know, because it did not, in fact, happen. I had only the vaguest image of my own grandfather's return to London, to his family, to his future wife and my unborn father, to his career in MI6 and all that that entailed – delivering Enigma-decoded intelligence to Montgomery in North Africa, rising to the rank of major, retiring to run a canal-side pub – all that I knew, after a fashion, but could not see. It was not in the diary, of course, but it was in the story. The story I knew I would not write. Aleks Overand, on the other hand, who if he was in the story at all, was there only as "the brave Norwegian", answered the question for himself.

What would he have done?

He would have turned back to his boat, his father's boat, the ugly, battered, fish-less fishing boat, the *working* boat, and set a course due east, back across the U-boat-ridden sea, back to a Norway run by German occupiers and home-grown fascists. To a home that was no longer his home.

It must have been a second slow, anxious journey through the unusually settled weather and quiet spring sea, his boat crawling eastwards at two knots, the steady thrum of the engine merging with his pulse, familiar, relentless, inaudible until a cough, a stutter suggested something wrong and Overand waited, praying to a God he'd long foresworn, not daring to breathe, until its rhythm settled, he checked his bearing and his thoughts returned to a steady course: what had he done? He had plenty of time to think, to imagine what might have happened while he'd been at sea. As dawn broke, touching the battered boat with thin red light, the question slowly shifted tense: what would he do?

Dusk was gathering again by the time he spotted the low grey smudge of warships anchored outside the harbour at Haugesund. The sky ahead, behind the mountains, was already black. Astern, an outsize sun dipped slowly through a cloudless turquoise sky into an oily sea; it seemed to gather pace once it was half-submerged, to drop so quickly he could almost see it move; he half-expected to hear the sizzling scorch of red-hot metal tempered in cold water. He chugged on, heedless of the mines Oskar had been so eager to tell him about when he arrived from the capital, only a week or so – was it? – ago. If he hit one, he hit one, Overand thought. At least that would be an answer of sorts.

The eight men billeted in the empty shop and in the flat above spoke only German. The radio played jazz, and two of the men were dancing, one pretending to be a woman. Overand saw another wearing one of his jackets over a collarless shirt. The man in his jacket offered him a beer, but Overand declined. He apologized for disturbing them.

Outside, the empty streets were dark. There were no lamps. His car was not where he had left it. He tried to remember if he'd given the keys to Kirsten. He was probably breaking a curfew: if he just stood still long enough, someone would arrest him. He wondered if that might not be simpler.

And do what?

The voice came to him from an Oslo window. Two weeks ago? Three? It seemed impossible it was not longer. He found himself thinking not about Kirsten, not about Elda and Oskar, not even about the Englishmen he'd saved, but about Abi. He wondered if she'd made it home.

There's no way to lock a fishing boat. If someone wants to come aboard, he will.

Overand woke in his clothes an hour before dawn, his head pressed against a bulwark, one arm dangling from the narrow bunk, certain he was not alone. He did not move.

"Herr Overand?"

The accent was local, the words an urgent whisper, not a peremptory demand for his surrender. A moment later a weak torch beam scoured the bulkhead until it caught his hand, trailed up his arm and came to rest on his face. "Herr Overand, you have to leave."

Overand raised his hand to shield his eyes. He could see nothing behind the torchlight. He remembered Oskar once telling him that when moths flutter round a candle they aren't flying towards the light, but trying to get to the deeper darkness beyond.

"Who . . . ?"

"Herr Sher . . ."

Something wasn't right. "You're not Sher."

"Herr Sher said if you came back, I should tell you to sail to Molde."

"If I came back?"

"He said it was not likely. He said you would almost certainly have more sense."

The voice from the darkness was relaxing, becoming more familiar. Another sentence or two and Overand would place it. He said, "Where else would I go?"

"You might go to Molde."

Almost. "But my family, Herr . . . ?"

There was a pause. The torch dipped and illuminated the deck. As his eyes adjusted, Overand could just make out the glint of spectacles on the speaker's face.

"Your family is no longer here."

He had it: the greengrocer.

"Where are they, Herr Marthinsen?"

Marthinsen sighed. "I didn't think you'd recognize me. You spend so little time here." He sat on the bunk opposite Overand. He stood the torch on its base so that they were both lit from underneath, their elongated, pantomime shadows stretching above and behind them both. Then he changed his mind and switched off the torch. In the dark he said, "The Germans still trust me."

Overand waited.

"They say Fru Overand and the children have returned to Oslo."

"Do you believe them?"

"It is possible."

Possible, thought Overand: anything was possible. "But not likely?"

"I . . . I don't know what to think, Herr Overand. If they had wanted to make an example . . ."

"They know about the Englishmen? They know I took them?"

Marthinsen said, "Of course."

"How? How did they know?"

"Because I told them."

Overand started. He sat upright, but Marthinsen continued, "You were here, remember? You were on my form. And then you were not here, and neither was your boat . . ."

"But the Englishmen?"

"They knew there were Englishmen here. There had been a bomb. A ship was scuttled in the fjord. Then there was the radio transmitter. They knew that we Norwegians were not responsible."

To Overand, he sounded bitter.

"You will need fuel," Marthinsen said. "Then you must leave."

Overand did not know Molde, but imagined it would be much like his father's coastal home: a fishing port, a harbour ringed by wooden buildings with steep roofs, a sharp-spired church. By the time he got there – towards the end of May, perhaps – he guessed there would be daffodils and primroses in the window boxes, but that it would still be cold, the weather shifting rapidly from storms to clear, liquid sunshine. In the event it took three days of slow coastal sailing, crawling past endless gnarled fingers of mountain, sometimes skirting between the islands, sometimes passing farther out to sea, his route intricate and crab-wise, avoiding, had he known it, the port to the south of Molde where the British had landed, but from where, less than a fortnight later, they had evacuated, leaving the country in German control.

When he arrived nothing was as he had expected.

To begin with it was warmer: he had never in his life been this far north, and had not anticipated the mildness that came with proximity to the ocean. The daffodils had come and gone, the primroses were dying back in the few window boxes he could see. But mostly there were no window boxes: there were no windows. Two-thirds of the town had been destroyed, the wooden houses burnt to their foundations, stone buildings collapsed in on themselves, roofless, with blank walls – where walls still stood – propped up by shattered, blackened beams. The air smelled of charcoal and burnt grease.

As he picked his way into the razed centre of the town Overand found himself following a group of women – eight or nine, in heavy woollen coats and plain felt hats – as they trailed from ruin to ruin, like starlings flitting between trees. They paused by each shattered building, their bodies still, listening. Overand could hear nothing. One lagged slightly behind and Overand caught up with her. He asked what had happened. She turned, and he saw that she was younger than he had supposed, her face pale but heavily made up.

She said, "The King was here, and the Crown Prince. The Prime Minister. They were all here."

From the middle of what had been the town Overand could see out across the slick black water of the fjord to the islands and mountains beyond. Behind him rose the mountains that would have protected the town in the past. It seemed an unlikely place to find a government; but now, at least, he thought he understood why he was there.

"Then the aeroplanes came."

The Germans had bombed the town all day, she told him. All day. There was nothing to stop them. The King hid in the woods above the town.

"When was this?"

"He's gone," the woman said. "They've all gone. The King. Prince Olav. The British took them. There was a ship. Perhaps now they'll leave us alone."

For the first time she looked into Overand's face. "Do you think they'll leave us alone?"

He could see how much she needed him to agree.

Instead he asked where he might find the cathedral. Marthinsen had passed on Sher's instructions. He was to meet a man there: a man called, at least for these purposes, Andreas. Andreas would attend each evensong until Overand arrived. That was the plan. Overand was no believer, but he assumed, even now, that a cathedral would be a solid building: not indestructible, of course, but even amidst this devastation something would have survived; the woman simply laughed. There was no cathedral. It had burned down fifty years before and they'd rebuilt it out of wood. Now it had burned again. She directed him to what remained, then hurried across the rubble-strewn street to join the other women, who were paused before another ruin, listening.

When he reached the cathedral site his watch said nearly six. If that were right, it would not be dark for several hours yet, but evensong would be due soon. He slipped between the fallen walls. A huge iron bell, cracked and deformed by the heat of fire, lay in a tangle of burnt beams. The marble font was blackened but intact. He found a scorched pew still strong enough to bear his weight and sat down. He tried to remember when he had last eaten; he hoped that Andreas would have food.

Some hours later, a young man picked his way fastidiously through the rubble. He had pale skin, exuberant black hair that refused to lie close to his scalp however much Brylcreem he applied, and a long leather overcoat that Overand would later say attracted too much attention, but which Andreas would refuse to abandon.

"Thank Christ you're here," the younger man said.

Overand hauled himself to his feet.

"Now we can get out of this dump."

As they left the ruined church, Overand saw a large black car in the street outside, and pulled quickly out of sight. Andreas laughed and walked past him.

"It is your car?"

Andreas said, "Of course." He stepped onto the running board and swung back the passenger door with a flourish. "Your chariot awaits."

"Where are we going?"

"Ålesund. Delightful place."

Overand pictured the charts he'd used to navigate the intricate coast. Ålesund was out towards the sea: west and a little south of Molde. It was not far as the crow flies – perhaps fifty kilometres – but there was a great deal of water in the way. The journey would take all of the short night and more. He suggested sailing there – "I have a boat" – but Andreas would have none of it.

"You have your luggage?"

A small canvas knapsack hung limply from Overand's shoulder. It contained little of any use, now: a toy battleship he and Oskar had carved from driftwood several summers ago, a scarf and a pair of stockings that might have been his wife's, and his father's leather toilet case, with its cufflinks and collar studs and old-fashioned, cut-throat razors.

"But my boat . . ."

"Will be safe here. It will be of use."

Of use to whom, Andreas did not say.

While the younger man drove, navigating his way without headlamps past bomb craters, past relics of the brief British expedition and out into deserted countryside down ever-smaller roads, Overand tried to sleep; but Andreas wanted to talk. He complained about having had to attend so many services. The cathedral was not a patch on the church at Ålesund. And the congregation? "You'd think, wouldn't you, that a war might bring a few more . . . interesting people into church?"

Overand said, "Interesting?"

"I mean attractive." The young man laughed. He took one hand off the steering wheel and clapped his arm around Overand's shoulders, feeling the hardness beneath the cloth. "I mean good looking."

Overand asked about the bombing.

"It was a bit of a relief, really. No more Evensong."

Overand assumed there had to be more to this young man

than flippancy. Why else would Sher have put the two of them together? He described the woman he'd spoken to, repeated what she'd said about King Haakon and the government. Andreas simply nodded.

Through most of the night their road hugged the dark fjord on their right, clinging to the edge of a mountainous peninsular only barely connected to the mainland at its eastern end. In the early morning the thread of rock narrowed until, at times, Overand could see water on both sides of the road. The sun had long since risen, but still hung low in the sky behind them, when they rolled over the bridge to Ålesund.

Andreas parked on the waterfront and steered Overand into a café. Overand said he had no money; he needed to sleep. It didn't have to be a bed: anywhere out of sight that didn't move with the swell of the sea would be enough. Andreas insisted they should drink, to celebrate his safe arrival – though it was only nine o'clock in the morning. He said there would be time enough for sleep; that Overand would stay with him. And money wasn't a problem.

Later, Overand thought he should have noticed that.

There were a few other customers, all men, mostly with the red, abraded faces, the slow squint and the easeful silence that comes from a lifetime of sailing small boats at sea. In their company, Overand's new companion seemed more than ever loud, brash, out of place, like a peacock in a dairy farm. He wished the man would quieten down. Instead, Andreas called out to the barman, ordering tumblers of oily, colourless liquor that smelled of fish and tasted like diesel. Andreas drank his in one swallow and gestured to the barman for another. The barman poured, then held the bottle out, waiting for Overand. Overand swallowed his drink but put his hand over the empty glass. The alcohol scorched his throat, plunged to his stomach: now he felt it begin to spread, to warm and soften him.

"Another time," he said.

The room above the bar showed little sign of Andreas' presence. There was a bed, a chair, a basin, but the blankets were smooth, there were no clothes hanging on the chair, no flannel on the basin; nothing but a small, leather suitcase in one corner. The fireplace was clean, empty. Overand, approving, said, "How long have you been here?"

It took the younger man a moment, but then he laughed. "Good God," he said. "This isn't my room – it's yours!"

Overand had not expected the luxury of privacy. He nodded towards the suitcase.

Andreas said, "Yours, too. Just a few things. I thought you might not have been able to bring much . . ." – he nodded towards Overand's dirty knapsack – "and, besides, I thought, life doesn't have to be so completely Spartan, does it? Just because of a war?"

Overand wondered what this young man had seen, what he had done, in the month since the Germans arrived.

When he left, Overand stripped off his clothes and climbed into bed. He had forgotten to draw the curtains, but doubted they would make much difference. He slept for eighteen hours.

The following morning he rose and shaved, standing naked before the basin, his father's razor in his hand. The water was warm, a pleasant surprise, but there was no soap. It was only when he had finished, and dressed, that he remembered the suitcase. He swung it lightly up onto the bed and popped open the brass catches. Inside he found two white poplin shirts, a pair of trousers and several pairs of socks and underpants. There were paisley silk pyjamas, a pair of hairbrushes and a small soft velvet case that proved to contain a shaving brush, a bowl of soap, a mirror, an ivory-handled safety razor and a packet of blades, each wrapped in its pristine wax paper. Overand dusted the back of his hand with the brush: its bristles were soft but springy, almost alive.

He wondered where Andreas had found such things.

He took his father's cutthroat razor from the basin, washed the soap from the blade and wiped it dry. The flat of the blade was mottled, but the edge remained sharp. He folded it closed and slipped it into the pocket of his greatcoat where it hung on the back of the bedroom door.

The shirts were too large; Andreas had clearly been expecting a taller man. Overand had to roll the cuffs over two or three times before fastening, to prevent them flapping around his fingers. By the time Sher first arrived with their orders, he had worn and washed each shirt a dozen times, rinsing them out in the basin in his room along with the socks and underpants, hanging them to dry over the back of the wooden chair. For almost a month he had waited, wondering what he would be required to do here. He explored the town, which did not take long; he climbed the hill behind it, as everybody does, stumbling slightly with his flat-footed gait, then turning back to be astonished by the perfect view: the old town filling the small island, the harbour bar jutting out to the right, its lighthouse winking in the early morning light, and, beyond the town, the massive bulk of Heissa and Godoya and countless other, unnamed islands, between which one could thread a route out to sea. He continued on, walking every track he could find, absorbing the mountains' contours as another man might explore the body of a lover. He walked, mostly, with his hands in the pockets of his overcoat, turning over keys to locks he presumed he would never see again, pebbles he picked up at the shore, fingering his father's razor, its handle smooth and comforting. He frequently felt breathless, light-headed; he would eat an apple, or one of the plums Andreas seemed to have no trouble procuring, and then, a few moments later, keep walking.

Andreas preferred to drive, and to talk.

As Andreas was the contact, the one supplied with money and petrol, Overand had little choice. But Andreas did not want to talk about their work. Every day, around lunchtime, when Overand returned to the café from his exploration, Andreas would hail him from the bar, insist he have a drink and perhaps some herring. While he ate, Andreas would talk – about food, about the university he had left, about the comrades he had loved there. About Ålesund. Like Molde, he told Overand, Ålesund had been destroyed by fire, before the last war. It was the greatest gift the town could ever have received, he said. Ålesund had been the ancient seat of Viking kings, but it was not an old town at all. It had burned down in 1904 and been rebuilt, all at once, with the most exquisite taste. Had Overand not noticed the consistency, the perfection of the architecture?

He had not.

"You have visited the church?"

He had followed the Kirkegata from the waterfront café to the island's tip and had, of course, seen the church. To Overand it looked much like every other stone church, larger than many, but essentially the same: a solid, square tower the colour of iron, low walls, rounded windows and a heavy sloping roof.

"But the frescoes?" said Andreas. "The stained glass?"

When Overand admitted he had not stepped inside the church, Andreas called the barman over urgently. "Can you believe?" he said, throwing one arm around Overand's shoulders, laying his other hand on Overand's cheek. "Can you believe that such a perfect philistine exists?"

The barman merely shrugged.

It was far earlier than he would usually leave the bar, but Andreas insisted that they go at once. On the short walk to the church, he tugged at Overand's sleeve. He talked endlessly about Thomt, who had painted the frescoes. When they arrived he pointed out the carved inscription: King Haakon had laid the first stone on July 7th, 1906.

"And now where is he?" Overand said.

Andreas said, "It gets better."

Inside, it seemed dark at first. Overand could just make out row upon row of wooden pews – seating for hundreds of worshippers, although the church was empty now. Then the sun broke through the clouds and the church filled with light. Overand stood before the small organ, the window behind it painting him and everything around him with splashes of tremulous colour.

Andreas stood beside him, looking up at the window, too. "A gift from Kaiser Wilhelm."

Overand turned to look at him. His face, usually so pale, was washed blood red by the stained light.

"Yes," Andreas said. "That Kaiser."

Later, as they stood either side of the font, Andreas leaned across, his long leather coat falling open. He was much the taller of the two and had to stoop a little when he took Overand's face in his hands and pulled it towards his own.

Overand did not assist, but neither did he resist. Andreas kissed his mouth.

"There," he said.

Overand saw Abi, then, walking slowly around the kitchen table in the house on Inkognito gate, in a grey shift dress that might have been his wife's.

They talked sometimes, he and Abi, he and Andreas, about what might happen. If I am wounded. If you are wounded. If one of us is going to be captured.

"We cannot be captured," Andreas said. "We would betray each other. Even you, Aleks, you would betray me."

That afternoon, when they returned from the church, Sher was waiting for them in the café. The Germans would soon be fortifying Ålesund and he brought orders. Andreas had been quieter than usual since he and Overand left the church, apparently content for once just to be with the older man, not to instruct or entertain him. Now, seeing Sher, something of his former manner returned. He called for drinks, for pickled fish and black bread. He asked too loudly for the news from Oslo, from Trondheim.

Sher led them to a table in the corner. The precaution was barely necessary: the fishermen had long since learned not to hear Andreas, just to nod when he paid for their drinks.

Overand told Sher what they knew; Sher told Overand what they were to do. Andreas excused himself: he needed the toilet.

Sher watched Overand's face as Andreas walked away from their table. He said, "You can trust him. Absolutely."

"You are sure?"

Sher nodded.

Overand said, "You understand that he is homosexual?"

"Of course."

Sher held his glass out to Overand.

"National Socialists are not fond of homosexuals."

As they touched their drinks together, the thick glasses made a muffled clink, like heavy coins knocked one against the other.

That night, after Sher had left, chugging lazily in Overand's father's boat past the lighthouse into a calm sea, Andreas came to Overand's room. Overand was already in bed. From the doorway Andreas said, "You are not wearing the pyjamas I bought you."

"No."

Andreas smiled. "If I bring my pillow, can I sleep with you?"

It was Overand who insisted that they prepare more thoroughly than ever before, than Andreas ever would; bringing to the task all the forensic attention to detail of the lawyer he had been. In court he tried never to ask a question to which he did not already know the answer; now he wanted to know all the questions the mission might ask of them. He insisted, in the teeth of Andreas' complaints, that they drive out hours before the time Sher's intelligence indicated would be necessary, hours before the convoy would clear the pass and begin the descent towards the bridge; he insisted that they strip and test their equipment again, in the field, before laying the explosives and the fuses; that they scour the surrounding hillside for the little cover it could provide, memorizing the terrain of half a dozen tracks that would take them back to the road on the other side of the peninsular, to the car, until they could find their way in the dark without a torch, without a moon.

The hillsides here were hard, basalt, granite. Thick tongues of rock probed cold salt water. The little vegetation there was lay thick, wiry, close to the ground: gorse, a windswept hawthorn, its barbed-wire branches all shoved over to one side, like the hair of a balding man. For two hours, Overand lay beneath that tree while Andreas, despite his leather coat, complained about the wind. Then the convoy arrived early – a whole hour earlier than their intelligence had said it would – but, thanks to Overand, their bombs were ready anyway.

The moment they blew the bridge, he knew for certain Andreas had betrayed them both. He had not known it before, whatever he might have told himself afterwards. But the revelation was perfect, complete, indisputable. It was not shock that he saw on Andreas' face - paler than ever, his mouth hanging slack - while the girders buckled and shrieked, and a tank, and then a truck, with soldiers spilling from the back, twisted slowly, pitched up on to their sides and seemed to cling to the frayed remnants of the suspension cables before plunging downwards, turning slowly end over end in the black air. The vehicles, and then the men, hit the deep, dark water of the fjord and were gone. It was not shock. On Andreas' face, it was not shock. It was fear.

They were supposed to have been too late.

After the bridge blew, Andreas was silent. Overand grabbed his coat, pulled him to his feet.

"Did you see that?" he shouted, knowing the question was redundant. "Did you *see* that?"

He whooped, loud enough to be heard if anyone had been listening. He grabbed Andreas again, dragging him along the path. As they scrambled up the hillside, rain began to fall, heavy and cold. As they crested the hill, wind off the sea hit them like a kick in the chest. The bridge was on the sheltered lee; a storm had been born and they had not even seen it. As they ran, slithering over wet rocks down towards the car, Andreas for once as flat-footed as Overand, it was the older man who talked, despite his lack of breath, his dizziness, Overand who shouted and laughed, excited, reckless in his own success. He talked like Andreas might have talked.

When they got back to Ålesund, they would go straight to the café. They'd celebrate.

Andreas said, "But Sher said, the boat . . ."

"I know. But we're early, Andreas. An hour early. The boat won't be there yet. We've got time."

They had left the hotel that morning, cleared out their rooms. They were not supposed to return. The boat – Overand's own boat; his father's boat – would take them further north, to Tromsø. Sher had arranged it.

Overand drove back to Ålesund, the car buffeted by the growing wind, the wipers barely coping with the rain. Generally, his driving was precise and efficient; he was careful not to waste the petrol he assumed was difficult to find. Now he drove stupidly fast, like Andreas might, scraping rocks and thumping into craters.

At the waterfront he slammed on the brakes, skidding to an untidy stop outside the café. When the barman offered to pour two glasses, Overand told him they would take the bottle.

He led Andreas to a table, slipped into a bench with his back to the wall, his face to the door. Andreas sat opposite, but Overand pulled him to his feet, pulled him round the table to sit beside him. He poured their drinks, one arm round Andreas' shoulders. They both swallowed and he poured again.

"We did it, Andreas!"

He slapped the younger man's back, then put his hand on Andreas's thigh.

Andreas said, "You did it."

Overand looked hard into Andreas's face, then turned to lift his drink.

"You did it, too."

Andreas nodded, saying nothing.

Overand took his face in his hands and kissed him.

There was a shout from another table. The barman said, "Now come on . . ."

Overand reached into his greatcoat pocket and pulled out his pistol. He slapped it onto the table with a noise that silenced the room. He poured two more drinks. "Andreas and I are going to celebrate."

One of the other drinkers put down his glass and left. Silently, with gathering momentum, the others followed, draining glasses, shrugging on coats, slipping away until they were alone: Overand, Andreas, the bottle, the gun and the razor they both knew was in Overand's pocket. It was better that way.

Overand was not surprised when the soldiers came, although he was surprised there were only two of them. They stopped in the doorway, not expecting to find the bar so empty. Overand grabbed his gun and hauled Andreas to his feet, knocking over the table, sending the bottle and glasses flying. He shot one of the soldiers: for a moment the man looked startled, then irritated, as if someone had spoken crudely to his girlfriend; then he collapsed. As the second soldier raised his pistol, Overand pulled Andreas across in front of him, awaiting his moment.

The soldier fired, his arm shaking visibly: the bullet hit

Andreas' thigh, high up near the groin where Overand's hand had gripped him minutes earlier. Overand shot the soldier twice, in the face.

Rain blew off the sea. The waves battered the harbour bar, then hauled themselves reluctantly back with a noise like shackles dragged across stone floors. There was no way the boat could make it now, whatever the time.

Andreas lay on the cold stones, blood soaking through his trousers, puddling around his groin. Overand lifted the younger man's head and laid it in his lap. Andreas said something he couldn't hear. He shouted, and Overand shouted back, but they were facing the ocean and neither could hear the other's words.

He knew what Andreas wanted to say, however. He was begging Overand to help him die. To kill him. The way they'd discussed. He stroked Andreas' hair: even this wet it would not lie flat. He traced a line across Andreas' throat with his finger.

"Why?"

He knew that Andreas couldn't hear above the sound of the storm, wouldn't answer; knew he wouldn't hear an answer anyway. But it didn't matter. He knew why. Andreas had betrayed him – betrayed them – for the usual, the *only* real reason there is for anything we do: fear. Not of pain, or death, exactly, although they were both bound up in that broader, all-embracing fear: of failure, of hope, of guilt, of seeing oneself in the eyes of others, even – especially – the eyes of those who love us, who place that intolerable burden upon us. The fear we once called God, that makes us invulnerable.

The landlady's nice eyes.

That same fear now made Andreas ask Overand to kill him. To save him.

Mrs kissed and said she would pray.

The same fear guaranteed he wouldn't do it.

All personal papers burnt.

3
RECONCILIATION

§

TRINITY BEGINS. IT is always a quiet term: your third-year students are revising for their finals, while, amongst the first years, ordinary girls from respectable state schools in Lancashire discover a taste for Pimms and methamphetamines. Your lectures on Rochester are not well attended.

You meet Walter for a drink, apologizing for not having responded to his text. You tell him your battery must have died, that the text arrived, for some unknown reason, three days late, that you had been busy. He does not believe you, but he smiles and says it does not matter. He tells you about his holiday in the Lakes. Once or twice, referring to things he has done or seen, he says 'we'. You do not point this out. You return to your flat, both of you, to your bed, but somehow it doesn't work, your bodies do not seem to fit. In the morning you say little, and what you do say concerns your work. You leave Walter drinking tea to check your email.

That evening you call your father. He tells you that retirement suits him. You don't believe it.

"You'll never retire."

"But I have, Hannah. I'm here."

"You can work in Scotland just as well as you did in London. Probably better. You can argue with the Government just as much."

"I could. But I don't."

"What do you do all day then?"

"I walk the hills. I sit and look at the lochs. I saw an eagle – did I tell you that? It was huge."

"You told me. What do you do when it gets dark?"

"I nurse a whisky in the local hotel bar and read . . ."

"Hah! Law reports, I bet."

"Novels, Hannah. Right now I'm reading *Middlemarch*. I haven't read it since I was at school. It's a completely different book."

"It's not my period."

"But you've read it? You should re-read it."

You said you would try, but you knew you wouldn't.

You said, "I'm glad you're enjoying it."

"I'm still going to die, Hannah."

Of course he is. We all are. You know that isn't what makes him special.

"But not just yet, Dad."

You hang up and check your email. You call Ben, but get Alice. Ben is at work, an evening committee. Alice tells you about the girls, your nieces. You tell her to give them your love.

You check your email again.

You read the newspaper. The civil war in Sudan that you had forgotten about has ended. A Chilean court has stripped Pinochet of immunity from prosecution. The "Corrections" column confesses to an extra nought in its reference to the deportation of French Jews: the correct figure is not 750,000 but 75,000. You had read the article without noticing the error, and you realize with some uneasiness that you would have believed either figure – or anything in between – because neither meant anything to you. What are seventy-five thousand people? What do they look like? You know the war's big numbers – six million Jews, twenty million Russians – but you know them as abstractions, as propaganda points. You have no sense of how they were made up, of how the French

– or Polish, or German, or, for that matter, the British or Norwegian – victims fitted into the greater scheme of twentieth-century atrocity.

The reply arrives at the weekend.

Re: re: re: Not in my name
Dear Hannah,
This is better, but the issue is perhaps more complicated than you suggest. There is much in your account of my country and my family that is inaccurate, but which I nonetheless find fascinating. The barest bones of your story are true: my grandfather Aleks Overand was a lawyer who saved your grandfather's life by sailing him across the North Sea in his father's boat. My grandmother and my aunt Elda disappeared, executed in reprisal. My grandfather returned to Norway, to fight. All this is familiar. How could it not be? It is the story of my family.

The inaccuracies, however, are what interest me.

As far as I am aware, there was no 'National Defence Union'. It was the National Union (*Nasjonal Samling*, NS) my grandfather joined. You must know this, as it is so easily verifiable. I assume therefore that you have changed the name of the party out of some fictional conceit – to demonstrate to your reader perhaps, that your rendition is fiction, despite the historical and biographical paraphernalia you deploy? Or perhaps out of concern not to alienate the sympathy of your reader, or of some residual squeamishness of your own: as you know, the NS was Quisling's party. Is it possible that you did not want to suggest – or even to think – that the man who rescued your grandfather from the Nazis might himself have once been a fascist?

Of course, 'Quisling' is now an English synonym for 'traitor'.

175

But Vidkun Quisling was a very particular kind of traitor. When the Germans invaded he accused King Haakon and the whole Norwegian government of treachery, and declared himself in charge – which must have confused the Germans. It also confused his party, which splintered as so many small parties do. Some members were shocked: Quisling pretended that there was no war, but it was obvious that peace was not an option, and in the choice between the Germans and the British it was not clear where their sympathies or their loyalties should lie. Some followed Quisling into puppet government; others, like those my grandfather must have met, decided to defend Norway against the more immediate aggressor. When he reached the coast, they were already there, the Englishmen with them.

All this I know from my father, Oskar Overand.

With kindest regards,

Paul Overand

PS Your final inaccuracy interests me also. You sign your email 'Holly', and yet your name is Hannah. Why is that?

You are furious, too angry to ask yourself why. You reply at once:

– You sign your email 'Paul Overand' and yet your name is Martin Pollitt. Why is *that*?

Even as you press 'send' you know instant replies are rarely wise.

A moment or two later you have worked out why you are so cross, which merely compounds your anger, because it is so obvious. You are angry for the most basic, most childish reason: because I am right.

I do not reply.

During the following weekend, however – which you spend with Walter, who seems not to have noticed the cooling of your relationship, and has invited you to dinner so innocently, and with such an absence of either righteousness or entitlement, that you cannot refuse – you find a new voicemail on your phone. You play the message, fearing that it must be your father, and that something is wrong.

I announce myself as Paul Overand. I say I will be coming to Cambridge for a couple of days at the end of May and would very much like to see you. I have much to tell, I say, about my father, much that you could not know. Could you please confirm that a meeting would be possible?

My voice is precise, accentless, unrecognizable.

This time you do not have to resist the temptation of an instantaneous reply, for at this moment, as you hold the phone to your ear, Walter returns from the kitchen, standing naked in the doorway, a mug of tea in each hand. Walter is thin, his limbs are long, precisely and visibly articulated and you could count his ribs from where you stand, yet he bears an undeniable pot belly, as if someone had strapped a well-stuffed cushion to his skeletal frame: standing upright, there is a crease in his flesh where it overhangs his pelvis and obscures the grey tangle of his pubic hair. It is the crease, more even than the greyness, which makes you realize that he – and therefore you – have passed the age where physical change brings any prospect of improvement. You are of an age. The downhill race towards decrepitude and death has already begun.

He waits in the doorway, apparently believing he is owed an explanation.

You gesture with your phone. "Just checking messages."

"Anything important?"

"No. Just my father."

Walter steps into the room, apparently reassured.

"How is he?"

"Not dead yet. Obviously."

Walter hands you a mug of tea and carries his own back around to what has already become his side of the bed. He climbs back in and sits up, his back against the headboard. He holds out a hand for yours and you sit together, duvet pulled up to your chests, sipping tea and holding hands. You cannot decide whether this makes you feel more like children or like grandparents, a married couple approaching your golden anniversary.

The thought makes you uncomfortable, and you let go. You push back the duvet and swing your legs out of bed. Your legs are thin, like Walter's, but pale, almost white, with a faint blue tracery at the back of the knees and ankles. At what point, you wonder, does alabaster skin become varicose veins?

Now, you think. *This* is the point.

Walter says, "Are you ready for some breakfast?"

"I have to go."

He makes a face that, on a puppy that had lost a toy, might be considered cute, but which, on a grown man, is not attractive.

"I have to work."

He reaches out and strokes your back, the way I used to, tracing your spine. "It's Sunday."

You stand up. "I still have to work."

At home you email:

178

– No, it is not possible for us to meet: you do not exist.

A few minutes later you receive a reply:

– And yet I email you. You email me.

– That proves nothing.

– Perhaps. Do you know Turing's test?

I know you do: I had once explained how Alan Turing argued that we would know we had created artificial intelligence when a man (you said: naturally, it would be a man) could hold a conversation with a machine, and not know it was a machine.

You write:

– Was your grandfather a fascist?

– He joined a fascist party.

– Did he switch to the resistance?

– The question is not that simple, Hannah. In Norway, as in so many countries, there was more than one resistance.

– ?

– My father told me that by the time my grandfather finally arrived at the family house on the coast, the two men you called Sher and the two Englishmen were already there. He remembered my grandmother was angry with him. She wanted to know where he had been, and what had happened to their housekeeper, and to the servant, Abi. In response my grandfather asked how long "these men" had been in the house. It was to fill the silence that followed that my father began talking about the German ships in the harbour, about the mines he had seen the British and the Germans laying.

It was my father who told Sher about the boat.

They had just finished eating. The Shers and the Englishmen, my grandfather, my father and my aunt Elda were all crowded around the table. My grandmother had put a kettle on to boil and was piling dishes in the sink.

Sher said, "It's a boat my friends could sail home."

My grandfather stiffened, but said nothing.

Oskar, my father, said: "But it's our boat. Farfar's boat. We should sail them home."

"That's right," my grandfather said, "we should. You and me, eh, little man?" And he ruffled Oskar's hair, something he had never done before.

My grandmother said she would not allow it.

When my grandfather said he was going, she stepped away from the sink towards Oskar's chair. She put her hands on his shoulders. "You will do as you please, Aleks."

Oskar felt his mother's grip tighten.

He wanted more than anything to hear his father say, "Don't worry, Oskar. I won't go without you."

But instead my grandfather turned to the Englishmen. He told them they would sail the next day. In the meantime, they were his guests. They had plenty more beer.

Sher said they should wait for fog before they sailed.

My grandfather ignored him and began handing round

bottles. He spotted an accordion one of the Englishmen had brought and demanded that he play it. Sher said they should not make too much noise, but my grandfather insisted. He kept encouraging the men to drink, pushing bottle after bottle across the table, and drinking more than anyone. He told the accordion player to play faster and faster. He told the other Englishman to dance with my grandmother. When she refused he shouted at her. The British were our friends. They were going to save us. He told his daughter to put her blasted notebook away and dance with the men who would save us from the Germans.

Then, according to my father, my aunt Elda said that wasn't what he used to say. That he'd always said the Germans were strong, while our King was weak. That the King was too close to the British, who were weak themselves.

My grandfather reached across the table and slapped her face so hard she fell off her chair. The accordion wheezed into silence. My grandmother led the children out of the room. As they left, my father heard Aleks encourage the men to drink more, play more, sing their national anthem, but Sher said they should go to bed: they should sail as soon as there was fog.

They waited three days during which, my father told me, he pleaded constantly with his mother to let him go. He begged Elda to argue his cause, too, but Elda said he was a fool if he thought they could sail the boat that far. They'd never been out of sight of land before. The Englishman, Jan, was a real sailor. He said Elda was in love with the Englishman and she hit him with the back of her hairbrush.

There never was any fog. But after three days, it was obvious they couldn't stay any longer or they'd have killed each other. My father would go with them.

He wondered what had made his father change his mind: Elda said it was because their mother kept insisting he shouldn't go; she had overplayed her hand. Then Elda opened her notebook, the one in which she wrote her poems and little plays, and began to write.

When they left, his mother kissed him. Elda hugged him, too. Then she hugged the Englishman he'd said she was in love with, and he saw her slip the notebook into his jacket pocket.

It was my father who first spotted the submarine, Hannah, not my grandfather. Oskar who thought it was a whale.

They landed at Lerwick, not Kirkwall; and they returned at once to Norway, not to Haugesund, but to the north.

So you see, Hannah, this is your greatest inaccuracy: when my grandfather sailed yours to Scotland, my father sailed with them. If he hadn't, I would not be here to tell the tale.

Regards,

Paul

§

I WAS TEN years old when my father left me with the
family of our former maid somewhere far to the north,
somewhere between Bodo and Narvik. Bodo was and is quite
literally the end of the line, where the Norwegian railway
network peters out: a separate line to Narvik runs up through
Sweden and across the narrow northern tip of our country;
from either it is a difficult drive or, in those days more likely,
a ride by horse and cart, over the mountainous coast road
to the small town where Captain Arne Burre was the most
senior policeman in a force of three, where Anna Burre was a
solid and respected presence in the lives of the women of the
town and where their eldest daughter, Abi, had grown taller
than her mother before leaving, at the age of fifteen, for a life
of domestic servitude in Oslo. Whether she remained in my
family's employment then was not entirely clear to me, and
perhaps not clear, either, to my father, the last of us to have
spoken to her; or to my mother, who had not now seen Abi
since before Easter, when she and I and Elda left Oslo for the
apartment on the coast, a thousand kilometres south of here,
and where, for all I knew, my mother and Elda remained,
sharing the flat and the empty shop below with eight loud,
over-large Bavarians; it is likely that Abi herself did not know
quite how things stood.

We had arrived at the town, however, my father and I, not
by train and car, or cart, but by boat, having sailed directly

from Orkney in the rusting, rolling tub we had inherited from my grandfather. Captain Burre was not at home when we arrived. The house was larger than most of those around it, and built of stone, not wood; it had been ferociously maintained. There was no trace of peeling paint, no glass cracked and papered over, no roof tile slipped and threatening to fall upon our heads; the small garden was staked out by a painted picket fence, and displayed all the colours one might reasonably hope for in that remote, inclement environment, with its salt sea wind and thin, acidic soil. A blonde girl about my own age opened the door and led us into a parlour where the polished wood of a piano glowed like the heart of a furnace and the armchairs all wore anti-macassars. She left us, promising to fetch her mother. While we waited, I played a scale until my father shook his head. The piano was almost in tune.

When Fru Burre entered the room I was surprised. She looked too young to be Abi's mother. Abi was grown up, an adult: her mother must surely be ancient? This woman was no older than my own mother and, if not quite as pretty, still the sort of person I could imagine holding my hand as we walked to the park, or playing tag for a while before laughing and saying she was out of breath, or reading stories to me at bedtime while Elda scribbled in her notebook and made that breathing noise in her throat that meant she thought I was being a baby and ought to be reading to myself and not disturbing her. Fru Burre did not look like her house, like the drawing room with its immaculately polished mahogany, its potted plant and its stuffed linnet in a glass bell.

My father explained why we had come.

At first Fru Burre listened politely, seriously. She said, "But why here, Herr Overand. Why this house?"

"I was given your husband's name. I was told . . ."

She interrupted my father, then. "Were you told my husband is a policeman, Herr Overand? That it might not be safe here, for your son. We are not exactly invisible."

My father ran his fingers through his beard. It was only a fortnight since we had sailed out of the dark harbour with the two Englishmen below deck while I, terrified, but proud as a peacock, stood in the bows watching for the mines I had seen being laid; only two weeks since my father had stopped shaving and, in the last few days, as we chugged slowly back across the grey cold oily sea, begun to complain of the itching.

He said, "Nevertheless . . ."

Fru Burre looked at him for a while, and at me, and then nodded, once. It was decided.

But my father seemed not to notice, to think he still needed to ingratiate himself. He said, "And then there was the connection with your daughter, of course. I never knew . . ."

"Where is Abi, Herr Overand?"

We both - Fru Burre and I - saw my father hesitate, I am sure.

He said, "She may be with my wife."

I was so surprised I said, "She wasn't there when we left, Pappa."

My father told me not to interrupt. To Fru Burre he said he hoped she might have arrived at the coast while we were away. It had been two weeks. He asked if Fru Burre did not also have a son?

She seemed to gather her thoughts before saying, "No. I have no son. Only girls."

"I'm sorry. I must have been mistaken. I thought . . . I only thought another boy might be good for Oskar to play with."

He had promised me there would be a boy, when we talked on the boat about what would happen when we returned to Norway. A little older than me, he said. The boy even had a name: Jørgen. This time I said nothing.

When my father left, I am embarrassed to say that I offered to shake his hand. He took mine, bowing slightly, and said: "My little man." He would return soon, he said, but he never did.

There were signs throughout the five years of occupation, had I but known how to read them, that he had not entirely forgotten me. From time to time, blue and white pennants fluttered from the fence posts or from the few, low trees that grew in the valleys; occasionally, packages would appear on the back doorstep of the Burres' house. Money, sometimes, or food: meat, butter, chocolate. One winter morning I stumbled face-first, blear-eyed, hands stuffed into my armpits for warmth, into a whole slaughtered pig, that might have been our pig but wasn't, strung up in the outside privy, its throat slit and dripping, still, into the toilet bowl. Captain Burre told me it was a present. Then he said it was not a present, exactly, more a bonus, from one of the landowners whose house had not yet been burned to the ground. I could see that he was lying. But that was later on, towards the end of the war, when we were all so much more used to lies, and I knew that this was not one I should question. I would perhaps never know who had given us the pig.

There was Aisa for me to play with, even if she was a girl. Even if, despite being less than a year older, she took it upon herself to explain the world to me. Her manner reminded me of Elda, but the explanations she offered were wildly different.

I liked her. She reminded me also of Abi, of whom I had been fond, although she talked rather more.

The first day, when my father left, Aisa took me out into the garden, and showed me the short walk into town. The walk crossed level ground at the head of a vast, steep-sided valley. Beyond the buildings of the town, the fjord glowed deep blue with the intensity of enamel. She showed me her school, and asked if I would be going there next term. I didn't know: my father had said nothing about school. She showed me the church. She said it had been built in the thirteenth century. I didn't know what to say to that, or whether I was expected to say anything. She showed me the police station. We could go in, she said, to meet her father, if I wanted to. I'd been in my own father's office, when it was closed. From the windows, I had looked down at the police headquarters. I told Aisa I could wait.

She shrugged. "Suit yourself. It's boring, really."

She asked if I had any money.

When we landed my father had given me the equivalent of six week's pocket money. "That should see you through," he said. Aisa took me to her favourite shop, where we bought boiled sweets, liquorice and fruit gums. The shopkeeper told us to make them last – there might soon be no more sweets – but we were ten years old, and we ate, dipping into the bags and feeding the sweets into our mouths in an almost continuous stream until we both felt queasy. Then we sat on the shore and threw pebbles at gulls.

Aisa said, "Does Abi have a boyfriend?"

I had no idea. Abi was a maid. She wore a black dress, a white pinafore and a pert cap over her short black hair. I liked her – she was friendly to Elda and me when our parents were not around. But how was I supposed to know what she did on her day off?

"Where does she sleep?"

"In a room in our attic. You can see the cathedral from the skylight."

"Could she take a man up there?"

I thought about it. "No. I don't think so."

"She had a boyfriend here. She was lucky not to get a baby."

I threw another pebble and, this time, hit a gull. It looked at me as if committing my face to memory, and then launched itself clumsily into the air.

When we returned to the house we entered through the kitchen door. Sitting at the table was a man I guessed must be Aisa's father. I had never seen anyone so big, or with such sharp edges: I can see him now as clearly as I saw him then, for the first time. He stood up when we came in, but stood at a tilt, one shoulder higher than the other, his enormous head cantilevered against the slope. His hair twisted upwards like black smoke from above a high, rutted forehead. His nose was large and predatory; deep grooves ran from beside his nostrils to the corners of his mouth; more creases ran downwards from his eyes across his cheeks and gave him the appearance of having been assembled from parts that didn't quite match. He had taken off his uniform jacket, which hung from the back of his chair, and I could see his braces stretched tight over his chest. His shirt collar was buttoned against his throat; his tie hung broad and stiff, the point a good three inches short of his waistband. His arms were angled awkwardly, crossed, the elbows cradled roughly in the palms of each hand.

To be honest, I was scared. The man stared at me, and seemed to be waiting for some mistake on my part. But when he spoke his voice, though deep, was gentle.

"You must be Oskar."

He held out a hand like a shovel that I could not get my own fingers around to shake. He laughed. "Captain Burre. At your service. Has Aisa been showing you the ropes?"

I did not know what to say.

The huge man put a heavy hand on my shoulder and pulled me under his armpit. It smelled like herring. He said, "Did she make you buy sweets?"

I tried to say that my father had given me money, but he didn't let me finish.

"Don't worry, little man," he laughed. "I just wanted to know if you had any left!"

He rubbed his knuckles across the top of my head, then whispered, *sotto voce*: "You don't have to tell me."

I pulled a paper bag out of my jacket pocket and offered him a liquorice tab, which he ate with theatrical relish, closing his deep black eyes and smacking his dry lips.

Fru Burre came into the kitchen folding a small towel and the captain, winking, let me go. Aisa asked if I were going to stay and, when her mother said I was, asked where I would sleep. Fru Burre looked not at Aisa, and not at me, but at her husband, as she said, "I thought he might sleep here."

"Here? In the kitchen?" I wasn't sure if he was angry or amused. "Curled up on the stove I suppose?"

She said nothing, but held her ground.

"Dear God, Anna, we're not peasants. The boy's not a serf."

He squatted down, his knees and elbows jutting out like the geometry problems I'd tackled at school, his huge face level

189

with mine. He said, "You'll probably be a bit lonely, to begin with. Aisa will look after you."

He straightened up and announced, "He'll share with Aisa. He can have Johanna's bed."

Fru Burre said, "If you say so."

"Oh, go on, woman. They're children."

That night, after she had drawn the curtains against a sun that still hung like a vast bauble above the horizon, after she had licked her fingers to snuff out the candle, in the faintly smoke-scented near-dark of the Arctic in early summer, Aisa told me that Johanna, in whose bed I lay, was her sister, her other sister. She was seventeen, and had been married almost a year, to Josef, who was a handyman, a carpenter and painter. He had painted their house, and the garden fence. She said, "Do you have any brothers or sisters?"

I told her I had a sister, Elda, who was thirteen.

"Where is she?"

I said she was at our grandfather's shop, with Mamma, and hoped it was true. "That's where we left them."

"You'll miss her."

"Maybe."

I wasn't sure. I believe now that I wasn't missing Elda, or my mother, that I had barely thought of them in all the time it had taken my father and I to sail to Orkney and back, other than to celebrate in my mind the fact that I was doing what my mother believed I couldn't, helping my father sail the Englishmen to safety. Whether this conviction is reliable I can't honestly say. It seems unlikely, from this distance, that a boy of ten, embarked on a perilous but also tedious mission in the company of two men whose language he did not speak and a father who was preoccupied and undemonstrative at best, that such a boy would not long for the comfort of a mother, or the companionship of a sister. But – what can I say? – that's how I remember it.

I heard Aisa's voice, in the dark. "You will."

We said nothing after that. I listened to the creaking and ticking of an unfamiliar house until I fell asleep.

In the morning Captain Burre – who insisted I call him Arne, which I never could – said I might play in the woods with Aisa, or down by the sea, or anywhere, really, but should keep an eye out for strangers.

"But Pappa," said Aisa, "everyone here's a stranger to Oskar!"

Burre thought for a moment. "I tell you what we'll do. This morning you can come with me. I'll show you around. Aisa can look after herself. Have you ever ridden in a motor car?"

I told him my father had two cars – a large German saloon and a small, green two-seater English sports car with a bonnet as long and thin as a coffin and a chrome rack on the back you could strap a suitcase to. When my father drove out to join us at the coast, it was in the two-seater. I had pictured Abi in the passenger seat, her hair tied under a headscarf, the way my mother sometimes wore hers, her mouth – Abi's mouth, my mother's mouth, I was no longer sure – open in a wide grin as they stormed the wind. When my father arrived, he was alone.

"But have you ever been in a *police* car? If you're good, I'll let you ring the bell. I'll let you stand on the running board like they do in the movies. You've been to the movies?"

I nodded.

"Of course you have."

We set off without breakfast. Fru Burre said I should eat something, but did not insist. Her husband said we would be fine.

When we pulled out of the yard we turned left, not right: inland, away from the town. Burre said he had visits to make. He would take me to the station later. I had imagined that there would be nothing this far north, nothing but rocks and snow and the dismal, ice-bound fishing ports and hydro-electric power stations we'd learned about at school. I was surprised to see the valleys so densely, richly, farmed. There would be ice and snow, of course there would – it was there, still, on the north faces of the mountains all around us – but now, at the end of May, there were crops and animals in every field. We drove for about thirty minutes, Burre explaining to me, as my father never had, how the gears worked, the clutch, and pointing out objects of interest: the Bergson's bull ("Stay away from him, Oskar. Gored a man to death last year"); the water tower; the hill with a sharp bend at the bottom where, as a boy about my age, he had fallen off his bicycle ("Second gear, Oskar, then step on it as you come out of the bend"); the road we didn't take that led to the barracks and the firing range where the army used to do manoeuvres ("When we had an army"). We pulled over a treeless pass where the rocks were emerald green with moss and into a low, wide valley and I could see the road scoured out ahead, what was left of it this far from town – two white tracks with stiff grass between, leading to a farmhouse, the only building I could now see in the entire landscape.

By the time we rolled into the yard a man was standing in the doorway, a mug in his hand. We got out of the car. I was careful where I put my feet. The yard and the man smelled strongly of animals.

He nodded. "Arne."

"Halvar. This is Oskar. He'll be staying with me."

The farmer looked my way, slowly scanning me from head to toe, then turned back to Burre and nodded again. Then he gestured with his mug.

"You'll want some coffee?"

The kitchen smelled almost as strongly as the yard. Halvar Madsen poured water into a kettle from a huge stone jug, put the kettle on the stove.

"She's at her mother's. They're trying to talk the youngest out of volunteering."

Burre said, "Peder?"

Madsen nodded.

"He can't be fourteen?"

"Same as Jørgen," Madsen said. "Birthday just before Easter."

He cut three thick slices of bread.

"Do you want eggs?"

By then I could have eaten any of the animals in the yard, so I was disappointed when Burre said we would be all right. The coffee tasted like hot tar. The bread was dense, hard to chew, but the dripping that Madsen spread on it was something I thought I could get used to.

As we ate, Burre said, "Any sign of them?"

Madsen shook his head. "Far as I can tell."

"They've not been up to the barracks?"

"No. Have you got orders yet?"

"Not yet. They'll look at their maps and get round to us in the end."

The two men finished their coffee. They stared for a moment into the bottom of their empty mugs. Mine was still almost full.

As we left, Burre said to the farmer, "If it helps, you can tell Peder we're stumped on the hayrick fire. Damned if we know who set it."

Madsen nodded. He said, "How's that garden of yours, Arne? Anna will be needing a little help."

They paused a moment, resting back on their heels. Even then, I'm sure I sensed an agreement had been reached.

When we returned to the car, Burre asked if I wanted a go at driving. I said I couldn't. He made me try, all the same, but I was right. My legs were neither long enough nor strong enough to work the pedals. Burre said, "Another time."

He drove back to the road. At a crossroads where, on our way out, we had driven straight across, Burre now turned left. A few minutes later, over another empty hill, the road again broke down into a track and ended at a farmhouse. Another farmer – a woman this time – was waiting in the doorway when he turned off the engine. Burre said, "This is Oskar, he'll be staying with us." The woman looked me over, as Madsen had; speaking to Burre not me, offered us breakfast. They talked about her family. Geir, her youngest son, had gone to Narvik to train as an electrician but had returned home, walking over the mountains for three days when the bombing started. What use was an electrician, she asked, here where there was no electricity? She enquired after Anna; Burre told her, briefly, such news as there was from Abi, in Oslo, about Johanna and her husband, and about Aisa, who was the same as ever, apparently. She was pleased to have a new friend, Burre said, seeking to include me in the conversation. After a while he talked about a brawl in town the previous weekend: a man – a stranger, who some witnesses said might have been German, or have lived in Germany, or at least been sympathetic to the Germans, or might have been a spy – had been injured, but no one had yet been arrested.

So the morning passed into early afternoon, at house after house, always the same words to begin with: this is Oskar, he'll be staying with me, sometimes with Anna and me, as if that were just the way it was. Burre offered no explanation and invited no questions. By the time we eventually drove into town and parked the police car in the tiny square, we'd eaten bacon, eggs, rye bread, smoked fish and biscuits, and I had even begun to acquire a taste for coffee.

I asked if we were going to the police station, but Burre said there'd be time enough for that, and led me to the single café on the square. I had been to cafés in Oslo with my father where there were mirrors on the wall and cakes in glass display stands. This was more like the one in Haugesund where I had spent my summers for as long as I could remember, but was plainer still. Two men stood at the short counter, behind which a couple of bottles stood on an otherwise empty shelf. Four more sat around the only table, playing cards. There were no women. Some of the men were drinking colourless liquid out of thick, stubby glasses. All wore hats or caps, and waistcoats over shirts of varying degrees of dinginess. Burre ordered a drink, asked if I would like lemonade, and bought that, too.

"Gentlemen," he announced indiscriminately to the clientele at large, "this is Oskar. He'll be staying with me."

I felt the eyes of seven men – the proprietor and all his customers – look me up and down the way Madsen and the other farmers had. One of the card players said, "How old are you, Oskar?"

I looked at Burre, who gave a slight nod.

"I'm ten."

A nodding of heads and a pushing out of lower lips followed, as if to suggest it had been a good answer.

"And where are you from, Oskar?"

The words were commonplace enough, but there was something about the way they were spoken that was neither friendly nor particularly polite, more as if the man were teasing me, or indicating that he did not believe Oskar to be my real name. Before I could respond, however, Burre said, "He's staying with me, Fischer." He paused then, as I understood afterwards, not to invite further conversation but precisely to underline the finality of what he'd said, to make sure there would be no more questions.

Burre swallowed his drink and placed the empty glass back upon the bar. "Now, if you'll excuse me, some of us have work to do." We left to the sound of laughter, some of it his own.

The following morning, Fru Burre told her husband that, as I was here, I would have to help out. I looked around the orderly kitchen and wondered what chore could possibly remain undone.

Burre said he had spoken to Esther Sarsen yesterday, that her boy Geir would be coming soon to wire the house. I could help, he said, it might be interesting for me; in the meantime I could play with Aisa.

"We'll have electric lights, Anna. And sockets in every room!"

His wife allowed the remark to die before saying sourly, "And nothing to power them with."

"It will come, Anna. After the Germans have gone, perhaps. We will be ready."

She shook her head. Aisa and I could do the washing up. Then we could weed the flower beds along the road, under the picket fence, but Burre said not to worry about gardening: Peder Madsen would be calling in the next couple of days.

Geir Sarsen arrived a week or so later, carrying a metal tool box that expanded upwards and sideways, displaying terraced scoops of nails and screws and cable pins and small glass tubes with metal caps that he explained were fuses. He was eighteen, and not a boy at all, his limbs long and hard, his eyes already squeezed into that distant squint I had learned to recognize in the faces of all the men and women Captain Burre had introduced me to. He did not want my help, which, with some justice, he believed would be no help at all. But I was keen to learn and, by the middle of the morning, he had me sawing through floorboards and feeding in the long stiff wire with a hook on the end that he used – and I soon learned – to thread cable under the joists from one side of the room to the other. By the time I had blisters on my palms, Geir had relaxed a little, enough to go easy on me. We had started at the top of the house, amongst the eaves, then in the bedrooms. I felt uncomfortable entering some of the rooms – Abi's, her parents' – as if I were intruding, and might be caught. Geir said he was used to it: I wouldn't believe some of the things people left lying around for him to see. In this overwhelmingly feminine house, one room seemed more familiar: from the few books left on the shelf and the pictures clipped from magazines pinned neatly to the wall, it could have been my room at home, in Oslo, if it had been a little better furnished.

A couple of days later, when Aisa snuffed out the candle, the wall behind the nightstand was scarred by the channel Geir had chiselled out of the plaster. Aisa liked to talk, I knew, but most of all she liked to talk when it was almost dark and she could only sense me lying in her sister's bed. Then she would tell me what was going on around us, passing on the titbits she had gleaned from her parents or the other adults of the town as if she were herself the fount of all knowledge. I knew before she told me that there were soldiers garrisoned in Bodo, that the railway bridge into Narvik had been blown up, but I did not let her know I knew. She would tell me about her father. He had joined the police straight from school, she said – as if she had been there to witness it herself, as if she were his sister, or his mother, even, rather than his child – after his father, a blacksmith and a drunk, but clear-eyed enough to see what the motor car was doing to his trade, told him to drop any stupid notions he might have had about taking over the family business, punctuating his point with a branding iron that glowed white and bent like putty when he smashed it against the bellows. Her father had done two years police training in Oslo before returning to Nordland to work his way up through the ranks. Not that there was much competition, Aisa said sagely, as if she were an old hand at office politics herself. She would tell me about her mother, who had been a cook in a rich family with a house in Oslo and a huge estate here that was mostly empty mountainside. Every summer they would charter an entire train to bring the family, its guests and servants up through Sweden to Narvik, then hire every car and cart and carriage in the town to ferry them all to the house amongst the trees that didn't belong here, trees the hall's first owner had spent a small fortune to nurture and maintain; here the gentlemen would shoot birds and the ladies would talk about the parties they'd go to and the dresses they would wear when they all returned to the capital. One year, there had been an accident. One of the guns had shot his own brother – by mistake of course, but a man was dead and the police were called.

"That's when my father met my mother," Aisa said.

Mostly Aisa was happy to talk, for me to listen, but sometimes she would ask about my family, about Elda, and about Abi. I always said they'd be all right, although I had no way of knowing. When the Germans left we would all find each other. One night, to avoid talking again about Abi – about whom, in reality, I had very little to say – I asked Aisa about her brother. In all the time I'd been there, nobody, not even Aisa, had said anything about a brother, but I had not forgotten what my father said he had been told, or the unoccupied room I had wired with Geir.

After a while, Aisa said, as if there were no mystery, "Jørgen? He isn't here."

I waited, but she said nothing more. I could hear her shifting in her bed, kicking out her legs to settle the blankets.

Our birthdays were close – within three days of each other, mine at the end of July, Aisa's at the start of August – and, when I was going to be eleven and Aisa twelve, her father said we should have a party.

"A party, Arne?" said Fru Burre. "Now?"

Soldiers in grey uniforms and round, coalscuttle helmets had finally turned up to occupy the old barracks. They commandeered the small town hall opposite the police station in the square. They stacked sandbags against the walls and hung heavy blankets over the windows. One night over dinner Aisa and I heard Captain Burre tell his wife he had been summoned to meet a fat colonel with sloping shoulders who had let him know he'd been a cavalryman in the last war and still, it was obvious, believed he looked good in a saddle. The colonel had shaken his hand and told him he knew this was a backwater; he invited Burre to agree that there would be very little trouble here.

"He assumed I knew all the likely troublemakers. He said he was sure I knew my job but, if I needed any help from the military, such resources as he had would be at my disposal."

"What did you say?"

"I thanked him. I thanked him and then I went to the café and ordered a drink. But before I touched it, I went to the toilet and scrubbed my right hand."

A week later we heard Captain Burre had been back in the town hall. Rationing was to be introduced, he had been told. Every citizen who could prove his identity would receive a card. The colonel was not a fool, he said – although Burre seemed to me less than convinced when he repeated the comment while Aisa and I ate quietly, hoping he would not remember we were there – neither, contrary to all appearances, the colonel had said, were his superiors. They knew that rationing would produce a black market and that, in a remote area such as this, where there were many farms, the opportunities for – how could he put this? – for *unofficial* transactions would be considerable. Captain Burre's task was to ensure that the consequences did not become . . . unmanageable. The colonel would of course do what he could to assist.

"I told him my job is to apprehend criminals. He laughed

and said how delightfully old-fashioned we are here. That's what the bastard loves so much about the place."

The profanity was greeted by a sharp admonitory hiss from Fru Burre, but she said nothing. Aisa and I held our breath.

"Apparently my job is to make sure anti-social elements don't spoil things for everybody."

The day of the birthday party was also the day someone drove a truck into the front of the town hall. The explosives in the truck did not detonate and the building survived, but, as three soldiers in grey uniforms ran out into the square, they were shot dead.

Aisa and I heard all this when her school friends' parents turned up early to take their children home. Captain Burre had stayed at home to help out with the party. He had risen early that morning, he told me later – much later, towards the end of the war when it was evident to all, not least the fat colonel who, by then, had been reassigned to the Russian front, that the Germans had lost – and had found on the kitchen doorstep a package of chocolate bars, eggs, sugar and flour, and a wooden boat carved from driftwood; that evening, walking home, he saw blue and white pennants tied to the lower branches of the one tree in the square, to the fences, and to the sign that welcomed visitors to the town that, until now, had had almost no visitors. At the time he simply told us all not to worry.

On the first day of September I went with Aisa to join the class for older children – there were about a dozen of us, none older than fourteen – who shared one of the two rooms at the school and were taught arithmetic and poetry by Froken Dahl. There was a red flag in the corner of the room, with a black swastika on a white circle and that first day – and all subsequent days – began and ended with a declaration of allegiance to our new leaders. Froken Dahl explained that this was necessary, and that nobody would think any the less of us for repeating the words.

At the end of September, we heard that the house of the family Aisa's mother used to work for had burned to the ground. The family, their guests and a handful of servants died; most of the household staff had been holding a dance in one of the estate barns, and survived. When Burre told his wife, she was surprised to hear there had been a party there at all: what did they think they were doing? How had they even travelled here? Surely they could not have chartered a train now?

Burre had been summoned to the scene in the small hours of the morning, and had spotted half a dozen red pennants tied to the cultivated trees on the avenue that led up to the house. He told us that the colonel had insisted on referring to the tragic fire as a crime "of no military significance". But that did not mean, the colonel pointed out – obviously pleased with his own wit, Burre said – that it was of no significance to the military. News of the fire had reached the capital – not just our capital; his capital – and examples would be made. This was an opportunity, the colonel said, that we could be sure his superiors would not let slip. The District Commissioner would be paying us a visit.

One wet October morning – I was still surprised that we were not buried six feet under snow and ice, and that the sun barely rose above the hills behind the town – when Fru Burre told me to answer a knock at the door, I found a soldier with a rifle held diagonally across his chest. The soldier stood aside to reveal a man in a full-length leather greatcoat with the swept-back hair, the strong jaw and the bearing of a film actor, an effect not wholly undermined by the weakness of his mouth – his cheeks seemed on the point of collapsing into a lipless hole – and the fact that he was barely taller than me. I directed him into the parlour while Aisa fetched her father.

The Commissioner complimented the Captain – and his good wife, of course – on the elegance of the house, the prettiness of its garden, the modernity of its light fittings (he had not been aware, he said, that mains electricity had reached this far) even on the beauty of the chaffinch on the mantelpiece.

It was a linnet, I said, and regretted it at once, for the moment Burre realized that Aisa and I were still in the room, he sent us out. Later that night, however, we crept downstairs to hear him tell Aisa's mother about the conversation. "Anti-social elements," we heard him say. "Trouble makers, obviously. Agitators, Jews; Communists, naturally. But also people of no use, he said – homosexuals, idlers, grocers, bank clerks, teachers – people of that sort.

We heard Aisa's mother say, "Teachers?"

"That's what he said. People of that sort."

"What's going to happen to them?"

"They'll be sent off to work. He said the fatherland had more important ways to use such people's energies. He said they might yet learn to become useful."

There was a silence. Outside the door, squatting awkwardly on the lower steps of the staircase, we held our breath.

Aisa's mother said, "What are you going to do?"

Another silence, then her father, again. "We are an experiment. I'll get a quota. It seems they know in advance how many anti-social elements there will be, how many will be adults, how many children. All I have to do is find them. If it goes well, they will do the same in other districts."

"And if it doesn't?"

Aisa's father did not answer.

He said, "The Commissioner said he would not presume to teach me my job. But I should set an example. Then he asked about my son. Our son."

Through the door, we heard Aisa's mother gasp, and Burre say, "He may have meant Oskar."

"Please, God. What did you say?"

"I said he's eleven. They're only taking boys from fourteen. The bastard just smiled at me."

"You told them Oskar is our son?"

To me, she sounded angry.

"I didn't say he wasn't."

Another silence. Once again, we tried not to move.

"He can't stay, Arne."

"What else can he do?"

"He's not our son."

A pause, then Burre said, "It might help if they think he is."

"Do you think no one will tell them?" Fru Burre was almost shouting now. "His father brought this upon us. Do you think no one's going to tell?"

"It was the communists who burned the hall. Not Overand."

"You don't know that."

"I do know that, Anna. Just as I know our son is with them."

She said again, more quietly, "You don't know that."

After a while, Aisa's father said, "You're right, I don't know for sure. He could just be dead."

When her mother began to cry, Aisa tugged at my pyjama sleeve and we crept silently back upstairs. When we were both in bed, I asked what her mother had meant about my father. She said the blue and white pennants meant the resistance had been there - the nationalists, she said, chewing her way uncertainly through the word as if it might contain an unpleasant surprise, like a brazil nut in an otherwise perfectly good piece of toffee.

"And your brother?"

"When we heard about the invasion - before you came - Jørgen said he was going to fight."

"With my father?"

Aisa hesitated. "I don't know. Perhaps."

When I said nothing, she said, "Do you think they'll take Froken Dahl?"

They didn't, not then. But when the first truckload of labour conscripts left town, just before Christmas, it included Geir Sarsen, who had managed to get into another drunken brawl, this time involving four soldiers from the barracks, and was lucky, Burre said, not to have been beaten to death. There was not much he could do about it. The boy was an electrician, he said: useful. They would want to look after him.

That night we were woken by a rifle shot, close by. Poachers, Aisa's father said, nothing to worry about. But I heard him rise early the next morning and, pulling trousers and a jumper quickly over my pyjamas, I followed him downstairs. He was standing at the open kitchen door, a sackcloth package in his hands. He leaned his forehead against the thick oak door. Later that morning I noticed a jagged hole in the door, perhaps two feet above my head, filled with putty and sanded smooth.

Over breakfast Burre reminded Aisa and I to keep an eye out for strangers – "You know who's strange now, don't you, Oskar?" – for anyone wandering in the fields close by and especially for anyone approaching the house or its outbuildings. There was nothing for us to worry about, but he would like to know.

On Christmas Eve, Aisa's mother gave her a doll's house, with hinged walls that swung back to reveal the richly furnished rooms within; she gave me a catapult. Captain Burre gave me a book of Greek myths retold for children and a packet of chocolate coins, which Aisa coveted and which I shared with her. I heard Fru Burre ask where he had found such things, but did not hear his answer. Johanna and her husband Josef came. No one had heard from Abi, and no one mentioned it, but I had the sense they all hoped she might arrive. During dinner, Josef talked about the work he had been doing, helping to refit the town hall and the barracks. Shelves, he said, he had never seen so many shelves. The Germans had files for everything.

Before school began in the New Year, Burre said, he would take me out in the car again. I should take my catapult, he would take his gun: we might stop off to hunt. I wondered what there could be to shoot, or how we would see it in the dark that had lasted now for weeks. Aisa begged to be included. She did not want to play with her dolls' house, she said: she wanted to come with us.

Halvar Madsen greeted us as he had before, standing in the unlit doorway, mug in hand. Burre said, "You remember Oskar?" Madsen nodded, and mentioned how much Aisa had grown. The mug in his hand was empty: he was sorry but he could not offer us coffee. Burre asked if Peder had volunteered. Madsen couldn't say. He wasn't there. He couldn't say.

Burre seemed irritated. "Can't, or won't?"

Madsen caught and held his gaze, but did not answer.

At eleven o'clock the morning was still thick, viscous, Stygian.

We couldn't find anyone at the Sarsen farm. The gloomy barns were empty, their roofs thick with snow. When we knocked on the farmhouse door, nobody answered. Burre shook his head and steered us back to the car.

He drove further than he had the previous time, with headlamps on throughout, visiting farms and cottages I had not seen before. Some were empty; some we could not reach because the roads simply disappeared in snow; in others family members – sons, fathers, sometimes wives – that Burre had hoped to speak to were not there. We were fed – bread mostly, some eggs and cheese – and given tea brewed from hedgerow plants. By the time we turned back towards town it was late afternoon, but the hour meant little when the darkness never thinned. The headlamps – large chrome bowls bolted to the car's front wings – threw a weak yellow puddle of light before us. Where the road straightened, Burre switched them off: we could see just as well by the light of a half moon in a clear sky.

We were still a few miles from town when we spotted a stationary car, leaning off the road at forty-five degrees, two wheels in the ditch, and, just ahead of it, heavy wooden blocks laid across the road. Burre swerved to avoid them, running off the road himself. We cleared the ditch but hit a fence post on the other side. We were thrown forward violently, then dropped back into our seats as the bonnet burst open and a huge cloud of steam erupted underneath. Burre asked if we were hurt, then told us to get out and away from the car as quickly as we could. I scrambled over the frozen ditch up onto the road; Aisa ran the other way. I looked back and saw Burre open the boot of the car. The moon was bright enough to cast shadows. He pulled out his hunting rifle and I heard him load it in the dark. I walked over to the other car. It was not empty. The driver's door was open, the driver hanging out, head and arms in the ditch, his left foot caught between the pedals – I remember noticing it was his left, the foot that would control the clutch; there are few details of that scene I have since forgotten. There was a second man in the passenger seat. Both had been shot in the chest and the head; their faces and clothes and the seats of the car were stained and sticky with coagulating blood. In the moonlight the blood looked black against the men's clothes, not red, not like I imagined blood might look. The second man, the passenger, was Josef. I lurched backwards, away from the car. I had never seen a person dead before. The indicator arm stuck out at right angles from the open driver's door. Tied around it was a small ribbon I thought was blue. In the moonlight it was hard to tell, but it did not appear to be the same iron non-colour as the blood where Josef's face should have been.

I felt a strong hand grab me by the scruff of the neck: Burre hauled me away from the car just as I began to vomit.

We would be all right, he said. We just had to walk home. It was a good night for it. When I could stand upright he asked if I could name the stars. His tone was light, as if this were some educational outing he had arranged. Aisa had run the other way, away from the road, but had not gone far. He called her back, climbing over the roadblocks so that she would join him ahead of the car. As we began to walk I saw a light flash briefly on the hillside, then a second, further down the road. Burre pointed out the Plough. Aisa knew Orion. A hoot that might have been an owl, if owls lived this far north, sounded behind us. It was answered from somewhere in the darkness up ahead.

An hour later, we were home.

The labour scheme was a success, I overheard Burre tell Aisa's mother. The colonel had said his superiors were pleased. They wanted a second batch.

Fru Burre asked what he was going to do.

"What can I do?"

"You could give them Overand."

I was stacking logs against the leeward wall; they were in the kitchen, the window left open to clear the steam.

"Would it be so hard?" I heard her say. "They could use the boy to get to him."

It was Fru Burre, who had been in town at the time, who told us all about the second truck. This one detonated successfully, taking the front half of the town hall – including the sandbags and the colonel's office – with it. Sadly, Fru Burre said, the colonel had not been in it at the time; her husband did not respond. He did not stop Aisa and I running to the square to see for ourselves. With the façade gone, the rooms at the rear were laid open, like Aisa's dolls' house, the fireplaces and urinals, the desks and clocks, the shelves that Josef had built, all hung exposed to view; the files had been ripped apart by the blast, their contents scattered across the square like betting slips

– Like betting slips?

– Is that wrong?

– For an eleven year-old? In rural Norway?

– I am an adult, writing in recollection.

– You are an adult trying to avoid writing "like confetti", which is understandable. But "betting slips" is worse.

like the soft leaves of ash that clung to the foreign trees and floated to the ground for two days after the estate hall burned.

The Commissioner returned. I showed him into the parlour again, and this time there were few niceties. He wanted to know what Burre knew. He did not believe that Burre knew nothing – Burre was a policeman, after all – but neither did he much care. Burre could deliver him the culprits or not, as he chose. If he did not, one in ten males in the town would be executed. If that failed to produce the culprits, they would have to consider the females.

Burre gave him names – the names of men who had not been there when we had driven out to visit them, the names of men who had already disappeared: some of them, in all probability, the names of those responsible. But it was not enough. The Commissioner wanted bodies. Burre had one week.

A few days later, sitting again on the stairs outside the kitchen door, I heard Fru Burre crying. Before I could leave, I heard her say, "Give them the communists."

Burre said, "It wasn't the communists who shot Josef."

"Does it matter? They've been to Johanna. Did you know that? The communists. Josef's barely dead, and they told her to take another one in. Some troublemaker they want to hide."

"Anna, you're not yourself."

"She had no choice. He'll be living with her. As if he were her husband."

She was sobbing now, between words: deep, visceral groans wrenched from her body by grief and fear and anger.

Burre said, "Did it occur to you she might have had a choice?"

I heard a grunt, a muffled slap, then Burre speaking quietly again. "Sit down, Anna. Sit down."

The sobbing resumed.

"And if I did, what then? Who else, Anna? He won't take just one. So who else? Peder Madsen? Jørgen?"

"You don't know that."

Burre said nothing.

"You don't."

Still Burre was silent.

"Oh, give them somebody, Arne. Anybody. I don't care. Give them Overand. Give them the boy. Just give them somebody."

I heard a chair scrape on the stone floor as Burre stood up. I climbed quickly, silently, back up to Aisa's room, to bed. I did not tell Aisa what I had heard.

In the morning, to get us out of the house, Fru Burre told us to clear out the old cowshed. It had come with the house, along with a small barn and half an acre of rutted pasture, but the Burres were not farmers, and had never used it. Now, perhaps, Fru Burre said, they would have to think about keeping a pig. We would find the shed full of old tools, she said, and rubbish that had been there since the Day of Creation, in all probability. We should sort out anything worth keeping, and take the rest to the dump outside town. She had been meaning to ask Peder Madsen to do it, she said, but . . . She did not explain, and we did not ask.

The cowshed was fifty yards behind the house. The doors were padlocked, but the hasp had rusted and become detached. We prised open the door and were assaulted by the stench of animal decay. Mice? Rats? Flies hummed thickly in the gloom. To the right was a workbench, a vice clamped to its front edge, its surface piled with old carpenter's tools – planes, saws, hammers and drills, an awl and a long square – the metal components mostly rusted beyond use. To the left was a stack of wooden crates and, propped against them, gardening tools – hoes, a scythe, sickles and pruning shears. Between them, down the centre of the stone floor, was a shallow gutter; lying in the gutter was a turd, slick and fresh. Further back, two or three more, older and drier, then more, until, up against the far wall where the gutter should have flowed out into the yard, a mound of shit, brittle as old pine cones, and another of clean bones, and feathers, and the heads, feet and viscera of small animals.

I said, "Foxes?" knowing that it couldn't be.

"Perhaps," Aisa said, her hand over her mouth and nose muffling the word.

I had read the book Burre gave me for Christmas. I said, "Is there a river nearby?"

Aisa asked what I meant, but before I could enjoy explaining something to her for once, we heard a scraping sound, brief and harsh, then silence again. There was something alive amongst the crates. Aisa grabbed a sickle and held it out in front of her, the curved blade pointing down towards her toes.

"Come out."

There was no movement, no sound.

"Come out!"

There was the scrape again, then a dull thud. The end of one of the crates swung open and a boy crawled out. I now know that he must have been fifteen, but he looked much older, like a feral version of the child-men you see in Renaissance paintings. His hair was long, matted and grey with dirt, almost the colour of his skin. He was thin, worse than thin. His eyes were red, his hands scarred, the knuckles over-large where the flesh had shrunk back against the bone. In Oslo I had seen men who looked like that, sleeping in doorways. I have seen them since.

Aisa lowered the sickle.

I said, "Should I call your father?"

"There's no need."

"He said to tell him about any strangers."

Aisa said, "This is Jørgen."

Then, waving her sickle towards the piles of shit and bones, "Jørgen, what are you doing?"

The boy shrugged, grabbing the lapels of his coat and wrapping it tighter around himself, crossing his arms, saying nothing.

In the kitchen, Burre said, "We thought you were fighting. Resisting."

"I was."

Jørgen's mother put a bowl of porridge in front of him. "We're just glad you're alive."

Jørgen picked up a spoon, then put it back down, gently. "I was scared, Pappa. I came back, and I was scared."

Burre left the room, left the house.

I never knew what he told the District Commissioner. I never asked and he never offered to tell me. Aisa and I stopped creeping down to sit outside the kitchen door at night; in any case, for the most part, Burre stopped speaking to his wife. So I have to imagine him returning to the Commissioner's office, the office at the police station that had once been his, but I cannot be sure that is how it was. I imagine the District

Commissioner stubbing out a cigarette in a thick glass ashtray on the desk and saying, politely, without inflexion, "Your son?"

I imagine Burre closing his eyes before saying, "He is not my son."

I imagine the Commissioner waiting, perhaps lighting another cigarette, perhaps studying his fingernails, before he says:

"And who else?"

§

You write:

– And after the war? What then?

– When the war ended, Aleks Overand, my grandfather, was a hero. He returned to the law, helped prosecute those who had collaborated with the German occupiers. After Nuremburg he returned to Oslo and recovered possession of the family house, and the office on Møllergata. His practice flourished. He wrote to Burre, summoning Oskar, my father, back to the capital. But by then, my father said, he hated my grandfather, who had abandoned his mother and sister, and then abandoned him. The wooden boat, the chocolate coins, the eggs, the book, the pig – the butchery, even – were not enough. He felt his dislike, or perhaps distrust, was reciprocated. After five years in Nordland, living with the family of their former servant, my grandfather thought his son had grown up a peasant. He was sixteen. The two of them met once, in the study of the old family home, and never met or spoke again.

There were Norwegians who did not resist. Most Norwegians, like most Danes, most Dutchmen, most Frenchmen, did not resist. Most Englishmen will never have to know that they, too, would not have resisted.

A few – we call them traitors, now – volunteered to fight the Russians on the eastern front, just as my grandfather, the hero, had volunteered to do in Finland. But that was before April the 9th. Before the invasion and the occupation and the war that Quisling said was not a war.

My father joined the Communist Party, which was popular for a while.

My grandfather became famous. The conscience of a nation, the obituaries said. He represented the wrongfully imprisoned, trades unions, political campaigns, the governments of developing nations. He advised on legislation and treaties. He wrote standard texts on the philosophy of law. He chaired committees and led inquiries. He was offered and accepted a newly-created Chair of International Jurisprudence at the University of Oslo, and when he died, a decade ago, at the age of ninety-three, the President himself led the eulogies.

My grandfather used to say a nation gets the cemeteries it deserves. He first said it in an article about our country's most prominent mass grave: a dismal, exhausted strip mine on the outskirts of a provincial town with little to distinguish it, other than the prison camp that had fed the graves and was by then a monument to remembrance. It is possible that is where my grandmother and aunt ended up, too – that, at least, is what my grandfather seemed to believe – but no one knows for sure. My father, Oskar, did not attend the funeral, or the memorial service a month later, at which the President called my grandfather's choice of burial ground "his last act of resistance, of identification with the victims of repression". He called for a final reconciliation, a simultaneous acknowledgement and forgetting of all the crimes committed during the war. Committed against us, committed by us. Forgive us this day, he said, our daily trespasses, as we forgive those who have trespassed against us.

When I told my father this he said he would not be so sure.

Some might think, he said – and he was certainly among them – that Aleks Overand died as he had lived, appropriating other people's tragedy.

Best wishes,

Paul.

§

'RECONCILIATION' CAN SIGNIFY the outbreak of peace between enemies; for Catholics it is a sacrament, comprising confession, penance and restoration to the community of the church; more neutrally, reconciliation can simply mean agreement, a tallying and verification of the facts. An auditor's reconciliation tests whether two accounts arrive at the same version of the truth, that the data coming out of one system equals that entering another. That the salary payments recorded in your employer's payroll, for example, equal the money that turns up in your bank account.

You write that your father has to agree, that we can publish nothing without his consent. You tell me to meet you in Inverness the following weekend. We will drive over to your father's house together.

I do not reply.

I am there, though, as you know I will be, when you get off the sleeper train in the grey light of dawn.

You spot me immediately.

"Martin," you call, as if there could be any doubt. In my opinion, I haven't changed.

I say, "Paul told me you'd be here."

We kiss, on the cheek. I ask after Walter; you say Walter is none of my business, and you are right, of course. I ask after Ben and Alice and the girls. You tell me to stop pretending.

I've hired a car, I tell you, picking up your suitcase. It's a Land Rover.

You say, "There's a perfectly good road."

Your father looks old. He *is* old, of course. But for all his talk of dying, neither of us has seen it before. There is a stoop to his spine, a way his head hangs from his shoulders that wasn't there the last time I saw him.

He transfers his walking stick from right to left to shake my hand. He says it is good to see me again. To see us together.

You let that pass.

You say we have something to show him.

He says, of course, but to come in, come in: have we had any lunch?

You have the manuscript of *Reconciliation* in your shoulder bag, in a sealed manila envelope. When you pull it out and give it to your father, I notice you have written his name on the envelope, as if you had not intended to deliver it yourself. We walk through to the kitchen and he places it on the counter between the kettle and the bread bin. He says, "Is bread and cheese all right? We can stock up this afternoon."

After lunch we get into the hired Land Rover and drive down to the village, to the stores. We buy food, and whisky. We drive out to the point, for the view of the islands and the coast past Ullapool. We walk along the beach, your father struggling with the sand, the way it shifts and sucks the energy out of every step.

How beautiful it is, here. I say I'd never known.

Despite the food we've bought, your father suggests we have dinner in the pub, and we agree.

When we get back the envelope is still there, unopened, on the kitchen counter.

It is still there when you go to bed, leaving your father and I and the unfinished whisky bottle.

It is not there in the morning, however. It is in your father's bedroom, beside the bed, ripped open, the pages scattered across the floor. Beside your father's body, which is curled into an inflexible question mark on the carpet.

The obituaries concentrate on his illustrious legal career, on the commitment he'd shown, the principles he lived by. None mentions suicide.

4

OTHER PEOPLE'S TRAGEDY

§

HANNAH MARTIN PUBLISHED *Reconciliation* in April 2005. It was her third novel. The previous two – *Life's Work* and *Coward Angels* – had been well received, and began to sell steadily, albeit unspectacularly, after *Coward Angels* made it on to the Orange prize shortlist. Her publishers were hopeful that *Reconciliation* would prove to be her breakthrough book, but were quickly disappointed. The reviews were poor; the early talent she had shown seemed to be faltering, they said: the book was an uneasy mix of fact and fiction, of history and imagination that did not quite cohere into either novel or family memoir.

Bill Martin ordered a copy on Amazon anyway; he had not spoken to his daughter since 1974, not since she was twelve and he'd left her and her mother in the house he always regretted buying and which, it turned out, Hannah's mother could not afford to keep alone; but he had followed Hannah's career all the same. He read the reviews, and bought *Reconciliation* in spite of them: she was his daughter, after all. He thought the reviewers mostly missed the point. He was not surprised to find that he was supposed to be dead – Hannah's previous books had both featured deceased fathers – but he did work up a witticism to the effect that, whilst once might be misfortunate, to kill him off twice in the same novel looks like vengefulness. He tried out this *bon mot* on a consultant cardiologist, who, at the time, was smearing jelly on his chest, and had asked whether Bill had experienced anything like this before; he was not rewarded with a laugh. The cardiologist had been referring to his recent collapse outside a Costa coffee shop in Fleet Street. Bill said he hadn't. The scan showed nothing untoward, apparently.

It was not his death that bothered him.

He left the hospital simultaneously deflated and curious about his own reaction. He had found the experience of passing out interesting. He had lately fallen into the habit of contemplating his own mortality with increasing frequency and decreasing concern, and had, indeed, begun to tell himself it might prove after all a consummation devoutly to be wished; nonetheless, when it came to a situation in which he had sufficient cause to believe he might be about to die, he had found himself, to put it mildly, fucking terrified. He had always disliked the smug aphorism that there are no atheists in foxholes, and was pleased to detect no trace of spirituality in his own reaction. But, as his vision collapsed and the world span and his legs somehow just wouldn't . . . and he couldn't . . . he found that he did not actually want to die. He was only sixty-two, for pity's sake. He had work to do, cases to finish; he had a daughter with a career teetering on the verge of failure and he wanted to know how that story ended. He knew of course that, barring tragedy, he never would. She would outlive him whether or not he survived this particular incident. He knew that. But only afterwards, only when a helpful passer-by had loosened his collar and asked if he were okay and should she call an ambulance and could she at least help him to a nearby bench, where she advised him to sit with his head between his knees until sufficient blood and oxygen had reached his brain to restore its cognitive functions and he had thanked her and assured her he would be all right, really, he was fine, it was just one of those things, a "funny turn" they would have called it once, and he'd be fine; only then did he identify his dominant fear: not dying, not even being dead *per se*, but being dead before he'd finished. Of failing. Of *that* being the meaning of his death.

He was fine. Hadn't the cardiologist just said so? He should be relieved. Grateful, even; albeit without conceding the existence of any power or supernatural being to be grateful *to*.

So why did he feel such a sense of anti-climax?

That was what most interested him.

It had been ten days since his brief collapse, nine since his GP had referred him to the cardiology clinic at Guy's Hospital. He had been surprised when the appointment came through so quickly. Surprised, but also gratified: whatever was wrong with him must be serious, something to be investigated with a flattering degree of urgency.

Except that now it evidently wasn't.

There, Bill Martin thought, he knew he'd crack it. Just takes a little applied reflection. Always on the nose.

If he felt deflated it was because, while he didn't exactly want to be dead, and didn't want to know for certain that his heart was about to kill him, he nonetheless did not want the whole incident to have had no meaning, either, to be a random but unthreatening event of no personal or medical importance. For ten days he'd lived with a sense of drama, of imminent, significant change, and now it had evaporated. Nothing had changed, or was about to.

Back to work; back to life. There could be another thirty years of this.

He'd wanted there to be consequences.

Then he remembered *Reconciliation*: there were consequences.

§

H ANNAH READ THE first couple of reviews su-
perciliously ("He would say that, wouldn't he?") the
next combatively ("That's the fucking point, you moron!")
and thereafter guiltily, knowing she shouldn't read them at
all, wondering if they might be right, wondering what the
point was anyway, knowing that none of this would help her
complete the next book, the one she really should be wor-
rying about now, because it was too late for this one, for
Reconciliation, which was done and dusted and would have
to make its own way in the world with little more help from
her than the occasional signing event her agent Frankie would
organize and her habit of moving as many copies to the display
tables in Heffers as she could get away with every time she
visited.

Of course there were positive responses, too. Friends and
fellow authors filled the Amazon review pages with briefly
literate, encouraging noises. Meanwhile, people she'd never
heard of posted reviews that said she was "utterly brilliant"
or "so-so" or a "pretenchius TWAT thats WASTING MY
TIME", which depressed her even though they meant nothing,
no one believed them, they carried no critical weight, because,
after all who *were* these people?

Her colleagues at the library were supportive, again. They
liked the idea that one amongst them did something else. But
Hannah knew that although they might congratulate her and

ask apparently admiring questions about how on earth she found the time, and might go so far as to place her books prominently by the library's check-out desk, they would feel no obligation actually to *read* them, much less purchase copies of their own.

One day, she even asked Beverley why not. She had made tea, dunking the bags in their mugs, then flicking them, dripping, into the blue food waste bin in the staff kitchenette. Beverley was young and fairly new. She was bright and not yet cynical about the library's management. Hannah liked her, and occasionally caught herself behaving as if she were Beverley's mentor.

"Does a baker eat bread?" Beverley said. "Does a miner burn coal?"

"Yes."

"Okay. Bad examples. But you know what I mean."

Hannah didn't, not really.

"I spend all day lugging books around, answering stupid questions, about books. Last thing I want to do when I get home is *read* one."

"What? Never?"

Beverley looked surprised at Hannah's surprise. "Are you okay?"

She was not. Of course, she'd known in theory there must be people who never read – she had the sales figures to prove it, after all – but they were *other* people, no more real to her than the sub-atomic particles that made up her world in ways she simply could not conceive. She found herself clinging to the rocks, peering over the brink of a precipice, incapable of imagining the void below. *Never?* She could no more create a character who never read than one who never had to defecate.

They might not do either on the page, but you knew they had to. What would such a person think about? What would she *do*?

"Oh, you know, stuff."

Well, we all do *stuff*, Hannah thought, but it's mostly just stuff that gets in the way of reading more.

They finished their tea in silence.

Afterwards, although the effort cost her dearly, she resisted the temptation to suggest books Beverley might like; she would never again regard herself as Beverley's mentor.

It was a Thursday morning coffee break when she read the review in *The Independent*: Jay had put aside the arts supplement while he sat reading aloud snippets about the election campaign. A young woman described as a disillusioned Labour supporter, although she was too young to have voted before, had berated the Prime Minister.

She plucked the supplement from the chair next to Jay. "Do you mind?"

She read standing up, leaning against the melamine counter by the kettle. The review was polished, elegant and brief, albeit not quite as brief as the online abuse, but its message was essentially the same: why are you wasting our time, woman? She wondered why her being female seemed so important to readers of *this* book in particular. Reviews of her previous novels had occasionally mentioned her gender, but more by way of simple biography than explanation. She supposed this was another twist of the knife of failure she would have to get used to: now she was to be punished not only for failing, but for having had the temerity to try. She was one of Dr Johnson's dogs, not walking well on her hind legs, but attracting attention for doing so at all.

"Are you all right?"

Jay put his paper aside and rose to his feet. She realized she was crying, that a tear was inching down each cheek and that Jay was hovering beside her, evidently wondering if he should hug her, or pat her at least, wondering if that was something a concerned colleague could do in the workplace without its being misconstrued.

She wiped her left cheek with the back of her right hand, the right cheek with the palm and said: "I'm fine. I should know better."

She held out the review. Jay scanned it quickly. "Bastard. Sexist bastard. I wouldn't take any notice of that pillock, Hannah." He put his hand on her arm. "I bet your book's great."

He bet.

"I'm fine."

She'd been angry about being criticized for being a woman and how had she reacted? She'd cried. Dear God.

She returned to the check out desk, told Beverley she could have an early break.

"Are you okay?"

"I'm fine."

And she was. She took the copy of *Reconciliation*, in its shiny un-creased plastic library cover and shelved it between *Coward Angels* and *A Storm of Swords*.

§

B ILL'S CHAMBERS WERE located in a narrow time
warp just off Fleet Street. On an average working morning
he could pinball through the centuries in minutes, emerging
from the Royal Courts of Justice to elbow through gangs of
students and tourists searching for Aldwych or the Courtauld,
then ducking into the mediaeval alley where porters guarded
doorways and his name was painted on the board at the foot
of his staircase: Wm. Martin, QC.

Queen's Counsel was a preposterous phrase, he often said,
though somehow marginally less pompous and self-satisfied
than silk. He'd met the woman a couple of times, but never
in circumstances conducive to his offering her advice. What
would he say if the opportunity ever arose? That her Prime
Minister was a war criminal who had brought her nation
and her armed forces into international disrepute, and that
she should order his immediate arrest for treason? It might
be interesting to watch the glint he felt sure would appear in
the royal eye before she closed the conversation with some
well-rehearsed banality. Or perhaps he would advocate her
abdication? Not in favour of her long-suffering son – he had
no desire simply to become a KC instead – but in order to
force her subjects to accept the responsibilities of citizen-
ship? It was a thought he imagined she must have enter-
tained repeatedly herself – how could she not? – if only in
the dyspeptic aftermath of yet another state banquet. She

could simply step away, and at the same time secure her place in history. How many of us could say the same? *Après moi le déluge.*

That morning he was not in court but in committee, considering applications for new tenants. He shuffled the *curricula vitae* of a dozen indistinguishably bright, personable, highly-educated and impeccably-motivated young people and wondered how, in this fifth year of the third millennium since the birth and slaughter of Our Lord, we had still not managed to crush such baseless optimism out of each successive generation? Had they not been paying attention?

According to the BBC, it would be the queen's birthday on Thursday, two days from now: she'd be seventy-nine. Maybe next year? He had no desire himself to be working at eighty, even if his apparently healthy heart allowed it. He had no desire to be working now.

The selection committee comprised the most senior members of the set, and was chaired by Sir Robert, whom Bill had first approached for pupillage himself in 1966. Getting on for forty years ago. There were marriages that didn't last that long, Bill thought – including his own, of course; whole lifetimes lived with greater dispatch, and many of them to greater effect. *Set.* It was another of those complacent, insider words Bill despised but used anyway. He liked to say it made him think of badgers. Looking around the table now that seemed apt: burrowed away in this silent, panelled room, the six of them ringed around a scarred and polished walnut table, sleek, well-fed and exquisitely tailored, with chins disappearing into their waistcoated chests, their white, unruly eyebrows sprawling above small, sharp eyes that missed little.

So, they were all agreed? Sir Robert asked. They were. Of course they were. They knocked their papers into tidy piles and stood, pushing back the heavy chairs with the usual effort. Sir Robert asked if he were free for lunch?

"Sorry, Bob. Con at two. I'd better have read some of the brief."

"What's the case?"

There was no conference, no case in particular; he just wasn't in the mood for Bob's war stories. He'd been in the trenches for most of them, after all.

"Wrongful imprisonment," he said. "Same old, same old."

He had no desire to be working now.

The thought had surprised him. He had not intended it, did not know if he even meant it. Was it true, or merely a product of rhetorical suggestion? The trouble with having been a barrister for so long was that the boundary between rhetoric and fact became so permeable: an argument that persuaded its intended audience was a better argument than one that didn't. Truth was not the point. But the thought existed now, whether he'd intended it or not, whether he believed it or not.

He would be sixty-three in October: surely too young to retire, particularly from a profession that was structured, as he liked to say, around the belief that its practitioners entered their prime only in their seventh or eighth decade, like popes or school crossing-keepers. The work was fascinating, varied, intellectually stimulating, socially useful and hugely remunerative. It brought him into daily contact with a wide variety of bright, and frequently attractive, young people. Young women in particular. Why would he not want to continue as long as he was physically capable?

2000 *Completed my destruction*
2100 *All personal papers burnt*
2230 *Sardine supper.*

§

SIX WEEKS LATER, Jay asked again if she were all right. They were in the pub this time, buying leaving drinks for Stephanie, the head librarian, who had been promoted to manage the Council's entire Library Service following the previous incumbent's arrest.

The pub was crowded. There were only half a dozen of them from the library – seven including Steph's husband, who had looked awkward from the start and was the first to say no when Beverley suggested tequila shots – but it was early on a Friday evening, and the town centre pub was full of men with loosened ties and sweaty faces and women mostly trying not to get too close. Their party was packed around a table meant for two, their glasses jostling for space between the empties, the ash trays and the crisp packets that wouldn't stay screwed up, but even so it was hard to hear what anyone was saying unless they were sitting right next to you, or you leaned across the table and risked knocking a wine glass into someone else's lap.

Jay and Hannah were sharing the bench seat at the back, his left thigh squeezed up against her right. He was wearing jeans, though Steph had often told him they were not appropriate for work. He cocked his head up and to the right to avoid blowing smoke at her, then turned back and said, "I always thought there was something wrong about him."

Peter, who had worked at the library longer than anyone, began folding each empty crisp packet in turn, knotting each one carefully in the middle.

Tony leaned across towards Jay, knocking a bottle off the table. Luckily, it was empty. "About who?"

Whom, thought Hannah, despite herself.

Jay said, "You know."

"You're only saying that because he's looking at fourteen years."

Tony was older than Jay, older than any of them. He'd been a Mod the first time round and still dressed sharply. He checked out the library's copy of *The Outsider* every couple of years.

"No," Jay said. "I knew. It was the beard."

"The beard?"

"Yeah."

"You reckon he's a menace to society because he doesn't shave?"

"That and the praying."

Tony mimed disgust, or perhaps he was disgusted: Hannah couldn't be sure. He said, "That's borderline racist, Jay. Not even borderline. Someone call HR."

"Fuck off is it." Jay stubbed out his cigarette and lit another. He read a lot of James Ellroy.

Steph was making a circular gesture with an empty glass. They nodded and she sent her husband to the bar for another round. Beverley went to help him carry drinks and Hannah found room to shift along the bench, opening up an inch or so between her thigh and Jay's.

Jay turned to her. "Are you all right?"

Peter had finished knotting the crisp packets and was

standing them carefully, like sugar sachets, like cigarettes, in an empty beer glass.

"Only you've not said much."

"I'm fine."

"Fine?"

"Fine."

Jay blew smoke again. "Fine-fine, or fuck-off-I'm-not-talking-about-it-fine?"

Hannah was actually just fine but even so she didn't want to talk about it. She was watching Beverley at the bar, who was not exactly flirting with the boss's husband, but was not exactly not flirting with him, either. Beverley was the reason she was fine, in a way. She'd been half way through a new novel when *Reconciliation* came out, but she'd parked it for now. A new book was forming in her mind. At its centre was a black hole, a character none of the others could understand. Perhaps not the centre, but the engine, the energy that would drive the book. The narrative would be random, unpredictable. She was not sure how it would work, yet, but it was coming together. She knew the gun in the first act would not go off in the third.

Frankie might not be too pleased about her abandoning the work-in-progress she'd already promised, but what else could she do? The new book was what she could work on now.

She said, "Are you going for Steph's job?"

"Me? No. No way. You?"

"No."

He looked at her cautiously. At least one of them was lying; Hannah knew it wasn't her. Was not *she*.

Jay said, "They'll give it to Peter, won't they? He's been here the longest."

"I don't think that's how it works."

"No?"

"Good luck."

She hoped Jay wouldn't get it.

Beverley and Steph's husband carried drinks back from the bar. There was no space on the table to put them down.

Hannah took a glass of wine. Jay took his pint. Hannah said, "I used to think one thing led to another."

Jay swallowed a mouthful of beer. "It generally does."

"No. It doesn't. It really doesn't."

"Yes, it does. One drink; another drink." He lifted each hand in turn towards his mouth as he spoke.

"One drink *follows* another drink. It doesn't cause another drink."

"But if we hadn't had a drink we couldn't have another. And we usually have another *because* we've had the first."

Hannah pushed aside the ashtray with the base of her wine-glass. "We have another because we want another. We only blame it on the first because we're spineless. And we only want a drink at all because it helps us to forget we're spineless."

"Speak for yourself."

"I speak for my generation. It said so in *The Independent*."

"In 1997. You showed me the clipping."

He offered her another cigarette; she refused again. He said, "What changed your mind?"

"What?"

"You said you *used to* think . . . Now you don't."

She wasn't going to fall for that. "I used to. Now I don't. That's not a story."

"It could be."

"A then B; not: *if* A, *then* B."

Beverley squeezed back onto the bench seat beside Hannah.

240

"What are you two so deep in conversation about?"

"Narrative logic," said Hannah.

"Bollocks," said Jay.

They talked about other things. About the Library, about the council, about who might have slept with whom. About computers, about the Internet, and what it might do to libraries: the consensus was, not much. Computers were tools or toys; readers wanted books. You could smell books. You could riffle the pages and feel the weight of the words you'd read, the words you still had left to go.

Hannah didn't contribute much to the debate. It was a conversation they'd had before, and one she knew they'd have again. The familiar, comfortable, predictable opinions and jokes settled around her like warm bedclothes. The sound faded and she watched the gestures, the leaning forward, finger pointing, the rocking back, mouths wide open, teeth and fillings and scarlet throats on view like freshly-slaughtered animals, the shouted whispers in the neighbour's ear, eyes wide open, hands clasped tight around near-empty glasses.

The trouble with *Reconciliation*, the reviewers said, was that nothing much was reconciled.

She knew it wasn't true.

She kept starting novels – her own as well as others' – with the blind, pathetic optimism that this time it would be different. It never was. The random digression she'd enjoyed in chapter three was never random or, in reality, a digression, just artful foreshadowing of the event that would resolve the second sub-plot in chapter seventeen. She could recognize the author's craft, but still it made her want to scream. She felt cheated, manipulated, soiled and ashamed. She'd been sold a pup, *again*, and it was her own fault. She'd latched on to a detail, a trick of style, that promised to be a little bit like life, only to find that it was – again, always – art.

Reconciliation had been just as complicit as the rest.

The stuff that looked random – like dust motes dancing in a sunbeam – wasn't random at all. It was governed by the narrative equivalent of the laws of Brownian motion. If you had a computer big enough you could predict it all. Forget the Shakespearian monkeys, you could work out the end of every story ever told or ever going to be told.

There were only seven, after all.

The next book would be different; it would be different.

She was drunk. She was definitely drunk.

Steph said, "Are you coming, Hannah?"

"Coming where?"

Steph rolled her eyes. "For a curry. Haven't you been here at all?"

§

HAVING SHAKEN OFF Sir Robert, Bill spent half an hour in his rooms attempting nothing at all before heading out towards the modest restaurant he invariably chose when he wanted to eat without the encumbrance of company.

Over lunch it came to him: he would get back in touch with Hannah.

It was obvious: *that* was the consequence.

If his death was not imminent, it was no less true that he was going to die; it was ridiculous that the animus he'd once felt for Hannah's mother should have sundered so completely their life stories.

He did not delude himself that it would be a sentimental reunion. His daughter would be a woman of forty-three – considerably older than he himself had been when he left – a woman he had not seen or spoken to since she was a child. She would be curious about him, he supposed: she was a novelist, after all. But if he could infer from the regular appearance of father figures in her fiction that she had not forgotten him, their equally regular and untimely deaths suggested little fondness in her recollections. She held him culpable, that much was obvious. She had made no effort to contact him, just as he, apart from following her faltering career with something closer to forensic curiosity than fatherly pride, had taken no steps to re-establish their relationship. He was a public figure of some standing (albeit less flamboyant and publicity-seeking than some colleagues he could name); he would not have been difficult to find, if she had so chosen. She did not wish to know him; that much was evident.

Or was it?

She had not written to him or called, or emailed his chambers or even mentioned him, in the handful of interviews that followed the publication of her books, other than to say that he had left her mother. And yet, the more he thought about it, the more he felt she *had* written to him: what were those long stories in which a parade of fathers crashed and drowned or severed arteries and bled to death, but cries for his attention, calls for a response? Until he left, long past her babyhood, long past the age when she should have known better, at ten or eleven or twelve years old, she would wake sometimes in the night and call out until he – not her mother; never *she* – got up in the dark and stumbled along the narrow landing to her room to find her blankets on the floor, and she would say, "I'm cold."

So she would come, he thought, if he invited her to some neutral ground, but she would do so warily, notebook in hand. He would recognize her from the author photographs on the jackets of her books, provided they were not too old or too misleading. They would not hug. He doubted she would cry; he was sure that he would not.

On the strength of this new-found resolution Bill awarded himself an afternoon off work and ordered brandy with his coffee. He liked to say that he was not "a silk who drinks". He drank, of course – he also liked to say he'd never met a barrister who didn't, and staunchly to maintain, in the teeth of isolated counter-factuals, the spiritual if not literal truth of his assertion – but he genuinely believed he did not drink in the way that many of his colleagues did. These days lunch itself was an increasingly rare occurrence, and wine with it almost unheard of, restricted to receptions of one sort or another. After work was a different matter: although it was only two o'clock, he decided that work had finished, and a glass of brandy was in order.

Almost forty years a barrister, and still not over. Longer still since he'd married Julia. They'd met, he liked to say, after the Chatterley trial and before the Beatles first LP: if they did not personally invent sex, it certainly felt that way at the time. It was the coldest winter since sixteen-hundred-and-something, the loose and willfully myopic landlady of his Oxford digs had told them, winking moistly. No wonder they never went out. The river froze solid for months; some damn fool drove a car across it. They spent whole days beneath the threadbare blankets, making their own heat, knowing it was already too late, that the damage had been done before they even moved in. By Christmas 1961 she was five months pregnant and there was no longer any hiding it. By March they were married, Julia sighing heavily at the altar, her hands pressing away the all-too-familiar lumbar pain, her shoulders arched back to brace the weight of her protuberant belly as the vicar asked if anyone knew of any just cause or impediment, and William Charles Albert Martin thought: I do.

She was seventeen, for a start. He was nineteen, his best man a fellow undergraduate. His parents paid for the wedding; hers thought she had struck gold. The reception was a brief and quiet affair in the tea room of the Randolph Hotel, with sandwiches and Earl Grey, champagne and bottled Bass, most of which Bill's father and the best man drank between them.

They moved into rented rooms in Headington, where they

at least had their own bathroom. Hannah was born three weeks later. Bill's father paid a year's rent in advance and somehow squared things with the College; that Michaelmas Term, while Julia fed Hannah her first solids, Bill returned to the weekly round of lectures and tutorials as if nothing had happened. Julia bought a Dansette to fill the vacuum with sound. The following spring he wrote a dissertation on Milton while Julia sang *can't buy me love* to Hannah when she couldn't sleep. By Hannah's first birthday he'd passed his Finals and was singing *it's all over now,* strutting like Mick in the privacy of their bedroom, while Julia preferred *I just don't know what to do with myself.* When they split, a decade later, he left the Beatles and the Stones, but took the Animals and Dusty Springfield.

After lunch he clawed back up through narrow alleyways to turn right on Fleet Street, then south towards Blackfriars. Downstream the dull truncated orange pegs of the old railway bridge stood like stranded soldiers, tea-brown water shoving back and forth around them like schoolboys in a crowded corridor. Halfway across, he leaned deftly into the vacuum slipstream suck of passing cars, ignored the hollered abuse of a tattoo-calfed cyclist, and skipped, almost, onto the upstream pavement. Not bad, he thought, for a well-lunched lawyer of sixty. Sixty-two. He leaned on the parapet. Somewhere beneath the bridge, he knew, the old Fleet River – so filthy it had been a sewer since the thirteenth century, a natural home for lawyers and journalists – discharged its effluent into the Thames. To his left, the kitsch of the Oxo Tower, and, beyond that, the smug South Bank where his father, despite occasionally musing that they should *take it in,* and outright promising more than once that they would do just that, had not taken the eight year-old Bill to see the Festival of Britain. To his right, behind the hardened scar tissue of the Victoria Embankment he could make out the Inner and the Middle Temple gardens, and home.

Herbal tea, he pondered briefly. Would that do for Clive? It was not really up to scratch. Nothing wrong with tea, of course, but he struggled to dredge up a truly positive connotation for *herbal*. Too hippie/Rastafarian. *Mint tea?* Possible, but still not top flight. Besides, they'd ruled out foodstuffs years ago, after Clive's *Vaseline ice cream*. Food was just too easy, they'd decided. Going back to drinks would be . . . going back.

He turned northwards, back the way he'd come, back towards chambers. Where else was he going to go? When you got down to it, there were no afternoons off.

He tried to slip past Clive's room on his way up stairs, but the old boy called out, "I've got one for you, sir." *Greek cinema*, Bill thought hopefully, but Clive had meant a brief.

§

S HE WOULD HAVE phoned in sick – she was sick, after all, even if the sickness was self-inflicted – but it was Saturday, and she knew that Jay and Beverley would feel just as ill, and would know exactly why she was calling. So she drank a lot of water and swallowed a couple of ibuprofen and co-codamol, and washed them down with coffee that had the tiniest hint of calvados, just enough to lift a corner of the thick curtain she'd found wrapped around her nervous system, muffling the synapses' fizz, slowing the transition from sensation to thought and thought to action. Food would come later.

At the Library it turned out Beverley had bottled it – food poisoning, she claimed, in the voicemail message she'd left so early she could be sure no one would be there to answer. "Lightweight," Jay said, when he broke the bad news. "That's the trouble with young people today . . ."

Hannah tried to visualize the day ahead. The view was bleak, by any standard.

C follows B follows A. Insufferable working day follows hangover follows too much alcohol. Narrative logic. Why had she not foreseen this when they left the pub for the curry house? Because, frankly, who does? *Homo sapiens*, she thought: so desperately keen to link the past to the present, such experts at explaining how *that* led to *this*, but, really, when it came to exploiting that knowledge to control, or influence their own futures . . . really, quite remarkably, crap.

How else could you explain all *this?*

"I can't do it."

"Yes you can. We can. We're not lightweights."

"No. Not today."

"Sure?"

She nodded, and he nodded back.

"Okay," he said. And at two minutes to nine, two minutes to opening time, he lit a cigarette, climbed up on to the check-in desk and stood, head close up against the ceiling, blowing smoke into the detector until the red, blinking light stopped blinking and an electronic howl curdled the half-formed objection in Hannah's throat and trashed her brain as surely as if he'd plucked it out and chucked it in a blender.

"*Et voilà!*" Jay pirouetted, unlocking the glass doors to let them out into the street, not to let the punters – with their greasy, overdue thrillers, their foul-smelling sandwiches and their idiotic questions – in.

They called the fire brigade from the café across the road.

Jay said, "We should call Stephanie."

"She's not the boss any more."

"But she's the not-yet-appointed boss's boss."

Hannah had watched Steph's husband – she'd never worked out his name – loading her into a taxi outside the club they went on to when the restaurant threw them out. She knew Steph would feel even worse than she did, except that she'd be feeling it in bed, with hubby on hand to bring her cups of tea and wipe the 40-proof sweat from her pale and clammy brow.

"You're right. We should call her."

The café had huge windows and faux-leather bucket chairs that weren't as comfy as they looked but, nonetheless, they found they could sit happily watching through the window as the fire brigade arrived, all large slow men exuding un-hurried calm. Shortly afterwards Stephanie, blear-eyed and anxious, sweating despite the cool of the morning, climbed out of a taxi, eyes closed and breathing deeply as she waited for her change, then turned to cast a dull, malevolent glance not towards the library, but towards the café window, where they sat, milk froth and chocolate dust still clinging to the dark hairs on Jay's upper lip, muffin crumbs scattered across their table. Just when Jay said, "Perhaps this wasn't such a good idea," Hannah's mobile rang.

"Don't answer it."

But Hannah scrambled through her handbag, and Jay watched Stephanie speak to a fireman who was carrying, but not wearing, his bright yellow hat; watched her turn to face, and point, towards the café window, towards them – "Don't answer it," he said, uselessly – towards him and towards Hannah as she finally located her phone, lifted it to her ear and said – uselessly, pointlessly, for who else would the caller expect to answer her mobile phone? –

"Hannah Martin."

§

PREDICTABLY, THE BRIEF had turned out anything but: a front sheet, yes, and a small sheaf of papers tied in traditional pink ribbon, but behind that lay half a dozen lever-arch files, three thousand pages of leaden interview transcripts, painstaking chronologies and psychiatrist's reports that doubtless added up to some poor sod – or some poor sod's questionably competent parent – remaining in the chilly, medicated embrace of the state, or not remaining in said state's embrace despite that being the poor sod's fervent wish, or that of his exhausted, exasperated offspring and their weary, over-worked solicitor.

"Can't Emma handle it? Or Ashok?"

"Ms Hartington has already given it a pass through this morning, sir. That's her skeleton there. But it's from Prosser's. Charlie asked for you himself."

Charlie would, Bill thought; although, to be fair, he rarely did, and Bill *had* told him that he should, years ago, long before the Queen had ever sought his counsel. Whenever the need arose, he'd said.

"When's it listed?"

"Monday morning, sir. Hillingdon."

Hillingdon? For fuck's sake.

So Bill had been gainfully employed post-lunch on Friday, after all, and would likely be for most of Sunday, too. But today, Saturday, was sacrosanct, and had been all his life:

family time, despite the absence of a family, a Sabbath-sense imbued not by any synagogue, or mosque or church, but by his father, who had always maintained an absolute, unbreakable distinction between the working week and home. Returning from Cheltenham, or London, or Washington, DC, there'd be gin, and music, and – later, when Bill was already an adult – television, but there would be no talk of work or the office, of what the higher-ups or the lower-downs had done now, no gossip or complaint, not a word of what on earth did Mrs Martin – Miriam; Bill's mother – make of that? What Bill's mother made of it Bill never knew, because it was a subject they simply never touched upon, not even when, with the Americans back from the Moon, the VC in the Mekong Delta and Nixon out of the Whitehouse, with Heath and Wilson swapping jobs like party games and the lights going out and the weekend not always coming at the weekend after all, his father, Albert Charles William Martin, died. Bill was thirty, a barrister with a wife and a daughter he loved more than he could say, or at least more than he ever did say, and a mother who would live quite comfortably on her widow's mite for a decade more. Not even then would they discuss what it was his father had done to earn the pension he passed on to her or why it was that he would never talk about it, on a Friday night, when he got home, and poured himself a gin, or on a Saturday morning, when he read the *Times* and cleaned his shoes and his pipes, or, once in a while, watched Bill play rugby, a game about which he knew nothing, he said, but which he could see built character. When Bill asked what games he'd played at school, his father said only that he hadn't been much interested in sport, preferring books, although he had enjoyed fishing, sometimes, with his own father, Bill's grandfather, who had died during the war, before Bill was even born, he said.

What better time, then, than Saturday morning, this Saturday morning – now, in fact – for Bill to fulfill his promise to himself, to make the move demanded by his little heart problem (which the doctors said was not a problem), to make sure it did not pass unnoticed, unremarked, without consequence? What better time to put down the paper, to finish that second cup of coffee, and call his daughter, Hannah, to whom he had not spoken in three short decades, but whose career he had followed, whose books he had read and recommended to his friends and colleagues, and of whom, when those friends and colleagues said that he must be very proud, he had replied, modestly, but with more accuracy than they knew, that, yes, indeed, he was proud, but that it was none of his doing, Hannah Martin was very much her own woman.

He would call her now.

§

"GOOD AFTERNOON, MS Martin. My name is Jobina Sørensen."

The name meant nothing to her.

"Yes?"

"Jobina Sørensen."

"You said."

Through the window, out on the street, Steph was gesticulating, beckoning them outside. Jay stood up, banging the table between them clumsily. "Come on," he hissed.

"I would like to talk to you about your book."

This happened, sometimes, although less so since the Orange thing had faded. Readers who enjoyed her books, but wondered why they couldn't have different, happier endings; readers who wanted to point out errors of fact, mostly harmless. Generally, they emailed, because email addresses are easier to find, but sometimes they tracked her number down. Nobody had wanted to talk to her about *Reconciliation*.

"I would like to translate your book."

That was different; it was also not right.

Hannah said, "That's great. But I'm sorry, you have to talk to my publishers first."

"I did. They are very keen. They gave me your number. I hope I am not interrupting you?"

That wasn't right, either. Her publishers should have spoken to Frankie, who should have spoken to her.

Jay was outside, now, trying to look defiant as he spoke to Stephanie and the fireman. It was probably the worst thing he could do.

Hannah said, "I'm sorry, this isn't a good time. I'll ask my agent to contact you."

She hung up. She did not move, however, did not go outside to face Steph and the fire brigade, not straight away. She sat with her hands in her lap, gazing down at her mobile phone. She had not "hung up", she thought. She had pressed a button that was not a button but a rubber nub much smaller than her fingertip, printed with a tiny red silhouette of a mid-twentieth-century telephone. Hannah was intrigued by the way words and signs survived the demise of their referents, living a ghostly life in a world that seemed, objectively, to have left them far behind.

Jobina Sørensen.

"Bina".

Hannah's agent was a blowsy, over-familiar throwback who still called herself Frankie in her late sixties: Hannah could easily picture her on a bar stool in the nineteenth hole of a Home Counties golf club, G'n'T in one hand, menthol cigarette in the other, mascara smudged, screeching with laughter at her own off-colour jokes before driving home in the two-seater Mercedes she'd accepted in part settlement of her second or third divorce. She was old enough to be Hannah's mother, but came on more like a cheerily disgraceful aunt, bullying and chivvying, coaching and nursing her charges through deadlines and blank pages, through all the inevitable tedious adolescent angst that came with her job and which she never admitted to resenting. She had, Hannah was happy to tell anyone who cared, done a fantastic job; the Orange nomination had all been down to her, and if *Reconcilation* wasn't selling, that wasn't Frankie's fault, it really wasn't.

On Monday she answered Hannah's call on the second ring.

"Don't tell me, darling, I know. You've been *approached*."

"You know?"

Frankie's laughter turned into a cough. It was still morning.

"I had hoped it might be Hollywood, but never mind. It will be. Honestly. This will help."

Hannah was accustomed to Frankie's flights of baseless grandiosity. When she wasn't about to win the Booker she'd caught the eye of whichever A-list actor it was that year who'd decided to take up directing in order to maintain creative control. It was just Frankie's way; Hannah had never taken it seriously, and always assumed she was not supposed to.

"She's a translator, Frankie, not a film director. At least she says she is."

"She's a *Norwegian* translator, Hannah."

There was what passes for silence on the line.

"You didn't even ask, did you?"

On the line, Hannah thought: another homely twenti-eth-century ghost for a technology that bounced Frankie's voice from phone to mast to satellite to mast and down to earth here, where she was speaking, in the staff room at the library, her break almost over, the coffee mug in her left hand almost cold. She had asked, of course she had. It was just that she'd only asked herself, and not the woman who'd called.

"You should call her. Really."

So that evening, after work, after she and Beverley had locked up and said goodbye, see you tomorrow, she paused and gazed blindly at the displays in two or three shops and dodged bicycles and traffic and crossed the Green to an empty house, the woman in the flat downstairs not yet home from her bookshop, which was unusual. She made supper – not made, really, reheated something a bit like shepherd's pie but with a fancier name that she'd bought ready-made at the weekend and only eaten half of, plus a salad that was just some leaves out of a bag, a few cherry tomatoes, she didn't bother with a vinaigrette or anything – and ate it listening to the news about the Foreign Secretary, who had used a peculiar form of words not to admit or deny that his Government, its territories or armed forces, had been involved in the extraordinary rendition of terrorist suspects. She wondered if now, nine-thirty, wasn't too late politely to ring someone she didn't know, and decided that it was, but that it didn't matter, because this was different: this woman would want her to ring. So she carried her empty plate and her empty wineglass back into the kitchen and refilled her glass. She burrowed past the keys and lipstick and the hand cream and the compact and the two-tampon leatherette tampon case in her handbag until she found her phone. She scrolled through the recent calls until she reached what she was looking for, a number from Saturday morning that she didn't recognize, her phone didn't recognize, just a number without a name, and, after no more than two or three minutes' hesitation, dialled it (did not *dial it*, there being no dial on a Nokia) and a voice answered. Not a real voice – well, yes, a real voice, but not live, not actually speaking to her, in particular – a recorded voice, a man's voice.

It said, "This is Bill Martin. Leave a message."

§

BECAUSE, WHEN YOU got down to it, she'd killed him, yes, or at least had some imaginary boyfriend have her kill him, and then made him kill himself, which wasn't good, he had to say, but wasn't news, either: she'd done it before, in her earlier books. Not suicide, actually, now he came to think of it. Suicide was new, and even if unlikely – at least as unlikely as driving a Land Rover into a loch – he thought it might represent some progress in her view, the basis of some reconciliation, albeit posthumous. Better still, it dawned on him that in *Reconciliation*, for the first time, it was the *mother* who had left, not the father: Julia, not he. Moreover, while the mother had cancer, she also had a mystical opposition to its conventional treatment that would both kill her and earn Hannah's contempt. Naturally, this was no more true to life than his own suicide. He had not spoken to Julia since the divorce, but was aware that she maintained a sporadic correspondence with Sir Robert – with whom he was not supposed to know she'd shared a drunken night or two, or six, in the early 1970's – who passed on occasional titbits to Bill, despite Bill's repeated requests that he not do so. As a result he knew Julia to be as hale as a carthorse, albeit in New Mexico. But truth was not the point. The point was that he was not to blame, in the story, in *Reconciliation*. Not to blame for leaving Hannah: rather, *she* was; her mother was. And what was that, Bill asked himself, if not a giant step forwards in their relationship?

So, yes, he'd called her right away, before he could change his mind. He'd called the number Julia had included in a letter to Sir Robert, to pass on to him, just in case. ("Why would I need that?" he'd said, but had stored it in his own phone, anyway.) He had called her but had not spoken to her because an automated voice that was not even her voice explained that the number was not available just then and invited him to leave a message. He did not leave a message.

Then, on Monday night, after a weekend's work and a successful hearing in which he'd convinced the court to compel an elderly and rather charming couple to relinquish their adult daughter with severe learning disabilities into the care of the local authority; after he'd returned to his rooms and worked on an article for the *Gazette*; after he'd eaten a solitary supper with a solitary glass of wine and watched the Foreign Secretary not acknowledge that British intelligence had knowingly used – let alone commissioned – information extracted under torture, she called back.

He missed it, of course, because she called his mobile – returning his call – which he almost always kept switched off, in case it rang in court, which would be unforgivable. Furthermore, he had left it in the pocket of his raincoat, which was hanging in the cupboard in the hallway, while he was in the armchair opposite the small television in the sitting room at the time, and did not hear it ring, or vibrate, and, in fact, he did not even notice the missed call until Wednesday afternoon, because although he carried it everywhere, he did not often use the phone, and did not remember to check for messages.

She had not left a message.

§

BY WEDNESDAY HANNAH had spoken to Jobina Sørensen both on the telephone and, again, in the flesh.

She had also, she thought, recovered from the shock of hearing what must have been her father's voice - she would not have recognized it, but who else could it be? - for the first time since she was twelve. He had rung her. He must have called when she and Jay were sitting in the café watching firemen attend the fire that wasn't a fire in the library and Stephanie arrived and summoned them out into the street to explain just what the fuck they thought they were doing. He had called while she was speaking to Jobina Sørensen for the first time - the call times on the phone confirmed it - but had not left a message.

"You wouldn't, would you? If you called someone you hadn't spoken to for thirty years. You wouldn't just leave a message."

Surprisingly - surprising herself - she'd told Jobina Sørensen about it, when they first met. It was Tuesday after work. It was the end of the day, the shops were closing and the café opposite the library was not busy. She'd asked Jobina if she wanted a cappuccino and Jobina had said no, cappuccino was for breakfast. Then she apologized, but Hannah said she was right, really; they both had espresso. She led the way to the table in the window, where she and Jay had sat three days earlier, when Jobina rang, when her father rang. Hannah had not intended to mention the coincidence, and did not do so immediately.

She said, "How did you come across my book, Ms Sørensen?"

The translator had already called her Hannah, but was much older than she - in her seventies, Hannah guessed - small, light as a wren, but just as sharp and with a bird-like habit of regarding people from one eye at a time. She wore a hat she did not take off in the café, a well-cut purple woollen suit with bone buttons on the jacket, and shoes with a heel that belied her age. She looked rich, Hannah thought, or at least very well off, but probably wasn't. Literary translation was no way to make a fortune. Perhaps it was not her primary source of income? She looked to Hannah like a retired, but very senior, civil servant. The sort who, in this country, might be made a Dame.

She flicked Hannah's question aside. "It is about Norway. My publishers spoke to your publishers at a book fair. The usual story."

There was no trace of an accent Hannah could detect.

"And did you enjoy my usual story?"

"To be honest, not much."

Hannah was caught off-guard. She had dealt with translators once or twice before, and they tended to be more deferential, or at least more enthusiastic.

"But it interested me."

"I . . ."

"It interested me very much."

She leaned back slightly in her chair, although her spine remained straight and you could not say she looked relaxed. Hannah did not know what to say. She said, "Thank you," which seemed not quite appropriate.

"I wonder," the older woman said, "how your father reacted?"

"I have no idea."

"You did not show him the manuscript?"

Hannah's voice remained as flat as she could make it. "Ms Sørensen, I do not know my father. He left when I was twelve. I have not seen him since."

But he had called; she knew that even as she spoke. And she had returned his call.

The old woman set down her empty cup with a click. Outside, a boy leaned against the café window, holding his hand over his eyes to see past his own reflection in the evening sunshine, his shadow sprawled across their table.

"I did not know."

Hannah said, "There's no reason you should have done."

That wasn't altogether true. Hannah wasn't famous - her private life of no real interest to anyone, not even herself - but she had been interviewed, there had been profiles in the literary reviews and she had told the story then, when her first book came out, of her parents' separation. If this woman had done her research, she would have known. It wouldn't have been that hard.

The boy, evidently not seeing what he was looking for - a girl, Hannah assumed: the usual story - stepped back from the window and made a show of consulting his watch.

"I don't know my father. My books are not about him."

"I doubt that very much, Hannah. Our books are always about our parents."

Hannah laughed, and relaxed a little. "Oh, in some trivial Freudian sense, I dare say."

The boy outside looked at his watch again.

"And what about Martin?"

"There was no Martin."

"Well, it is your name, so obviously it is not his name, his real name. But there was someone? A man?"

"You mean a man I loved who disappeared and wrote something like my family history and posted it back to me? Is that what you mean?"

Jobina Sørensen uncrossed and re-crossed her ankles.

"Ms Sørensen, my book is not a memoir. I am a novelist. I make stuff up."

Novels are not true. A translator who didn't know that wouldn't be much of a translator. Perhaps Frankie had been wrong after all?

"Yes," Jobina was saying, "your Norway, for example. It is certainly not true. It is very made up."

This was definitely turning out to be a wasted evening. "I don't write travel guides."

"Although you know where Åland is. And Haugesund. And Molde and Bodo."

"I have an atlas."

She did. It was a huge beast, too large for her desk, too heavy for one person to lift comfortably. She'd had it since she was a child; it had been her father's, but neither that nor its cumbersome bulk had deterred her from carrying it to each new home, however temporary.

"And yet you know so little about Norway."

"Ms Sørensen, I see you are not interested in translating my book."

"Please, call me Bina. And I am, I am. Didn't I tell you so? It is just . . . There is no President in Norway."

The woman's English might be perfect, but that didn't make her easy to follow.

"In the early part of the book you have your Aleks Overand petitioning the king. And that is right. King Haakon IV. That is right. I expect not many English people would know that, at least not of your generation."

"It's basic research. It isn't hard."

"And yet, at the end, when your Overand dies, you have a President speak at his funeral. Which is unlikely enough, and not really necessary for your story, but what is it, I wonder, that made you think Norway does not still have a king?"

"Does it matter?"

It mattered.

"There was a time when editors would have corrected such things. I remember . . . " She paused, then pointed at the window. "Perhaps we should buy that young man a coffee?"

She really was like a bird, Hannah thought. You never knew where she'd land next. "I don't think he wants coffee."

"No?"

"I think he's been stood up."

Hannah was pleased the idiom seemed to challenge the older woman's perfect bloody grasp of the lingo.

"Boy meets girl. Boy likes girl. Boy invites girl to coffee shop. Girl agrees. Girl gets cold feet. Boy doesn't really like coffee anyway. Boy gets drunk and picks a fight. Boy goes home and masturbates furiously at some sickening thing on the Internet."

Bina smiled, which surprised Hannah, who had hoped she might be shocked. Instead, she twitched her head again and said, "You *do* make stuff up."

Hannah said, "Not that. That's an old, old story. Apart from the Internet bit, of course."

"And Overand."

She was at it again.

"No one in Norway is called Overand. But perhaps that was your point?"

Hannah said, "Would you like another coffee?"

Of course it was the point. The woman might be maddening but she was obviously not stupid.

There had been a time, and most of a draft, when *Reconciliation* had not been about Norway at all, not even loosely, but had been transposed to a fictional, nameless eastern bloc republic, which must have been where the president had crept in. Overand was not an eastern European name, either, of course. It might be Dutch, she thought, or Afrikaans. She could no longer remember where she'd picked it up, but suspected Radio 4.

"When I translate your book the main character will not be called Overand."

There were so many things wrong with that sentence, Hannah barely knew where to start. She picked the least offensive. "You think Overand is the main character?"

Bina ignored that. She behaved as if she were speaking to Hannah – leaning towards her, holding her eye, at one point even reaching out a curled and desiccated hand to pat the arm of Hannah's chair in emphasis – but her eyes, though bright, were focused far away. "He will be Jacobson. Not Overand. Aleks can stay, I suppose, but there will be a better ending."

"Then it won't be my book."

"It will be a better book. Overand – Jacobson – will not fight for the resistance. He will not emerge a hero after the war."

Hannah felt a gnawing anxiety rising from her stomach. The light in the café seemed to fade for a moment. She breathed deeply. "But that's the point. Overand saves the Englishmen. He abandons his family, but he fights. He fights with guns and with the law. That's the story. Otherwise he's . . ."

"Jacobson does not fight. He does not return to Norway at all."

"Then what?"

Jobina closed her eyes, and was quiet, still. Hannah waited. She found herself leaning forwards, as if trying to hear the older woman whisper, or to hear her think. She stirred, opened her eyes and was brisk again.

"What do you know about him?"

Hannah said, "It's all in the book. What I put in there is all there is. He doesn't exist anywhere else."

"But the book is based on facts, Hannah. On your family."

Hannah sighed. "I made it up. That's what I do. I made Overand up. Like you said, that's the point."

Jobina said, "I wonder . . ." This time when she reached out her hand she made contact, holding Hannah's wrist firmly. Hannah felt like a child. The woman was older than her mother, old enough to be her grandmother, almost. Perhaps.

Her next question took Hannah by surprise, again. "What if the submarine wasn't British?"

"But it was. It's in the diary."

"The diary you made up?"

"The real one."

Jobina waited. "That your father gave you."

That my father gave me, Hannah thought, before he left.

Not Holly Stanton's father. Or Hannah Stanton's father. Her father.

Except it wasn't a diary, was it? It was a transcript of a diary; she'd had the publishers include a facsimile of it at the end of the book.

Jobina said, "Jan was never much of a name for an Englishman."

A woman in a brown tunic pushed a bucket on wheels towards their table, using the mop to steer, like a nurse wheeling a drip stand towards a patient. She lifted the mop and spread grey water across the floor.

Jobina stood up. She said, "There is something here. Something I can work on. But also something missing. I will let you know."

She held out her hand again, this time to shake. Hannah struggled to her feet.

"And I will correct the geography."

"You said that was the one thing I did get right."

"In Norway, yes." Jobina smiled and, despite herself, Hannah was grateful. "But the Scottish page of your atlas must be missing."

At home that evening Hannah poured herself a whisky, hauled her atlas onto the coffee table in the attic room, and searched for the very north of Scotland. There it was, Sutherland – the south land at the farthest northern tip of mainland Britain, but southerly to the Vikings (the Norwegians, Hannah realized, belatedly) who, more than a thousand years ago, had sailed down what her atlas called the North Sea and conquered most of what they found. Above the southland, Orkney. And, inset in a box of its own, Shetland. So far, so obvious. Except, she knew, if she'd been asked, if she hadn't had a map in front of her, she'd have said they were the other way around, that

Shetland was closer to the mainland, Orkney further north.

She plucked a pristine copy of *Reconciliation* from the shelf above her broad desk. It was her book, and she knew where to find what she was looking for. There, in the middle of Part Two, she found it:

The following morning they land, not at Lerwick, as they had planned, not in Orkney at all, the diary says, but a hundred miles north, at Kirkwall, in the Shetlands.

It was where the diary ended, and she'd got it right. Shetland *was* north of Orkney. Not only that, she sees now, looking at the map, it is north of Stavanger, north of Haugesund, even, while Orkney is just a fraction south. But she sees something else, something that tugs her memory. She turns to the back of the book, her book, to the facsimile that is not hers, to the final words of her grandfather's diary. She reads:

Remainder of trip tedious though anxious, stopped for two hours from 0000 to 0200, I slept from 0100 to 0400. On deck land just in sight, we had made perfect landfall & secure to Fish Market Quay Lerwick not Kirkwall at 7.00 May 18th.

How perfect could a landing be, Hannah thought, on the wrong island?

At the end of the transcript, her father had added:

Note: *Lerwick is in the Orkneys, Kirkwall in the Shetlands!*

and then at some later point had crossed out *Lerwick* and *Kirkwall* and had written by hand above them *Kirkwall* and then *Lerwick*. Kirkwall is in Orkney; Lerwick in Shetland.

How hard could it be? It was the sort of mistake she might

have made – had made – about Norwegian towns; she had
checked, those, though, and corrected them. But her corrections, unlike her father's, were not hand-made and were not
visible.

§

ON HIS WAY past the clerks' office on Wednesday evening he spotted Clive talking to Emma Partington, who looked up when she heard him, eyes wide beneath full brows. It was one of the ancillary pleasures of his profession – one of many, he would admit, today, when things had gone well – that it attracted more than its fair share of intelligent, articulate, opinionated and frankly beautiful young women and then required them, much of the time, to dress in formal, flattering black and to look up at him, a senior member of the bar, counsel to the queen, much as this young woman was looking at him now. He nodded and she paused, waiting for more. Such thoughts were not appropriate, he knew, not permissible. He was not a dinosaur.

Clive said, "Nabokov cocktail."

"Oh, that's good. That's clever."

But was it?

"No, that doesn't work. You could just have cocktail. There's nothing wrong with cock" – he glanced at Emma – "and tails are perfectly serviceable. Where would monkeys be without them?"

"Not all monkeys have tails, I believe, sir."

"But it's not a good one, though, is it? Cocktails are mostly just a waste of booze. Though I suppose a martini, a proper martini . . . but no. They're drinks. We said no food, no drinks."

He turned to Emma. "Too easy, you see."

"Vaseline ice cream," Clive said.

"Exactly. Shooting fish in a barrel."

Emma looked from Bill to Clive and back to Bill. She said, "I have literally no idea what you're talking about."

Bill nodded. "And I applaud your accurate use of the word "literally"."

Clive said, "It's a game, Ms Partington."

Bill explained. The aim of the game was to choose two nouns, two objects or concepts, each in its own way perfectly acceptable, but which together combined to create something unutterably hideous.

"It's called *Jazz flute*," Clive said.

"After my most perfect contribution," Bill added. "The essence of the game."

There was certainly nothing wrong with jazz – Bill was an admirer of Oscar Peterson, despite his being Danish or Swedish or whatever he was ("Canadian," Clive said. "He's still alive") and playing far more notes than most people could even *hear* – and nothing wrong with the flute either, of course – there were some Bach sonatas Bill would be happy to take to any desert island you cared to name. But jazz flute was an abomination, inflicted by a crazed, vindictive Mephistopheles on an undeserving world.

He and Clive had invented the game years ago, before Bill took silk, but had quickly ruled out food and drink and national stereotypes – German humour, Italian diplomacy, that kind of thing, along with mere oxymora – like military intelligence, Bill explained – that were not, in themselves, inherently evil. It made the game increasingly difficult – which was the point; they were clever people, after all – and their

271

moves increasingly intermittent.

"So, no, Clive. Not clever. Doesn't work at all. You see," he turned back to Emma again, "Nabokov cocktail is not a thing at all. Not something in the world. It's just a pun. Besides, I never much cared for Nabokov."

Too fussy. Too prim.

"No, sir? Not *Pale Fire*? Or *Pnin*?"

Emma said, "I've only read *Lolita*. My father gave it to me when I was twelve."

Bill couldn't stop himself. "Your *father*?"

"Well, step-father. But I always called him Daddy."

Bill held his breath, or stopped breathing; he wasn't quite sure which. This was some other game, not *Jazz flute*; it had to be. He was being teased, and would be magnanimous. He said, "*Nil point* for Nabokov cocktail, I'm afraid."

Emma smiled.

The thing was, it was true, the thing about young women barristers, whether he thought it or not.

Was that why he'd smashed up his life? Why he'd left Julia – and Hannah? And why, when it turned out he wasn't dying, he had no one else to tell but a daughter he hadn't spoken to for thirty years?

Not really. Or not entirely.

Back in his own rooms he pondered his next step.

§

MAN LEAVES GIRL. Girl grows up. Man calls girl/
woman. Girl/woman calls man. Neither call is connected. (Except to the fact of the other.)

Man calls girl/woman again.

§

IN HER ATTIC, upstairs, sitting at her desk bathed in her computer's blue antiseptic glow, trying not to think about Jobina Sørensen, about Overand, about Jacobson, about "Bina", trying instead to work on the next thing, on novel number four, as Frankie said she should, she answers. Her voice is not a voice he recognizes, but he knows it's her. Who else would it be?

"Hello, Hannah. It's your father."

"I know."

§

ON THURSDAY MORNING Hannah called her agent. "Frankie," she said, "what have you done? The woman's mad as a box of frogs."

But Frankie wasn't there, or wasn't answering, and Hannah was talking to a machine.

She told Jay, because she had to tell someone. They were in the staff room having lunch. Jay had microwaved a plastic tub of leftover curry; the smell was overwhelming.

"The woman's mad."

"So?"

"Not mad, really. Charming. Clever. Bonkers. I just don't know what she wants."

Jay forked food into his mouth. A chickpea rolled onto the stained carpet. "You said she wants to translate your book. What's the problem?"

"She wants to re-write it."

"Is that such a bad thing?"

He had a point. It wasn't like anyone much was reading it in English.

Jobina Sørensen called again that evening.

Hannah had gone back to working on the next novel, the one she'd promised Frankie she'd have at least a first draft of by the time they published *Reconciliation*, and was only half way through. The one she'd put aside in favour of whatever it was she'd thought more interesting a few days ago, in the pub. She gave up and went downstairs to pour herself a drink, changed her mind, and filled the kettle. She would keep trying.

While the kettle boiled, she turned on the radio. A business programme ended and the news came on. Dick Cheney had been interviewed on CNN about a comment he'd made three weeks earlier, about the Iraqi insurgency being in its "last throes". He'd said that that if you look at what the dictionary says about throes, they can still be violent – Hannah thought, in fact, that was the point of throes; it wasn't his use of "throes" that anyone disputed, just the "last" – but Cheney was as confident and idiotic as ever: the very violence of the situation signalled that it was going to end and that democracy would win inside Iraq.

"I have it," Jobina said. "Some of it."

Hannah thought: that thing he said, about known and unknown unknowns, it never was as stupid as people liked to say. There were things you didn't know you didn't know; that didn't mean you could ignore them.

"We must meet. Tomorrow, or the weekend."

That wasn't Cheney. It was the other one.

"I'm sorry," Hannah said. "I can't. I'm busy."

Rumsfeld.

The next day, Friday, she met Fiona, after work. Fiona was also a writer – short stories, historical romance to pay the bills: no competition for Hannah. They met in the Eagle and, even though they had tickets to see *Medea* at the Arts, they both had large white wines, then more white wine, and went for dinner instead, where they drank cava and two bottles of red; when the restaurant closed, and the pubs closed, they went back to Hannah's flat and drank what was left of her whisky, and, in all that time and all that alcohol, she did not once mention her father or "Bina" Sørensen (except to say there was a chance she was going to be translated into Norwegian, which was exciting, and a bit scary, it being a book, in part, sort of, about Norway).

For her part, Fiona did not mention her mother's dementia or talk about the man she'd met who was not her husband and was, in fact, the father of one of her daughter's school friends, or how, when they'd finally managed to engineer themselves into a situation where they were alone, with a bed, he had thrown her onto it, which had been all right; or how they'd torn at each other's clothes and then he'd put his hands around her throat and tried to throttle her and when she'd pushed him off and asked him what the fuck he thought he was doing he'd said he thought she would enjoy it, he'd read her books; or how, before he left, which was almost immediately after that, he'd said he was sorry and he hoped that they could still be friends and she didn't say another word, then, and not later, either, to Hannah, not about that.

And while they were waiting for Fiona's cab to come, they both said they'd had the best night they'd had for ages. Wasn't it great to have friends you could really talk to? Say anything to? They should do this more often.

On Saturday, despite all the wine and the whisky, Hannah rose early and tried not to think about her day. She ate cereal and drank tea and refrained from turning on the radio. Up in the attic, rain pattered gently on the roof. So much for summer. She booted up her computer. Five hundred words. She'd do it now. She might not have much time later.

They had not said much on the phone. What could they say? Hello? How are you? How have you been these thirty years? How's your mother/wife? (Ex-wife.)

They'd agreed they would meet, that he would come to Cambridge. It couldn't be Thursday (he had a chambers dinner he couldn't avoid) or Friday (she was going to the theatre with a friend, she said). The weekend would be better. She would not be working at the library. He would book into a hotel. They would have time. They would not have to rush, he said, or watch the clock. Or speak, even, if they did not want to. They could just see what happened.

"Yes," said Hannah.

She wasn't sure that time – time with her father – was what she wanted. But having come this far there didn't seem to be much else she could say. They agreed to meet for lunch.

In the meantime: five hundred words.

No: a thousand. (She had written nothing yesterday).

Go.

She opened the file, and made a note of the current word count. A succession of small boxes popped up in the bottom right hand corner of her screen. Spam, mostly, junk. At least it was easier to delete than the old-fashioned paper sort. One from a bank she didn't bank with, one from a company whose website she had once browsed for duvet covers, one from Amazon recommending coffee grinders. One from Bina, subject: Jan Sørensen.

No, Hannah thought. One Sørensen's enough.

She let the box dissolve.

She would read her email later. Right now, write: now.

(The phrase was printed in block caps on a postcard from Frankie she had pinned to the wall above her desk.)

But Bina's voice was in her head, saying: Jan never was much of a name for an Englishman. She pronounced it Yan.

It had been her grandfather's name, all the same. That's why she'd put it in the book. Not his real name - not any of them - not Albert Charles William or even Martin, four first names, four Christian names, even the one that wasn't, but none of them Jan. Also, it wasn't what she'd called him, obviously. She'd called him Granddad, if she'd called him anything at all. But when she was a girl her father said it was what his friends called him, his army colleagues, his navy colleagues, his colleagues in MI6. He pronounced it Jan, with a J, like Janet, and said it came from the West Country, where her grandfather grew up. Hannah had thought it was her father who'd grown up there, not her grandfather, but perhaps it was both, and anyway, it didn't really matter: she wanted to hear more about her grandmother.

The email began:

– You were right the first time.

No good morning. No, I know you're busy, but.
How could I not be right, Hannah thought. It's my book.
She read on:

– Oskar never sailed to England with his father; Oskar never sailed back to be abandoned in the north. (Of course there never was an Oskar in the transcript, but there was a "boy" and Oskar is as good a name as any other, I suppose. Better than Overand, certainly.)

There was only one Englishman, though, not two. At least, only one by the time they were in the boat: this is important.

279

It is important because the Englishman will not make it back to England, or even to Scotland. And you will ask: why not? Here's why -

But Hannah was ahead of her here. Bina was going to kill off the Englishman, kill off her grandfather and dump his body in the sea. Which made no sense. Her grandfather had survived the war. Survived long enough to meet his granddaughter, to visit at Christmas with a box of magic tricks all wrapped up for her.

You will remember the greasy woollen sweaters and the canvas jackets? They were good, well chosen, and right. The jackets were identical, one perhaps just a little older than the other. They had belonged to Jan's father (I told you Jan is not an Englishman's name) but no one buys two identical jackets at the same time. So one must have been older, but it does not matter. They were both weathered by the rub of ropes and the salt spray and the frost.

On the second morning at sea, it is still dark, Jan goes up on deck to relieve the Englishman at the wheel. He pulls on the jacket hanging on a rusty bulwark. It is not the one he has been wearing, he knows, because of the way it hangs down on one side. There's a weight, something in the pocket. It is a small dark blue notebook.

He assumes it is a diary – he has seen the Englishman writing each evening. He reads the last few pages by the weak light of his lantern. He puts the notebook back in his pocket. He hunts about for a weapon – perhaps one of those vicious iron hooks with a wooden T-bar handle (you could look up what they're called, but it will be something different in Norwegian) – then carries on up the gangway to where the Englishman is standing, almost asleep, in the wheelhouse, his half-closed eyes fixed on the point where he imagines the sky would meet the earth if both were not impenetrably black. It is cloudy and there are no stars, no moon.

He kills the Englishman. He hauls the body to the gunwale and, laboriously, pushes it up, and out, until gravity catches hold and swings it free. He returns to the wheelhouse and adjusts the boat's course by a degree or two. He ties the wheel in place and goes below to the cabin. He takes everything of the Englishman's that he can find – his pipes and tobacco, and his accordion; he takes the vicious iron spike with the wooden handle and the Englishman's jacket, the one he had been wearing and which, now, is stained with blood. He throws them all, too, into the sea. There is no trace left of the Englishman.

What was it, Hannah wondered, that he read? They would need to know, if this story were to work.

The following morning Jan makes land at Lerwick. He assumes the Englishman's identity (which, being a spy, is false anyway). His name is now Albert. Bert. But he is never comfortable with it. He makes his way to London where he meets a young woman widowed in the Blitz. They begin "stepping out". She asks why he has not been called up. He says he has, that he is working for Churchill. He says that if he tells her any more, he will have to kill her, and he laughs. He says, "Seriously, you must not tell anyone. If they ask you must say that I work in signals."

They marry and, late in the war, they have a son they christen William.

William's mother dies.

Later, when William is grown up, his father dies. (This is what happens in families, if not in novels, always.)

When William's father dies he clears out the family house. In his father's study he finds a small blue notebook, in which he reads about an Englishman's escape from Norway in April-May 1940.

It is a story William knows well, that he has grown up with, that, after his mother died, his father told him more than once. It is a story he has passed on to his own children, a story of who they are. He makes a copy, typing it out on the battered Olivetti he uses for all his stories –

He is a lawyer, Hannah, thought. You cannot make him a writer.

– and, much later, clearing out his own house, he gives the copy to his daughter, even though he knows it to be false.

The email ended there, without even a sign off.
Hannah typed:

– How would he know it is false?

and hit send before she could think long enough to stop herself.

There was no point trying to work this morning. Not on the next book, anyway. By the time she'd made a cup of coffee and found some ibuprofen for her head, there was a reply:

– If we knew that, we could finish the book.

Who did this woman think she was? She typed:

– I did finish it. The father died.

(Pause.)

– But why?

– Because he's old, because he's dying from the start, although no one believes him. Because he cannot bear what he reads when Hannah and Martin take their manuscript to show him.

(Pause.)

– But why not? Why can't he bear it?

– Why not? Because. Be-bloody-cause. Did you not read the book?

– I read it.

(Pause.)

– And?

– I told you. It could be better.

– Who are you? I mean, I know you're not Jobina. Bina. I'm not stupid. "Bina" is a name in the diary, in my father's transcript: you're not her.

– How do you know?

– You're not old enough, for a start. Bina would be about a

hundred now. So who are you?

(Long pause. Hannah wondered if she'd finally lost the old woman, but doubted it would be that easy.)

– Until I was thirteen my name was Aisa.

– No it wasn't. I made her up.

– Then, after I crawled out of the pit we'd dug on the edge of town, out from under my mother's corpse, and my sister's and my brother's corpse, and the corpses of our neighbours, I learned to call myself by many names. I had lain there for two days, feeling the bodies stiffen, smelling the urine and the faeces they gave up, listening to the town dogs fighting over the spoils and wondering why they bothered. There must have been plenty to go around. I was waiting to make sure I was alone, that there was no one left. I was Annette for a while, and Grete, after friends I'd left in that pit, and Sofie, after my sister, who had gone to Oslo before the war to work, and who, I hoped, was still alive. The one you called Abi.
Why did you call her Abi?

Hannah thought she'd been right when she told Frankie the woman was mad, wrong when she'd corrected herself.
She typed:

– It was a sort of joke.

– ?

– In the eighteenth century 'Abigail' meant servant girl. It spared the aristocracy the bother of learning their domestics' names.

– An English joke, then.

(Pause.)

– I'm sorry.

(Pause.)

– Tell me. When Abi/Sofie disappeared, in your book, had Aleks/Jan abandoned her? Betrayed her to the Nazis? Or murdered her?

Hannah felt both cold and sweaty. She typed:

– I don't know.

– How can you not know?

She was reminded of the readings she had given where there'd be half a dozen people in a cold library or a bookshop after hours, and somebody who'd read every word she'd ever written would fixate on all the wrong things. He'd want to know whether the train the protagonist took was diesel or electric, why a minor character's eyes change from brown to blue, or why the woman in chapter four doesn't seem to know her way around the town it later turns out she's visited before. She wanted Bina's questions to be like that: ordinary human madness – not the threatening kind, not the mania of someone who knew a secret that could tear your world apart, could take the person you thought you were and rip her into shreds before your eyes, the kind of secret that just happened to be true.

– I don't have to know. It's fiction. Those possibilities are all there, but I don't have to decide.

– Yes, you do.

– No, I don't. That's not my responsibility.

– Whose is it, then?

Just reading the other woman's words on her screen, not hearing them spoken, not knowing how they were said, it was hard to tell what species of insanity this was.

She typed:

– I have to go. I have to meet my father.

She logged off. If there was a reply, she wouldn't see it, she thought, until after she'd discovered a few more things about herself.

§

THE RADIO SAID, "Good morning, it is seven o'clock on Saturday the 25th of June. Here are the headlines . . ." and he switched it off.

He didn't need John Humphrys, not today.

He'd been up already when the radio turned itself on. He'd been packing, practising his lines. Talking aloud even though he was alone – a barrister's habit – listening for the false notes in his own voice.

"Hello, darling . . ." – he could not darling her. She'd been his darling, his sweet-pie, his pixie, his princess, but that had all stopped in 1974. He'd left.

"Hello, Hannah . . ." Serviceable, and probably best.

He would get to the restaurant first and sit facing the door, waiting for her to come in. He'd see her speak to the waiter, and walk towards him, an attractive young – no longer young, exactly – an attractive woman, threading her way through the tables. He would stand to greet her. "Hello, Hannah." And then what? Shake her hand? Kiss her cheek? Kiss the parting on the top of her head, like he had when she was twelve?

"I've read all your books." – a gushing fan? – "As you can see, I'm still alive."

He'd said they wouldn't have to talk, if they didn't want to, but of course they would. Human beings who had not spoken for thirty years could not sit through lunch in silence.

The kettle boiled and he made tea, a small pot.

Consequences. You do this and that happens. You do nothing and something else – not nothing – happens. Lear was wrong. Nothing never came of nothing, not since the world itself began. He'd had a scare, but that was nothing, the doctor said. Then out of it had come this . . . this what? This triumph. This reconciliation.

Or, no.

He was ahead of himself. He would have to see – *they* would have to see – how it went.

He had an overnight case he'd used for years when he was away at the provincial courts, but even that was barely full. A clean shirt, a change of underwear, the leather toilet case – one of the few things he'd kept of his father's, with its intricate velvet indentations for comb and brush, for nail scissors, toothbrush, collar studs and soap, for a shaving bowl and, although he'd never used it, for a cut-throat razor that he'd once told Julia he kept "for sentimental reasons". (She'd asked if that were some kind of threat.) His father said it had belonged to his own father, Bill's grandfather, and was designed for a sailor, a ship's captain, probably, to hold everything he'd need and yet be as small as possible. There wasn't much space aboard ship. They'd all been sailors on his father's side, all the men. He was surprised that Hannah had so obviously remembered it.

A book. He should pack a book for the train, and for the hotel room tonight. Or a brief. He was in court again on Monday.

An umbrella: they were just about due a thunderstorm.

It was only seven-thirty; his train wouldn't leave until after ten. He might as well read that brief now, then it would be done.

It was nine o'clock before he knew it. He pulled on a jacket, plucked a dog-eared copy of *Tristram Shandy* from the shelf, tossed it into the overnight bag and left. In his head he took the stairs down from his rooms two or three at a time. In reality he knew there was no need to hurry, and that tripping now, rolling and bouncing down four flights on his sexagenarian bones would be the worst possible way to assure a timely arrival. He reached the ground floor faster than usual, all the same.

Walking up the alleyway towards Fleet Street, he felt a little out of breath. He slowed down, for a moment, as the world slipped sideways, just for an instant, before snapping back into place.

He told himself there was no need to rush.

Fleet Street was thrumming with traffic, taxis and buses, mostly, at least a dozen, huge and red and shiny and sliding into one another and, strangely, silent. Then suddenly not silent at all, roaring, and rolling and roaring again like a pride of bored lions.

He flagged a taxi, stepping into the gutter, his left arm shooting up with practised authority.

"King's Cross," he said as the passenger window slid down. Listening to himself, though, to his own voice – a barrister's habit – over the roar of the feline buses, he wasn't sure it sounded quite like "King's Cross".

"Hrn, hrrrn, hrnff," the cabbie said, a Labrador chewing a pillow.

"Wrrrm, wwwrrrrrm," Bill said.

Then, just as suddenly, the buses stopped roaring and

rolling around and sat patiently, diesel-chugging at their stops; the cars pulled past politely and he was fine, absolutely fine. He'd never felt better.

"King's Cross, please," he said again.

"Not in my cab."

He watched the taxi pull away. There were plenty more, but he didn't need a cab. He was fine. He'd walk. It had rained in the night, but it wasn't raining now. His bag wasn't heavy. It couldn't be much more than a mile up the Gray's Inn Road. He used to walk it all the time, when he was younger, when he had first moved into the flat in the Temple, when he'd first left Julia and Hannah.

Hannah. He was going to see Hannah.

He'd walk. He had time. He had . . . He looked at his watch, and the curious thing was, he couldn't see the numbers. He could see shapes, squiggles, but he couldn't work out what they were. And the hands, the hands on the watch, they meant something, he was sure of it, but he couldn't quite remember what.

He noticed that his arm, his other arm, not the arm with the watch on – his *right arm*, that was it – felt numb. The fingers were tight and swollen, larger but less flexible than normal.

The shoulder strap of his overnight bag – light as it was – must be cutting off the circulation. He lifted his hand towards his shoulder to unhook the strap, but his arm was denser, heavier than it should have been. It felt as if he were trying to lift a chair, a log, or a tree trunk, something long and heavy and far, far from his body. He looked down at his hand and it was someone else's hand, some other species' hand, the fingers curled and clawing at nothing, at his face, but they couldn't reach his face because his hand was so heavy he couldn't hold it up to look at it.

Then it wasn't an arm, just shapes and colours, colours he wouldn't have expected, green and purple and blue – a deep, intense blue like the cloak of a renaissance Madonna – and there was no difference, no boundary at all between his arm and the pavement beneath it or the walls, or the people, they were all the same, all beautiful, and it didn't hurt and it wasn't heavy, his hand, his arm, his body, because it wasn't him, there was no him, just light and colour and stars that weren't stars, just energy and peace and silence.

The voice in his head that reminded him to do things, to get to the station, for example, to catch a train, to read a brief, to not always say out loud the things it said to him, the voice that came up with *jazz flute* and *life coach* and *daytime television*, the voice that reminded him Julia was still alive, that Sir Robert was still head of chambers, that the lying war criminal Blair was still Prime Minister (but only because the alternative had been Michael "Something of the night about him" Howard, and what kind of a fucking choice was that?) *that* voice, the one that told him he'd got things wrong, that he should be ashamed of himself, that he was on top form today, that, honestly, he should just rule the world, *that* voice wasn't there.

And it was bliss.

And then it *was* there, saying quietly: "You're having a stroke."

It said, "You haven't got time to have a stroke, you fool, you've got a train to catch."

It said, "Ring Hannah. Let her know you might be late. Sit down here, right here, on the pavement, yes, that's right, and ring her now."

He patted his jacket pockets with his left hand until he found his phone. He pulled it out and couldn't remember why.

"Ring Hannah."

But what was the number? What were numbers?

"Re-dial. She's the last person you spoke to."

Buttons too small. Fingers too fat. That was interesting. He could see his right eyebrow. It had slumped down over his right eye. He felt his face, it was thick and rubbery – or his fingers were rubbery; or both – and his mouth wasn't quite where it should have been. He could see as clear as day the Spitting Image doll of Margaret Thatcher, he remembered watching it with Julia and Hannah – which couldn't be right: he'd left them long before Thatcher, long before Spitting Image, he'd left in 1974 when he was just a junior, five or six year's call—

"Ring Hannah."

All right. Okay. All right.

Who's Hannah?

And for the next hour – was it? Two hours? Three? How was he supposed to know, when all he knew was that he was spinning slowly or the world was spinning, there wasn't any difference, and he was lying on the ground, then he wasn't on the ground, then he was; and there were people, sometimes, leaning in and leaning back, dissolving into the sky, the clouds, into the ambulance roof and the lights. Sometimes he thought they might be talking but he couldn't understand them and they couldn't understand him, if he was speaking back, which he wasn't sure he was. So, then, for however long it was, for as long as he had left, he was an infant, unable to walk or speak or do anything at all that would affect the way things turned out for him, but all the same, at the same time, an intelligent, articulate infant who could, when the voice came, watch and comment on what was happening. And the voice came, and went, and the bliss came, and went, and the voice came and the bliss came until he couldn't tell them apart and—

"And actually, what's going to happen now is that you're going to die.

"That plaque in your left carotid artery (the one the doctor said wasn't thick enough to be high risk) has choked off all the oxygen to half your brain; or perhaps a chunk of fat elsewhere – your heart, maybe – has chipped itself free and whooshed its way upstream, like a spawning salmon fighting through a waterfall until, at last, it's through, it's reached it's goal and – bang! – your brain's exploded like a firework.

"One or the other, it really doesn't matter."

What was happening was: the thing the doctor said wouldn't kill him, was killing him after all. And, after all, it wasn't all that bad.

§

HANNAH ARRIVED EARLY at the restaurant and chose a table in a corner where they would not be overlooked. She sat with her back to the wall. Her father would have his back to the restaurant. It would give her some kind of advantage, she thought.

She practised opening lines:

"Hi, Dad." Neutral.

"Hi, Dad. How've you been?" Neutral, shading to sarcastic.

"Mum sends her love." Not true, but would certainly throw him.

"Why did you leave?" Straight to the point.

"Why now?" Ditto, plus probably what she wanted most to know.

A waiter with an improbable French accent asked if she were ready to order. She explained she was waiting for somebody and he turned to leave.

"But I'll have a gin and tonic."

Best get prepared.

The opening exchanges didn't matter. They'd be awkward whatever she said, whatever he said. How could they be anything else?

She knew why this was happening now, in any case. It was *Reconciliation*. It had to be. Something beyond merely killing him off (she'd done that before) had caught his attention.

Could "Bina" – whatever her name was – be right?

The waiter brought her drink. She thanked him and swallowed half of it before he was back in the kitchen.

He ought to be here now.

If Bina wasn't right, what was she up to? Why re-write her story – Hannah's story; Hannah's father's story – like that?

Break it down, she told herself. First principles. What did she know?

Her grandfather was a spy.

No: she knew only that her father had told her Granddad was a spy. He'd told her that, in April 1940, her grandfather was in Stavanger, a port city on the southwestern coast of Norway, when the German army invaded. He had been in Berlin the previous September when Chamberlain declared war, and was well known to the German authorities.

Her grandfather had never mentioned it, to her, or in her hearing.

She'd only met him once or twice that she could remember.

He'd written it down, though. He'd kept a diary in a small navy blue notebook. Her father had transcribed it. Before he left, on her twelfth birthday, he'd given her the transcription. Years later she had used it in a novel (that much was true) which had prompted her father to contact her for the first time in three decades (speculation).

No. None of this was true, or at least not certain.

She had never seen the diary. She knew only that her father had given her a typescript. It began on April the 9th – her birthday, which is why, he said, he was giving it to her now but also the date of the invasion of Norway (and, coincidentally, of Baghdad, sixty-three years later). It began with the words *Up all night*; it ended on the 18th of May, the morning after Norwegian National Day, or Constitution Day, when her grandfather landed in Orkney. It said many of those who helped him escape were arrested by the Germans and never heard of again.

It said no such thing.

How could it? Her grandfather wouldn't have been there to record it.

But her father had said it. Hadn't he? It was part of the story he passed on, the story she herself had told many times before she ever decided to write about it.

Her father still had not arrived. She had finished her gin and eaten a small basketful of bread. She ordered olives, and another gin. She rang, but her call went straight to voicemail. He would be on the train, or in a taxi, now, on the way from the station.

The typescript said *Decision to run taken*. It said: *All personal papers burnt*.

It said the proprietor of a Norwegian Bed & Breakfast had *nice eyes*.

It said they ate *sardines*.

It said *Mrs kissed and said she would pray*.

It said they sailed from Haugesund in a fishing boat that was intercepted by a submarine, *most fearful moment of my live* (sic) but the submarine turned out to be British. It said they made *perfect landfall* at Kirkwall.

No: it said *Lerwick, not Kirkwall*.

Lerwick is in Shetland, not Orkney.

This much she knew. And it was precious little.

Also, she knew her father wasn't going to come. Not now. That much was obvious.

He'd said they didn't even have to talk if they didn't want to, but she knew – they surely both knew – that would not have happened. He would have had questions for her, no doubt, but she would have had more for him. It was his job to ask questions, if only those to which he knew the answers. But surely, if he'd come, he'd have had to answer some of hers?

§

"WHEN'S THE FUNERAL?"
    "Thursday week. The seventh."
"July already?"
"It will be."
"Where does the time go?"
She'd telephoned her mother. It would be summer in New Mexico, too, wouldn't it? Of course it would, and hotter than Hades, probably.

"It's at the Temple Church. I had a call from someone at his chambers. Apparently they used Sir someone's name to swing it."

"Sir Robert. That would have seriously annoyed your father."

She didn't ask why. She was surprised her mother knew the name. Although they talked, and met whenever she was in England, Hannah thought she probably knew her mother little better than she knew her father.

She said, "What's the weather like? Where you are?"

"What?"

"Is it baking hot?"

"Darling, it's two-thirty in the morning."

Of course it was. "I'm sorry. I forgot."

"Don't worry. I hadn't gone to bed. How's the book going?"

"The next one?"

"The last one. What was it called?"

Hannah guessed her mother knew exactly what the book was called.

She went to work, where Jay and Beverley found it difficult to talk to her. Tony told her to take some time off.

She said, "I'm all right. I hardly knew him. I didn't know him, really. I'm all right."

That evening her mother rang back.

"Wednesday the 6th. Meet me at the Aldwych hotel. You know the one. Bring your nightie and a black suit. I've booked you a room."

"You're coming?"

"Wouldn't miss it for the world."

"I'm not sure I'm even going myself."

"Of course you are, darling. He *was* your father."

The obituaries were respectful, some fulsome. The *Guardian* put him above Richard Whiteley (but below Luther Vandross). If there'd been a president, Hannah thought, he – or she – could have led the eulogies. As it was, the Prime Minister, long the target of her father's rare but vituperative public pronouncements, evidently had other business to attend to.

In fact, hardly anyone was there: Hannah and her mother; Clive and a handful of barristers who, like Bill, lived in the inns; "Bina" Sørensen. Hannah introduced her to her mother as "my translator".

"Bina's working on my last book. The one you haven't read."

"I didn't say I hadn't read it."

Clive said the church should have been packed. He said

there'd been some major fuck-up on the Underground, something about power surges, he'd heard. He apologized for saying "fuck-up".

On the way back to the hotel Julia said, "Is it always this quiet?"

They ordered sandwiches, and coffee. They had time to fill before Julia's taxi to the airport. While they waited, Julia dipped into her handbag. She said, "I brought you something of his. Of his father's really. I thought you might be interested."

It was a small navy blue notebook, old and battered. Inside the front cover, in the overly neat hand of a precocious child, was written *Elda Sørensen, Inkognito gate 15, Oslo, Norway.*

The book contained notes, poems, fragments of plays and stories, written in what looked to Hannah to be a mixture of Norwegian, Russian and English. There was a page that seemed to be about *The Seagull*. There was a sketch entitled, in English, *Bugger God: a Comedy*; another, also written in English, and in the same neat hand, appeared to be a diary. It began on April the 9th. The first entry read:

Up all night.

NEW FICTION FROM SALT

RON BUTLIN
Billionaires' Banquet (978-1-78463-100-0)

NEIL CAMPBELL
Sky Hooks (978-1-78463-037-9)

SUE GEE
Trio (978-1-78463-061-4)

CHRISTINA JAMES
Rooted in Dishonour (978-1-78463-089-8)

V.H. LESLIE
Bodies of Water (978-1-78463-071-3)

WYL MENMUIR
The Many (978-1-78463-048-5)

ALISON MOORE
Death and the Seaside (978-1-78463-069-0)

ANNA STOTHARD
The Museum of Cathy (978-1-78463-082-9)

STEPHANIE VICTOIRE
The Other World, It Whispers (978-1-78463-085-0)

RECENT FICTION FROM SALT

KERRY HADLEY-PRYCE
The Black Country (978-1-78463-034-8)

CHRISTINA JAMES
The Crossing (978-1-78463-041-6)

IAN PARKINSON
The Beginning of the End (978-1-78463-026-3)

CHRISTOPHER PRENDERGAST
Septembers (978-1-907773-78-5)

MATTHEW PRITCHARD
Broken Arrow (978-1-78463-040-9)

JONATHAN TAYLOR
Melissa (978-1-78463-035-5)

GUY WARE
The Fat of Fed Beasts (978-1-78463-024-9)

This book has been typeset by
SALT PUBLISHING LIMITED
using Neacademia, a font designed by Sergei Egorov
for the Rosetta Type Foundry in the Czech Republic.
It is manufactured using Creamy 70gsm, a Forest
Stewardship Council™ certified paper from Stora Enso's
Anjala Mill in Finland. It was printed and bound by
Clays Limited in Bungay, Suffolk, Great Britain.

LONDON
GREAT BRITAIN
MMXVII